"I always try to mix business with pleasure—"

Cole sank into an armchair and pulled Tess into his lap. His warmth and hardness sent heat shimmering through her. "Sitting is allowed during business transactions, isn't it?"

"I—I suppose so," Tess stammered. She couldn't think clearly while his hand was splayed below the small of her back and his handsome, virile face hovered near hers.

A muscle flexed in his jaw, and his hands tightened on her. His gaze touched her face, her throat...her breasts. When their eyes met again she nearly melted from the force of the heat.

"I want you, Tess. And business has nothing to do with it." He pulled her closer and kissed her—a possessive kiss that stunned her with its intensity.

"I can't do this," she whispered. "I've never been intimate with anyone I wasn't in love with."

"Then fall in love with me," he uttered against her mouth. "Fall in love with me, Tess."

Dear Reader,

I love when "sparks fly" in a romance. Sparks started flying between Tess McCrary and Cole Westcott when they were young teens...except those sparks had more to do with fury and spitfire than with romance. Their families have been enemies for so long, tour guides in Charleston tell the story of the century-old feud when pointing out their ancestral homes. Tess grew up knowing that a Westcott means nothing but trouble for a McCrary.

If she'd only known what *kind* of trouble Cole Westcott would cause her, she never would have agreed to his marriage scheme, regardless of all she stood to gain.

Then again, maybe she would have. The wickedly handsome scoundrel *does* have those sweet-talkin' ways. And he says some of the most irresistible things with no words at all....

Hope you enjoy the fireworks between Tess and Cole as much as I did. Come visit my web site at www.temptationauthors.com or write to me at P.O. Box 217, Auburn, GA 30011. I'd love to hear from you.

Sincerely,

Donna Sterling

HOT-BLOODED HERO
Donna Sterling

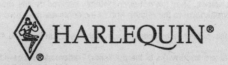

HARLEQUIN®

TORONTO • NEW YORK • LONDON
AMSTERDAM • PARIS • SYDNEY • HAMBURG
STOCKHOLM • ATHENS • TOKYO • MILAN • MADRID
PRAGUE • WARSAW • BUDAPEST • AUCKLAND

I dedicate this book to my boys—Chris, Nic, Sterling and Patrick. But still, don't read it until you're older. Much, much older.

My sincere thanks to my critique partners: Carina Rock, for never hesitating to "be *really* picky." Susan Macland Hardy Goggins, for all the DBMs. Jacquie D'Alessandro, for acting out the choreography when necessary. And Ann Howard White, for her emergency whirlwind critique.

I feel compelled to dedicate Chapter Three in its entirety
to Jacquie D.

RECYCLED PAPER · RECYCLED PAPER

ISBN 0-373-25877-1

HOT-BLOODED HERO

Visit us at www.eHarlequin.com

Printed in U.S.A.

1

"DON'T BOTHER TRYING to contest the will, Cole. The court will uphold it. The stipulation your father added is legal and binding."

Cole Westcott responded to his attorney's pronouncement with a soft, fluent curse into the cell phone. Sinking deeper into the lounge chair on the hot, sunny deck of his yacht, he squinted through his sunglasses into the Carolina blue sky above the Intracoastal Waterway. His father had obviously lost his mind before he'd died. All those years of cutting-edge business schemes, hundred-proof cocktails and gorgeous women competing for his attention had finally warped the old man's brain.

He cast a wry glance at the double martini on the table beside him and the three topless beauties sunbathing on the lower deck with his business associate. He supposed there *were* worse ways of warping one's brain.

"Damn it, Henry," he uttered into the receiver, "are you saying that I'll actually have to *marry a stranger?*"

The attorney who had served his family for forty-some years replied in his cultured southern tones, "If you want to inherit Westcott Hall, the townhouse, the businesses, the real estate holdings, the boats, the stocks, the bonds and the cash, then…yes. You'll have to marry in accordance with your father's will."

Cole cursed again. He'd spent his life building up the Westcott businesses and increasing the family holdings. As his widowed father's only offspring, he'd never questioned the fact that he'd inherit the businesses as well as the capital. He certainly hadn't doubted that he'd inherit Westcott Hall, the waterfront home in Beaufort or the house in Charleston, all of which had been in his family for over a century. He'd spent a lot of his personal time and money renovating them. "There has to be a way around it."

"There isn't. If you don't satisfy the codicil to your father's will within six months of his death, his ex-wives will inherit everything. And you've already wasted a month of that time trying to find a way around it."

Cole hissed out a frustrated breath. He knew without a doubt that his father hadn't wanted his ex-wives to inherit. He'd used that threat to force Cole's hand. It was a damn effective threat. Even if he hadn't stood to lose so much personally, Cole hated to think of the Westcott legacy torn apart by the old man's ex-wives.

None of the glamorous blondes his father had married had remained with him longer than a few months. They'd each collected a cool million or so in divorce settlements and never looked back. Until now, of course. The prospect of inheriting millions upon millions had united the three ex-wives. They'd banded together and hired a high-powered attorney. Cole knew he'd better act quickly or he'd lose everything.

"Read the stipulation to me again, Henry."

Obligingly the lawyer read, "'My son, Cole Westcott, shall fully satisfy the stipulations contained in Addendum A within six months of my death.'" After a pause, he said, "Of course, Addendum A contains the curse."

Cole closed his eyes in a pained wince. That had been the root of all this trouble—the so-called curse his father had found in an old family bible a couple of weeks before his death. How could he have possibly believed such nonsense?

"Until I learned about this curse, son," his usually well-balanced father had rasped from his hospital bed, "I thought I was just one of those people who was unlucky in love. But now I realize that I've been victimized. So were my parents, my brothers, my grandparents and *their* parents."

Cole had tried to make him see how ridiculous that idea was, but his father vehemently believed it.

"I was married to your mother for less than a year when she died in a plane crash...in her lover's private jet. She was running off with him," his father had ranted. "My mother left my father, too. My grandmother killed my grandfather by hitting him over the head with a whiskey bottle. All my brothers were either abandoned by their spouses, widowed or completely shunned by the opposite sex." Sullenly, he added, "I should have known a McCrary was behind it all. It's the curse, I'm telling you."

Cole had begun to understand. Rather than facing the fact that Westcott men simply didn't have whatever it took to sustain a long-term relationship, the old man found it easier to blame the McCrarys. Realizing that common sense wouldn't make him see reason, Cole resorted to a tactic that couldn't fail to sway him—or so he'd thought. "You can't really want me to marry a *McCrary*."

Though Cole himself had never paid much attention to the animosity between the two families, his father had always been an avowed McCrary hater, as his own father and grandfather had been. Nothing had pleased them more than besting their archrivals. And they'd been good at it.

"Hell no, I don't want you to marry a McCrary," his father had growled, "but I believe it's necessary—at least for a while. The curse doesn't say how long the marriage has to last. I'd say at least four or five months. That's a respectable time for a marriage nowadays, wouldn't you say?"

Cole had almost laughed at that. Three of his father's marriages had lasted about that long.

"When I die, son, you become 'Westcott of Westcott Hall.' You'll be the one named in the curse. Your happiness will depend on your satisfying its terms. Your cousins, aunts, uncles, and future generations of Westcotts will depend on it, too."

"That's crazy."

"Read it for yourself." His father had shoved the old yellowed bible into Cole's hands and pointed to the scribbling on the inside cover. Although the curse was written in some unrecognizable language, an interpretation and explanation had been neatly printed beside it.

The trouble, it seemed, had begun in 1825 when a McCrary daughter became pregnant by a Westcott son. The heads of both families—rivals in the shipping business—had refused to allow a marriage between them. The woman was pressured into marrying someone else, and in her grief and rage, she lost the baby. With the help of her Gullah maid's magic, she cursed both families. She wrote the hex in two bibles and sent one to the heads of both households, the McCrarys and the Westcotts.

"A sad story, Dad, but that's all it is," Cole had insisted. "A story."

His father had narrowed his eyes. "What about you? You're thirty-one years old and none of your relationships have lasted long enough to write home about."

Cole had shrugged, ignoring the discomfort caused by the observation. "Too many women in the world to settle for just one." It was the truth. Yet he couldn't deny to himself that a peculiar restlessness had replaced the thrill. Maybe the game had become too easy; the bounty too plentiful.

The thought brought to mind the giggling models awaiting him on the sundeck below. Reaching for his martini, he muttered into the phone, "Read the damn curse to me again, Henry."

"You, Westcott of Westcott Hall, must marry the daughter of your McCrary neighbor. Until the Westcotts and McCrarys are so united, you and your family shall reap only loneliness and heartbreak."

Ah. Loneliness. He couldn't deny that one. As the motherless child of a busy father, Cole couldn't remember a time he hadn't been dogged by loneliness. Even as an adult, he hadn't been able to shake the feeling for long. Perhaps it had become so deeply ingrained that nothing would ever rid him of it.

That prospect didn't bother him all that much. In fact, he preferred the familiar old loneliness to the smothering effect of a long-term relationship. His longest-running affairs had somehow increased his sense of isolation until he'd clamored for room to breathe.

He damn sure wouldn't attribute his wandering eye and taste for variety to the curse, though. "I can't believe my father took this nonsense seriously," he grumbled into the phone.

"Whether the curse is real or not," replied Henry, "your father's will is *very* real. You'll have to satisfy its terms or lose everything."

Cole glumly admitted he was right. With a nod at his guests who called to him from the lower deck of the yacht, he asked Henry, "Do I have to be physically present at the wedding, or can we do it by proxy?"

"I'd suggest you attend—and make every effort to give the appearance of an actual marriage."

"Meaning?"

"You and your, er, *wife* should live together."

"Live together?" He'd been hoping for a quick, impersonal paperwork transaction. "For how long?"

"That's a gray area, legally speaking. But I'd advise you to marry as soon as possible and remain married, cohabiting in your primary legal residence as husband and wife, for the remainder of the six-month period."

"So approximately *five months?*"

"I'd strongly advise it. Your father's ex-wives will have their attorney looking for ways to invalidate the marriage. They have a lot to gain if you fail to satisfy the conditions of the will."

Just his home and everything he'd always worked for. "Guess I'd better find a McCrary bride," he mused, resigning himself to the idea of a temporary marriage. A *very* temporary marriage. "I'll have my assistant research the McCrary families and make up a list of single females."

"Actually, I took the liberty of having *my* assistant do that very thing."

Cole raised his brows in surprise. He then remembered that his father had left a tidy sum to the old family retainer contingent upon Cole's satisfying the stipulations of the will. *Of course* Henry would be anxious for him to marry a Mc-Crary. The bequest would allow him to retire in high style. "What did you come up with, Henry?"

"Since the curse specifies 'a daughter of your McCrary neighbor'—and we want to satisfy the will to the letter—I ran a check on the descendants of the original McCrary clan in the Charleston area and came up with four single women. One is eighty-three. Another is a nun. The other two are daughters of Ian McCrary."

A humorless laugh escaped Cole. "Ian McCrary! He hates the Westcotts as much as my father and grandfather hated *him*. They basically ran him out of business, didn't they?"

"They came close."

"How close?"

"From what I've gathered, he's near bankruptcy. *And* having tax problems."

"Hmm. Could be useful. He has two single daughters, you said?"

"Yes. Kristen, who's twenty two, and Tess, twenty eight."

"Tess?" Cole quirked a brow. "Tess McCrary," he repeated musingly. "I met her once." He'd been sixteen, which would have made her around thirteen. He and his cousins had strayed onto McCrary land when their fishing boat capsized in the river. She'd appeared from behind a tree—a skinny little redhead with a BB gun aimed at them. *You're Westcotts, aren't you?* she'd asked. They'd laughed at her fierce expression. One of his cousins uttered a wisecrack about coming to gobble up little McCrary girls. She ordered them off her property. Cole had made a move to take the gun.

She'd put a BB in his shoulder.

Absently he rubbed the tiny scar barely visible on his bare, sun-warmed skin. That damn BB had stung like hell. And Tess McCrary had taken off running. "I'd probably have better luck with the nun or the old lady," he murmured, somewhat amused at the irony of the situation.

"You'd have to make the deal extremely rewarding to entice either of Ian McCrary's daughters, I'm sure," agreed Henry.

"I'll make the offer to Kristen. I'd like to keep this deal as simple as possible."

After he disconnected with Henry, Cole called his assistant in Charleston and instructed him to research the financial circumstances of Ian McCrary and his family.

Later that afternoon, his assistant called back with a report that Ian McCrary had fallen behind on certain business loans, which Cole's wily father had managed to acquire through the bank he owned. Glad for his father's insightful planning, Cole called an officer of that bank and instructed him to foreclose on the loans. "Demand full and immediate repayment."

He ordered the foreclosure with a clear conscience. After all, he meant no personal harm to the McCrarys. This was simply a matter of business.

He had to put his prospective bride in the right frame of mind for his marriage proposal.

TESS MCCRARY awoke with a start, raked a long, limp tangle of auburn hair out of her eyes and realized she'd fallen asleep at her father's desk, in the cramped, musty office of the bridal shop, sprawled out over the account books she'd been working on.

The account books.

She grimaced as the morning sun brought her to full consciousness. She'd worked all through the night trying to get the books straightened out in hopes of putting her parents' shop up for sale. But the books *couldn't* be put in order. Too much data was missing. Which meant she'd have a hell of a time selling the business. Her parents, therefore, would not be able to repay the delinquent loans.

They'd be forced to close up shop by the end of the month. And they had no other source of income.

Anxiety clawed at Tess. How could her parents possibly retire? Having been self-employed all their lives, they were depending on their savings to see them through. But they'd already spent most of their savings on medical bills incurred because of her father's heart attack.

Tess moaned and buried her face in her hands. She dreaded breaking the news to her father. He'd have a fit over closing the store...and maybe another heart attack.

If only she, her mother or her sister had realized sooner how much his mental acuity had been slipping, they could have prevented financial disaster. They'd known that he forgot things now and then—appointments, names, or where he put his car keys. But no one had realized that he hadn't been keeping the books up-to-date, managing his funds correctly, filing his taxes or paying certain bills. Tess still wasn't sure how much of that neglect had been because of memory loss.

Pure stubborn orneriness—and maybe a little paranoia— had accounted for some of it. He said he hadn't paid his taxes because the government was crooked. He hadn't paid the health insurance premium because he felt they were overcharging him. And he refused to make certain loan payments because he swore that the Westcotts had bought the debt, and he'd rather die than give them a penny. According to her father, *they* owed *him* much more than the balance of the loans.

The bank had notified them yesterday of foreclosure on three of their business loans, demanding full repayment.

Tess wished she had the money to bail her parents out of trouble, but she'd drained her own savings on investigators in an attempt to find Phillip. She'd also taken a leave of absence from her fairly well-paying job at the university financial aid office to run the bridal shop while her mother nursed her father back to health.

Things were indeed looking grim.

Rising stiffly from behind the desk and stretching her cramped muscles, she glanced at the wall clock. Eight-thirty. She had an hour to drive home to the apartment she shared with her sister, shower, change, drop in at her parents' house to check on them, and return to open the shop.

She was surprised Kristen hadn't called. Glancing at the desktop phone, she realized that she'd knocked the receiver off the hook some time during the night. Promptly she returned it to the cradle. Within moments, the phone rang.

"Belles and Brides Boutique," she greeted sleepily.

"Tess," came her sister's cry, "I *figured* you'd worked all night. I've been trying to call you. You've got to get home right away."

Her sleepiness fled at the panic in Kristen's soft, almost child-like voice. Either her father had gotten into more trouble, or something had happened between Kristen and her fiancé. Or...could news have come regarding Phillip? If so, it couldn't be good news, judging from the tone of her sister's voice. "What's wrong, Kristen?"

"It's Cole Westcott. He's coming over to talk to me. He'll be here any minute. Something about a business proposal. I don't want to meet him alone. I didn't call Mama because she'd tell Daddy, and he'd be here with his rifle."

"What?" Tess shook her head, certain that her all-nighter must have clogged her brain. She couldn't have heard correctly. "Kristen, you're not making sense. It sounded like you said *Cole Westcott* was coming over."

"I did. He called me this morning, and— Oh my gosh, there's the doorbell. I think it's him. Come home, Tess, *please!*"

The line went dead, and Tess frowned. Cole Westcott...going to her sister with a business proposal? She'd never heard of anything so ludicrous. Kristen was too busy trying to earn her degree in elementary education to get involved with business. She *had* been helping out on Saturdays at the bridal shop, but only in the past three weeks, since Tess had taken over the running of it.

With a growing sense of foreboding, Tess reached for her purse and car keys. What the hell did the Westcotts have up their sleeves now? The fact that it somehow involved her sister put her on immediate alert.

From a lifetime of hearing about their devious ploys and antics, she knew those Westcott men couldn't be trusted—not in business, and certainly not with pretty, naïve young women like Kristen. Cole Westcott had come from a long line of scoundrels notorious for breaking hearts, creating scandals and destroying the lives of enemies. The first Westcott to land in Charleston had been a thieving, womanizing pirate. It seemed that none of his progeny had strayed too far from that path.

Cole Westcott, alone with her sister. She had to get there.

She locked up the shop, hurried to her car and sped through town, across the grand sweep of Cooper River Bridge to Mount Pleasant, her thoughts racing as she drove. Had Cole Westcott learned of their financial trouble and hit upon some scheme to exploit the situation? If so, how did it involve Kristen?

Adrenaline pumped through Tess as it had the day a rowdy bunch of Westcott boys had surprised her in the woods. Kristen had been picking berries closer to the house. No one else had been home. Tess had been forced to put a BB through the biggest boy's shoulder.

She believed that had been Cole Westcott. Since the Westcotts and McCrarys never socialized in the same circles, attended the same schools or lived in close proximity, she hadn't known him personally. And she hadn't seen him after that day. But she *had* heard gossip about Cole, the heir to the largest of the Westcott fortunes. In fact, she'd heard something about him recently, she suddenly remembered. His father had died. Which meant Cole had come into full power.

He'd now pose more of a danger than ever.

She ran from the parking lot of the small complex, up a short flight of wooden stairs to her apartment. The first thing she saw when she pushed through the door was her pretty blond sister seated on the sofa, her blue eyes shimmering with tears, her lips trembling.

Concern and anger roiled in Tess. "What's going on here?" she demanded, her fists clenched at her sides, her body braced for confrontation.

A man rose smoothly, courteously, from a corner armchair. His sheer size threw Tess somewhat off-balance. Disjointed impressions flitted through her mind. *Tall.* At least six-foot-three. Wide shoulders. Muscular forearms beneath rolled-up sleeves. A hint of dark hair near the opening of his gauzy white shirt. A strong, tanned throat. Clean-shaven jaw.

Her mouth went dry.

He'd been too good-looking for comfort when she'd been thirteen, but nothing had prepared her for *this.* Between his deeply bronzed tan and the golden lights in his thick brown hair, he seemed to glow with the sun's own energy. A groove too long and masculine to be called a dimple ran along one side of his wide, firm mouth. But it was his eyes that held her entranced—a vivid sea-green, they were lit with keen intelligence, and focused intently on her.

"Tess, this is Cole Westcott," came her sister's soft, disembodied voice from somewhere in the room. "Cole, my sister Tess."

Neither of them offered a handshake or murmured polite banalities.

He raised a brow with mock wariness. "You're not packing a BB gun, are you?"

She supposed she should have expected it—the deep, gruff southern voice that could melt honeysuckle from a vine. The very sexiness of it irked her. "No, Mr. Westcott. Next time I feel the need to defend myself or my family against you, I'll pack something *much* more potent than a BB gun."

A rueful sparkle lit his gaze. "Somehow I don't doubt that."

"What did you do to make my sister cry?"

"Oh, no, Tess," protested Kristen, rising from the sofa, her face streaked with tears, but her eyes now dry, "he didn't...I mean, it wasn't..."

"I asked her to marry me."

Tess stared at him, thunderstruck. "You *what?*"

"It's true," Kristen said. "He asked me to marry him. Oh, are you okay, Tess? You look so pale. I know it's a shock. You'd better come sit down."

Soft, insistent hands closed over her arms, but incredulity kept her standing. "You asked her to *what?*" she repeated more forcefully.

"I think sitting down would be a damn good idea." He eyed her with that wary look again.

"I think you'd better start talking."

"Come on, Tess." Kristen tugged her to the sofa and pulled her down beside her. "I'll explain everything."

Dazed, as if she'd had a physical shock, Tess forced her gaze away from that Westcott man now seated in her armchair and turned questioning eyes to Kristen.

"It's for business purposes," Kristen informed her. "A temporary marriage. Just a matter of paperwork, really. And he's offering us money. A *lot* of money." Leaning closer, she whispered as if it were a secret, "A million dollars!"

Tess couldn't have been more stunned. *Or* more suspicious.

"Did you hear me, Tess? I said—"

"Yes, yes, I heard you." *A million dollars. More than enough to solve their problems.* She frowned at the man who watched them with cool, calculating green eyes. "Why are you doing this?" she demanded.

Again, her sister answered for him. "Because of his father's will. Before he died, Mr. Westcott came to regret the things he'd done to Grandpa and Daddy, and wanted to mend the rift. He tried to think of a way that would force the families to put aside their differences and unite in friendship."

"Unite in friendship!" Tess repeated, her incredulity bordering on scorn.

A flicker of unease crossed Cole Westcott's face.

"So he put a stipulation in his will," Kristen continued. "Cole has to marry a McCrary woman before six months have passed."

"He wanted you to *marry* a *McCrary*?" Tess asked Cole in stark disbelief.

He cleared his throat and avoided Tess's gaze.

"Oh, yes, he wanted that very much," Kristen assured Tess. "If Cole doesn't marry a McCrary, he'll lose Westcott Hall."

Tess gawked first at Kristen, then at Cole. "Is that true?"

"Absolutely," Cole confirmed.

Tess thought about it briefly, then shook her head. She wasn't buying the story. Cole Westcott definitely had some underhanded scheme in mind.

The Westcotts *always* had underhanded schemes in mind. They'd engineered a hostile takeover of her father's corporation, forced him out of the import-export business, financed a mud-slinging campaign when he ran for mayor, sabotaged his investments and bought up his assets as quickly as he lost them.

The worst had been when the Westcotts acquired her father's ancestral home in Beaufort—McCrary Place—with most of its original furnishings, for way below market value. She'd heard they hosted parties there just to flaunt the spoils.

How her father hated them! Of course, he *had* inflicted some damage of his own. Her mother had been engaged to Cole's father when Ian McCrary met her. Westcott had never forgiven him for stealing her away.

And now Cole expected her to believe that his father had added a stipulation to his will to force his son into marriage with a McCrary? She didn't believe it.

"A million dollars, Tess," emphasized Kristen. "That's more than enough to pay off Daddy's back taxes, the medical bills *and* the business loans. It'll even give him money to retire."

She winced at her sister's openness. Although Cole Westcott probably knew more about their financial state than Kristen did, Tess didn't like discussing their personal business in front of him.

"Mr. Westcott," she said with cool formality, "before we waste more time, please understand that I intend to go to the courthouse and look at your father's will. So if there's anything you haven't explained to Kristen regarding this offer, you'd better do so now."

A hint of amusement—and maybe respect—entered his gaze. "What? You don't believe my father repented his dastardly deeds on his deathbed?"

Tess managed to refrain from snorting. "Do *you?*"

He laid a hand over his heart. "I'm hurt that you doubt me."

Tess twisted her mouth to hold back a laugh.

"Don't be hurt," Kristen begged in her soft, kind voice. "Tess didn't mean to doubt you *or* your father. She's just surprised, that's all."

A somewhat sheepish expression doused his amusement. "Thank you, ma'am." He cleared his throat and glanced uneasily at Tess. "Maybe my father *did* have a little more motivation than simple regret when he added that stipulation to his will."

Tess raised her brow, waiting.

"Shortly before he died, he found a curse in an old family bible." He actually looked embarrassed. "The curse demands that the 'Westcott of Westcott Hall' marry the daughter of his McCrary neighbor. For some crazy reason..." he uttered a dry laugh "...my father believed it. He added the stipulation to his will in hopes of removing the curse from the family."

Tess stared at him, thoroughly surprised.

"I'll bet it's the same curse we found," Kristen theorized. "Remember, Tess? It said that the McCrarys and the West-cotts would find only loneliness and heartbreak unless a McCrary woman married a Westcott man."

A chill raced down Tess's spine. *Of course* she remembered the curse. She'd tried very hard to forget it since the day she'd read it in her grandmother's bible. But every time another tragedy struck, another heart broke, another bout of loneli-ness hit, she thought about the curse.

She'd thought about it too often.

"Why did your father believe it?" She hoped he didn't hear the tremor in her voice.

Cole shrugged. "Dementia, maybe?"

She bit her lip. She supposed it *was* crazy to believe in a curse. Crazy and pointless. "Were there...tragedies in your family?"

"Some."

"There've been quite a few in ours," Kristen confided.

An understatement. Every one of the McCrarys had suf-fered a deep, personal loss, including Kristen, their parents and Tess. Kristen's high-school sweetheart had died in a car accident. Her parents had lost a child to illness. And Tess's fi-ancé had never returned from an anthropological study over-seas.

Phillip. The old pain and anxiety swept through Tess. Had he fallen victim to the curse? Was he, even now, suffering somewhere because she, a cursed McCrary, loved him? Had he *died* because of it? But no, she couldn't allow herself to be-lieve the worst. Thirteen months had gone by without any word of his whereabouts or fate, but she refused to give up hope.

"Regardless of why my father put the stipulation in his will," Cole Westcott said, "I'll have to satisfy it." He no longer looked amused. "As I've told Kristen, I'll draw up a contract for her to take to an attorney. My lawyer has advised that we remain married for five months. He also advises that we, uh, cohabit in my legal residence for that entire time."

"Cohabit?" Tess narrowed her eyes on him, her suspicions flaring. "You expect my sister to *live with you* for five months?"

"In a purely platonic way, of course." Though he'd said it in a business-like manner, Tess didn't miss the wry curl of his mouth and the sardonic awareness in his gaze. He knew of the suspicions looming in her mind. Kristen was too beautiful a woman not to present a temptation to a man like Cole Westcott. "She'll have her own private suite in Westcott Hall. I'll even spring for a deadbolt if she feels...unsafe."

The wry note in that assurance caused Tess's jaw to square off. "Be sure to write it in the contract."

A small sob turned both their gazes to Kristen, who'd pressed a hand to her mouth as her eyes filled again with a liquid sheen.

"Oh, honey, don't cry." Tess slid an arm around her, and Kristen buried her face against her shoulder. Tess suddenly realized the reason for her sister's misery. She should have figured it out much sooner, but she'd been too stunned by the proposal to think clearly. "You don't have to do this, Kris. You know that, don't you?"

Cole frowned at Tess.

Tess frowned right back at him.

"But I *do* have to," Kristen cried against her shoulder.

"Let's go to the bedroom and talk, okay?" As she helped Kristen up from the sofa, Tess said to Cole, "Excuse us, but I'd like to have a word with my sister." He nodded, looking mildly annoyed, and Tess ushered Kristen to her bedroom.

"Don't you see?" Kristen whispered as Tess shut the bedroom door. "That million dollars is the answer to our prayers."

"But what about your wedding?" Tess said, broaching the topic that sat so heavily on her sister's heart. "It's all set for next month. You've already invited the guests. You've spent your savings on deposits for the hall, the cake, the caterer, the flowers. And Josh made non-refundable reservations for your honeymoon. You can't marry Josh if you're married to Cole Westcott."

"I know that," Kristen wailed with a fresh welling of tears.

"And how will Josh feel about your marrying another man? *Living* with another man? He's being transferred to Seattle in July. He'll have to leave without you."

"But what else can I do? Daddy and Mama need that money."

There was only one answer. Tess knew she should have suggested it the moment she'd realized her sister's dilemma. Her hesitation shamed her. Swallowing her trepidation, she said, "Let me check into the situation a little more closely. If I feel that Cole Westcott's offer is legitimate..." she paused, momentarily overcome by the daunting prospect "...*I'll* marry him."

Kristen blinked in surprise. "You?"

"Yeah, me." Her insides churned at the very thought. "*I'm* a daughter of his McCrary neighbor, the same as you. That should satisfy the terms of the will. And we'll still get the money for Mama and Daddy."

Hope shimmered through Kristen's tears. "Do you think Cole Westcott will allow it? The switch, I mean."

"I don't see why not." An outright lie. Tess saw very clearly why he might not allow it. He'd made the offer to her beautiful younger sister. Perhaps he wouldn't want his name linked to a plain-Jane type like Tess, no matter how temporary the arrangement. He did, after all, have a reputation as a first-class womanizer to uphold.

And then there *was* the fact that she'd shot him. Living with a trigger-ready bride who harbored unresolved hostility issues against him might not be particularly appealing.

Too bad. If he didn't want to lose Westcott Hall, he'd have little choice. As far as she knew, the pickings were slim when it came to single female McCrary relatives. "Forget about Cole Westcott," she told Kristen. "*I'll* handle him."

"Are you sure? I hate to saddle you with another problem. Besides, *you're* engaged, too. What if Phillip comes back?"

Tess stared at her in dismay. Although her fiancé had been missing for over a year, she prayed every night that he'd return to her. What if he *did* return and found her married to Cole Westcott?

She glanced down at her engagement ring, and doubt assailed her. Was she wrong to consider this deal with Westcott? No. There was too much to be gained by going through with it. "I'd simply explain the situation to Phillip, and he'd understand. It's not like there will be anything personal between Westcott and me. And five months isn't forever."

"Thank you so much, Sis." Kristen fervently hugged Tess. "I don't know what I'd do without you." As Kristen smiled gratefully at her, Tess was again struck by her beauty. In a cotton-candy-pink sweater and slim white slacks, her short blond hair glimmering around her heart-shaped face, she was the kind of woman any man would be proud to introduce as his wife—even a playboy tycoon like Cole Westcott.

Tess, on the other hand, was the kind of woman he might *not* mind introducing as his sister-in-law. She wasn't even too sure about *that*. She'd never been particularly pretty, and at the moment... She caught sight of herself in the full-length mirror and winced. She looked a wreck. She wore the baggy old jeans and roomy gray sweatshirt she'd worn last night while working on the books. Her hair streamed in untidy strands from her braid, and there were dark shadows smudged beneath her eyes from lack of sleep.

She could just imagine what Cole Westcott thought of her.

Not that she cared. She was very much in love with another man—a man who loved her for her mind and her convictions and the person she was. At least, he *had* loved her before he'd disappeared in some faraway land. *Oh, Phillip! I miss you.*

Gathering her composure with an effort, she encouraged

Kristen to go wash her face and calm herself. Tess then removed her engagement ring from her finger and tucked it away in her dresser drawer. It seemed somehow inappropriate to wear Phillip's ring while discussing marriage with another man.

Anxiety bunched and knotted in her chest as she headed for the living room. She dreaded the prospect of approaching Cole and proposing that he marry *her* instead of Kristen. *It's a business deal, nothing more.*

She found him standing near the fireplace in the living room where photos lined the mantle. He was studying one of Kristen in her high-school cheerleading outfit.

Tess cleared her throat nervously. He turned, and his gaze locked with hers. A disturbing warmth washed through her. He was just so big and solidly masculine and ruggedly attractive. Tess hadn't had much experience with that sort of man. She felt unbearably awkward.

She had to remind herself that Cole was, under all that virile splendor, only a Westcott. "I'm sorry, but my sister has decided to decline your offer."

He leaned against the mantle and hooked his thumbs into the front pockets of his jeans, letting his hands curl loosely on his thighs. Long, muscular thighs, from what she could make out through the tight denim. "May I ask why?"

"She's marrying someone else next month."

"Ah. So I've been thrown over for another man." The dry humor in his naturally gruff voice should have set her at ease. It didn't. "I must admit, I'm impressed. She's willing to kiss that million dollars goodbye, and all for love." He angled his head and regarded Tess with a slight frown. "She *did* understand it would be a marriage in name only?"

"Of course. But the timing was bad. Next month...a big wedding...a honeymoon...a move to Seattle..." She lifted her shoulder in a shrug. "Marrying you just didn't fit on the agenda."

The groove beside his mouth deepened, and his green-eyed gaze played over her face. In a softer, gruffer voice that sent spirals of warmth curling through her, he asked, "Know where I might find a single McCrary woman in need of a million dollars?"

"Well, I...I..." *Oh, come on, Tess. Spit it out. He's practically asking you, isn't he?* She bit her lip. Maybe he wasn't. Maybe he sincerely wanted her to recommend another McCrary woman. "I might know of one."

"Might?"

All her insecurities rose to her throat, preventing a single word from squeezing through. She wanted to slap herself. She couldn't believe she was even considering letting a million dollars slip through her fingers to avoid a possible rejection. Since when had her ego become so delicate?

Since when had a man's stare made her wish she was beautiful?

Alarms rang in her head. She couldn't allow herself any vulnerability where a Westcott was concerned. She would treat the matter exactly as she would any other business proposition. "If you're talking about me, Mr. Westcott," she finally replied, "I'm afraid I'll need *two* million dollars to make it worth my while."

He stared at her in clear surprise. "There *are* other McCrary women, you know."

She still wasn't sure if he *had* been talking about her. But she did know a bluff when she heard it. If he was so sure he could find another eligible McCrary in time, why had he bothered with Ian McCrary's daughter? "Yes, of course there are. Unfortunately, cousin Mary Francis's vows won't allow her to marry. And if you plan to ask Aunt Sophie, let me give you fair warning. She'll probably call you a whippersnapper and hit you with her umbrella."

Cole pursed his lips, rocked back on his heels and crossed his arms. How in the *hell* could a woman annoy him so much, yet still make him want to laugh? If he had any sense at all, he'd thank her for turning him down and saving them both five months of abject misery. "My father's will doesn't say the woman has to be related to you."

"The curse specifies 'the daughter of your McCrary neighbor.' Since the curse was written in the early nineteenth century, I believe the court will interpret that to mean a descendant of the original McCrarys of Charleston. You won't find many of those. With all the nuns, spinsters and childless widows among my ancestors, the family tree has been, shall we say, well pruned?"

He was beginning to consider that divine intervention. Who knew what fate would befall mankind if too many more women like Tess McCrary populated the earth? He had no trouble believing she was a direct descendant of the McCrary witch who had put the curse on the Westcotts in the first place.

"Funny," he replied, hating to let her get the upper hand, "the genealogist I hired drew up quite a list of eligible candidates." A lie. He wondered if she knew it. "And if all else fails, I know of one or two married McCrary women who wouldn't mind leaving their husbands for a million dollars...or for five months of my, uh, company."

Disapproval flashed in her wide gray eyes. One of her gleaming auburn brows then lifted ever so subtly. "I wish you the best of luck in your endeavor, Mr. Westcott." She made a graceful little flourish with her hand toward the door. "Godspeed."

She really was getting on his nerves. If he left right now, he could probably find "Aunt Sophie" before her nap time and brave the umbrella bashing.

Damned if he knew why, though...he wasn't ready to walk away from Tess McCrary. Maybe because she owed him. She *had* shot him with that BB. She'd also talked his prospective bride out of marrying him. Yes, indeed, she owed him.

He intended to collect, in one way or another. Squinting at her, he slid his hands into his pockets and sauntered closer. "*One* million dollars. Not a penny more."

Her lips bunched and shifted in eloquent disdain.

Full, shapely lips, he noticed with surprise. At least she had *something* physical going for her other than the vibrant color of her auburn hair. Too bad she'd tortured it into that ragged braid. As far as beauty went, she had little else to catch a man's eye.

Yet he found himself adding before she'd even replied, "And the deed to McCrary Place."

Her amazingly lush lips parted at that, and he actually heard the breath catch in her throat. "McCrary Place?"

He hoped, for her sake, that she didn't play high-stakes poker. The prospect of reclaiming her family's historic house illuminated her eyes like stars on a clear southern night. He swore they turned from gray to blue. Or maybe it was the rosiness now glowing in her cheeks that made her face seem so much more colorful. She looked...transformed.

No way would she turn him down now.

"Two million," she countered, "*and* McCrary Place."

His gaze shifted to hers in surprised admiration. He had to give her credit for trying. But not *that* much credit. "Don't push it, McCrary."

Her chin came up, but her eyes still shimmered. She looked so blazingly pleased with what she'd accomplished so far that he almost wanted to take back his offer. Almost. "One million dollars, then," she acquiesced, "and McCrary Place. And...and..." she searched for another demand "...the furniture."

"*All* of it?"

"All of it," she insisted, her tone ruthless.

He was very careful not to smile. He held out his hand to close the deal.

She shook it, her grip firm and dry, her gaze direct.

A heady sense of victory washed through him. *He had her.* His McCrary bride. The thought infused him with an unexpected rush. Something surprisingly primal and male stirred within him. Something that made him glance one more time at that soft, lush mouth and wild auburn hair.

She owed him.

"My assistant will fax you a copy of the contract this afternoon," he told her. "I'll apply for the license tomorrow. Blood tests aren't required, but you'll have to stop by the marriage bureau with your driver's license. I'd like to schedule the ceremony for Friday." He turned and headed for the door.

"If you will, Mr. Westcott," she called, remaining where she stood, "fax a copy of your father's will along with the contract. And have your accountant send me a certified financial statement. I'll need to know that you have the means to honor our agreement." He glanced back at her to see a prim smile. "And I'll be sure to check my calendar to let you know when I'll be available for the ceremony. *If*, of course, my attorney gives me the go-ahead."

Pausing near the door, he fixed her firmly in his gaze. "Pack your bags, Ms. McCrary," he drawled with deliberate softness, "for a five-month stay."

He had the satisfaction of seeing a subtle wash of color in her face.

And his resolve hardened. If he had to marry a damn McCrary, it would be this one.

2

"WE CAN'T TELL your father, Tess! His daughter, marrying Harlan Westcott's son. It would either kill him, or he'd kill someone else. That Westcott boy, probably."

Hearing her mother refer to Cole as "that Westcott boy" made Tess choke on her morning coffee. Her mother obviously hadn't seen him in a very long time, if ever. "I think we'd be making a big mistake not to tell Daddy. I'll be living in Westcott Hall for five months. He's bound to find out." At the apprehension in her mother's gaze, she added, "I'll tell him about the million dollars and the deed to McCrary Place *before* I explain the details of the deal."

"Money won't make him any happier about you marrying a Westcott."

"Please don't worry, Mama. I'll break the news to him gently—and not until it's absolutely necessary." Setting her coffee on the counter beside the cash register, Tess returned to her task of dressing a mannequin in a wedding gown. She'd arranged for Kristen to stay with her father while Tess brought her mother to the shop and broke the news of her possible nuptials. Buttoning a row of pearls on a lace-pointed sleeve, she said, "No sense in getting Daddy all riled up when I might not go through with it."

"Maybe you should call the whole thing off, honey. I'd be worried sick about you, living in Westcott Hall. As for your father's reaction..." Margaret McCrary shook her head in grim foreboding "...it won't be good. His temper has been so volatile lately. All this 'bed rest' wears on his nerves."

"He's been a bear," Tess sympathized. "I'm glad you're getting a break this morning."

"Oh, he hasn't been *that* bad. But I guess I am grateful to Kristen for staying with him for a couple hours." A huge admission for her mother to make. She'd always been the very model of wifely loyalty, never uttering a single complaint against her husband. "It'll be a pleasure to watch the store," Margaret said. "I miss working here."

Tess glanced affectionately at her mother. With her mild-mannered ways, her graying auburn hair and her wide blue eyes so much like Kristen's, she brought out the protective instincts in Tess. Hiding her own anxiety at the idea of marrying Cole Westcott, Tess looped an arm around her mother's thin, rounded shoulders. "If all goes well, Mama, you'll have the choice of keeping the shop open or retiring with Daddy to someplace nice. Like...McCrary Place."

"That would be wonderful, honey." For an instant, wistfulness settled over her gently lined face. "But I don't want you to get into any kind of trouble because of that Westcott boy. I'm not sure if he can be trusted."

"Of course he can't be trusted! That's why I'm checking out every possible angle of this deal before I say 'I do.' In fact, I intend to meet with Cole this morning and go over a few, um, details."

Such as the forty million dollars he'd failed to mention. From her visit to the courthouse, she'd learned that he stood to lose not only Westcott Hall, but also his entire inheritance. No wonder he hadn't faxed her a copy of the will. He hadn't wanted her to realize how strong her bargaining position actually was.

She'd also discovered that Cole Westcott himself had ordered the foreclosing of her father's loans. The thought made her blood boil.

His underhandedness made her question the marriage scheme itself. His father had named his former wives as his benefactors in the event that Cole didn't satisfy the conditions in the will. Were those women more deserving of inheriting the estate than Cole? It couldn't have been easy, being married to a Westcott. Had Harlan Westcott provided adequately for his cast-off wives when he'd grown tired of the marriages?

Determined to confront Cole with her questions, Tess took her mother up on her offer to watch the shop while she paid him a visit. His assistant had told her he was too busy to accept calls or visitors, but Tess had a hunch Cole would see her anyway.

She'd bet forty million on it.

After assuring her mother once again that she would use extreme caution while dealing with those wily Westcotts, Tess left the shop and drove to the Concord Inn, a historic building that now housed an exclusive restaurant owned by the Westcotts as well as Cole's office. She'd dressed in a tailored "power suit" of gun-metal gray and the highest heels she owned—high enough, she hoped, to allow her to glare at him eye-to-eye.

Her heels clicked against the stone walkway like the ticking of a time bomb as she strode toward the stately old harborside inn. When she drew near the entrance of the restaurant, however, her pace slowed. A crowd had gathered—a surprisingly large crowd for ten-thirty on a Wednesday morning. Wending her way through the throng, she pushed open the ornately carved doors into the plush reception area and noticed many individuals carrying cameras. And microphones. She recognized a local news anchor...and another. Why were news crews here?

"I don't care if he's busy. I'm not a reporter," insisted a tall, leggy brunette in a short black dress near the hostess stand. "I'm here on a personal matter. You tell Cole that Lacey La-Bonne wants to see him."

A stern-faced woman behind the hostess stand flatly stated that Mr. Westcott was taking no calls or visits *from anyone*.

Lacey cursed and hissed. A stocky, double-chinned man

nearly knocked Tess over to reach the curvaceous brunette. "Excuse me, Ms. LaBonne," he wheezed. "I'm Sam Stephanovich of the *Global Gazette*. Are you a friend of Cole Westcott's?"

"No, we're much closer than friends," she said with an angry sniff. "He promised to take me to St. Lucia next week. Then last night, he leaves me a message. He's postponing the trip. Not a word about his wedding. Men can be such pigs."

A cameraman aimed a lens in Lacey's direction and the reporter jotted down notes as he spoke. "So would you say his engagement was sudden?"

"I'd say it was. I'd never heard of this 'Tess McCrary' until I turned on my television this morning."

Tess shrank back into a shadowy alcove. These reporters were here because of Cole's marriage plans—and her name had been mentioned on television. Good Lord...had her father been watching?

Anxiously Tess headed for the telephone near the restrooms and called Kristen. Keeping her voice as low, she asked, "Kris, have you had the television on?"

"No. Daddy and I have been playing cards."

"Good. Don't let him near a television or a radio. Or a newspaper." After a brief explanation, she hung up and started for the exit. She had to get home and tell her father about her plans before he heard the news elsewhere.

Lacey LaBonne's voice carried beyond the reporters now surrounding her. "If Cole had dumped me for somebody *better*, I'd understand. But did you *see* the woman? She looked like a schoolmarm."

Tess winced. They'd apparently shown her photo on television. Probably the one from the university yearbook. Not the most flattering photo, but...a *schoolmarm?* Hah. Didn't Lacey LaFluff recognize a Financial Aid Director when she saw one?

As Lacey repeated her earlier sentiment, "Men can be such pigs," a bright-eyed young Jimmy Olson-type shifted into

Tess's path. "Hey," he said, his gaze narrowing. "Aren't you Tess McCrary?"

"Me?"

"She *is* Tess McCrary," confirmed an exuberant voice from her other side. With "ahs" and "ohs," the crowd converged. Lights glared in her face. Cameras flashed. Microphones jabbed toward her mouth.

"Tell me, Tess, how did Cole approach you with his marriage proposal? Were you aware of the terms of his father's will?"

"Were you acquainted with him before he proposed?"

"Did he offer you money to marry him, and if so, how much?"

"Will the marriage be in name only, or have you agreed to consummate?"

"Does he have to pay extra for that?"

Embarrassment warmed Tess's face. They were making it sound as if Cole were paying her to sleep with him. Clutching her leather handbag to her chest like a shield, she tried to think of a reply that would set them straight.

Before she'd uttered the first coherent sentence, though, a familiar broad-shouldered figure appeared at the edge of the crowd. Tess fixed her gaze on him in relief—an ally in this madness. At least, she hoped he'd be an ally. Then again, he *was* a Westcott.

She watched Cole force a path through the clamoring reporters, his sun-gilded hair glistening in the lights, his ruggedly appealing face exuding calm authority. He seemed even bigger, more muscular, more commanding, than he had yesterday in her living room. And he was headed straight for her.

Tess waded toward him, her progress hampered by the reporters who now divided their attention between him and her. Cole ignored the microphones thrust in his face, the questions shouted at him, the cameras flashing, and reached for her. She gave him her hand. He pulled her to him and slid a strong, protective arm around her. A cacophony of voices roared for his attention, but he set a steady pace toward a back archway where a burly security guard stood.

Tucked against Cole's side, Tess couldn't help wondering if the glamorous Lacey was watching. A silly thought. Unworthy of her. If Cole had had any choice, he'd have reached for Lacey. And rightfully so. What did Tess want with a low-down scheming Westcott, anyway?

"Sorry, folks, but we don't have time for questions now," Cole announced in his deep, smooth rumble of a voice. "Give me twenty minutes or so, and I'll meet you in the back dining room. I'll even spring for coffee and key-lime pie. Berta, show all card-carrying members of the media to the Magnolia Room."

A pleased murmur rippled through the crowd. Cole urged Tess past the security guard and up a carpeted flight of stairs, his arm strong and steadying around her. Her legs trembled slightly as she climbed, whether from the media's attack or Cole's overpowering nearness, she wasn't sure.

When they reached the upstairs corridor, he swept her into a large but surprisingly plain office, with worn oriental carpets on a scuffed hardwood floor, a paper-cluttered desk, oak filing cabinets, a computer and absolutely nothing to proclaim the room special except for the high, wide sliding-glass doors that led outside to a rooftop view of the harbor.

Tess immediately broke away from Cole. She leaned against the desk to catch her breath, gather her wits. She'd nearly forgotten the heady feeling of being held against a virile, muscular body; of sensing the strength coiled within a man. Or maybe she'd never known that feeling at all. Dismayed by that traitorous reflection, she assured herself that she was overreacting simply because she'd been without Phillip for so long.

Cole locked the office door and sauntered toward her with a glint of amusement in his eyes. "Hope you didn't mind my interrupting your moments of glory."

"Glory?" She welcomed the bracing rush of indignation. "You can't honestly believe I enjoyed that mass assault."

He shrugged, shifting wide shoulders beneath a soft blue chambray shirt. "Never can tell how a person's going to react to media attention. Take Ms. LaBonne, for instance. I'd say she was glorying in the spotlight, wouldn't you?"

So, he'd heard Lacey. Had he heard her comment about Tess looking like a schoolmarm? Not that it mattered. And what the heck did he expect her to say about his ditzy girlfriend, or their postponed trip to St. Lucia? "Men can be such pigs."

Cole crossed his tanned, muscular forearms and settled beside her, the back of his jeans-clad thighs resting against the desk. "So I've heard." The groove beside his mouth deepened in a lazy, appreciative smile.

Tess felt a purely feminine pull deep within her. No wonder he thought he could snap his fingers and have his enemy's daughter jump to do his bidding. That smile had probably been enslaving women from the time he'd been old enough to connive. Fortifying herself against his charm, she strolled away from him and asked briskly, "Why on earth did you agree to give that mob downstairs an interview?"

"Self-defense. If we don't talk to them, they'll interview everyone we know, everyone we've ever met, and some we haven't. Who knows what they'll say about us?"

The prospect of all that publicity made her insides clench. "How did the media get involved in this?"

"I have my suspicions. My father's will made it obvious that I'd be marrying soon. Someone probably bribed a clerk in the county marriage bureau to tip him off whenever I showed up. I applied for a license yesterday."

"But what's so newsworthy about a marriage?"

He shook his head as if the answer escaped him, but amusement glistened in his gaze. "There must be something about millions of dollars, a curse written into a will and a forced marriage between age-old adversaries that some folks consider titillating."

Tess ignored his good-natured sarcasm. His mention of "age-old adversaries" had reminded her of the reason for her visit. "Imagine their reaction when I explain that you foreclosed on my father's business loans to pressure me into marrying you."

The amusement left his gaze, and a slight flush rose beneath his tan. But he answered with his usual nonchalance, "There was nothing unethical about those foreclosures. Your father was behind in his payments."

"The loan officer admitted to me that they usually extend their grace period for a full month longer than they did for my father."

"That's merely a courtesy we allow some of our long-time borrowers."

"And my father certainly wasn't a long-time borrower of yours. You bought those loans from the original lender only weeks ago."

"Months ago. And my father bought them. I didn't."

"Oh, so he was looking ahead, was he?" She glared at him—not quite eye-level, despite her highest heels. "And you followed through by foreclosing."

"It was business. Just business."

"Yes—a maneuver designed to make the McCrary family desperate."

He pushed away from the desk and stalked closer to her. "If I'd given your father another month on those loans, would he have come up with enough money to bring them current?"

Tess hesitated. She dearly wanted to lie, but he probably knew the state of their financial affairs. "Probably not."

His gaze roamed her face. "Then I'm doing you a favor, Tess McCrary," he said softly. "You'll walk away from our marriage with a million dollars."

A million dollars.

Her throat constricted. She so needed that money. And as

much as she hated to admit it, he was right—his actions had not caused her family's desperation. Her father's poor judgement had caused his downfall, and her search for Phillip had drained her own bank account. A million dollars would make things right for her parents and give her funds to renew her search for her fiancé. But she could not, in all good conscience, ignore the questions nagging her. "I'm not sure I can go through with the marriage."

Cole's brows gathered. "What? You've already agreed. We have a deal."

"But that was before I knew the full truth about your father's will. You told me you only had Westcott Hall to lose. You never mentioned the rest of the forty million dollars. I thought I was simply helping you reclaim your home. But this...this is something much more. Who am I to say that you're the rightful heir to the estate?"

"The rightful heir?" He stared at her. "Do you mean you're ready to give up that million dollars if you determine I'm *not*?"

"What's right is right. I won't help anyone rob the deserving party."

He gaped at her as if she were some alien being. "How are you going to determine who's deserving? Do you expect me to tell you that *I* am? Do you really think that any-damn-body in the world *deserves* forty million dollars?"

Tess realized with a sense of shock that she'd managed to shake his calm. She'd somehow touched a sensitive nerve.

He gripped her elbow and steered her to the glass doors, then outside onto the rooftop that overlooked the shining green water of the harbor. He turned her away from the harbor, though, toward downtown Charleston with its historic houses, redbrick alleyways and picturesque steeples, his hands firm and controlling on her shoulders.

"Do you think I'm not aware of the poverty out there—of the families who wonder where their next meal is coming from? Do you think I don't know about the millions of people in the world who do without the most basic comforts? Am I supposed to tell you that I'm more deserving of money than they are?" The subdued passion in his voice stunned her.

"That's not what I—"

"Do you want me to tell you about charities that I've funded, or children I've sponsored, or the lives that my money has saved? Will that make me 'deserving' of forty million dollars?"

"Well, actually, that *would* weigh pretty heavily in your—"

"Even if I *could* claim that I was deserving of the cash, my inheritance is about more than just money." Tightening his grip on her shoulders, he whisked her into the office and parked her before a wall of paintings that depicted historic houses, shops, inns and plantations. "It's about places. Important historic places. Does any individual *deserve* to own pieces of America where wars were won and the country was born and history was made?" Again, his passion surprised her. "No, damn it, Tess." He dropped his hands from her. "I can't tell you that I deserve any of it."

She couldn't stop herself from watching him as he paced across the office, his face dark and troubled. This was not the Cole Westcott she'd believed him to be. Unless he simply had the knack of knowing what to say to win a woman over.

With an inner groan, she wrenched her gaze away from him. Of course he knew what to say. He'd descended from a long line of schemers and sweet talkers. As she opened her mouth to retort—just to let him know she hadn't fallen for his act—he held up a hand.

"Don't bother to answer. It doesn't matter what you say, or do, or think." He stopped before her, his gaze challenging, his masculine scent clouding her reason. "Whether I deserve my father's estate or not, I *am* going to claim it. With or without your help." His determined stare would have backed her up a step if she hadn't somehow become rooted to the spot. "So do you want that million dollars, or not?"

Tense silence settled between them.

"Of course I want it," she whispered, her gaze shifting beneath his. "But—"

"But what?"

"I have to do what's right."

Cole regarded her in utter disbelief. *She meant it.* The woman would turn down a million dollars if she decided he wasn't the rightful heir. He'd never have expected that from anybody, let alone from the McCrary who had tried to pin him to the mat during their first negotiation. How deep, he suddenly wondered, did her righteousness go? "Two million," he tested.

"Two million?" She frowned, as if confused. "You're offering me two million dollars to marry you?"

He nodded as an odd tension built within him. What answer was he hoping for—a yes or a no?

A *yes*, of course. The sooner he settled this matter, the better. The money and the property were unquestionably his. The Westcott fortune had always been there for him as one of the few constants in his life. Unlike the nannies, stepmothers, relatives—even his father—all of whom had come and gone, barely skimming the surface of his life, the house, the history and the wealth had always been there. An integral part of him. The *defining* part of him. He was the Westcott heir.

Tess McCrary was the only person he'd ever met who didn't seem to grasp the importance of that distinction. Inhaling deeply, she pressed a hand to her heart and gazed at him in wordless response to his offer.

He wondered what was going through her mind. He wondered what she'd decide. He wondered how she managed to look so feminine and vulnerable in such a business-like suit, with her hair pulled back in that uncompromising twist, her only adornment a slight glint of gold at her ears and throat. All that severity only made a man want to loosen her up. Peel away the armor. Find the softness.

"I'm afraid you don't understand." Her gaze locked with his. "It's not a matter of money."

"It's entirely a matter of money."

"Okay, maybe it is." She raised her chin—a stubborn chin with a cleft in the middle. A sexy little cleft. He imagined skimming the tip of his tongue over it...and then upward, to her mouth, her full, smooth, provocative mouth. A militant sparkle in her eyes brought him back to his senses. "But whose money should it be?" she demanded. "Yours, or your father's former wives? He named them as his heirs in the event that you don't marry a McCrary. By marrying you, I might be aiding and abetting in a gross miscarriage of justice."

He frowned. She couldn't be for real. She couldn't possibly be ready to give up millions of dollars for the sake of his wild-and-wicked stepmothers. If he wasn't so damn frustrated with her, he might have laughed at the very idea.

"It isn't always easy for an older woman to make her way in the world," she went on, "especially after she's been out of the work force for a while."

"Out of the work force?" he repeated blankly. She was obviously laboring under some serious misconceptions.

"I might not know anything about your father's wives, but I doubt that they held jobs during their marriages."

"They didn't, but—"

"Did they have children by your father? Grandchildren?"

"*Hell*, no."

"So they don't even have the comfort of family to fall back on." She looked genuinely distressed by that idea. "I only hope he allowed them enough money to piece their lives back together after he divorced them."

"What makes you think *he* divorced *them?*"

"Didn't he?"

"I believe it was by mutual agreement."

"Well." She tossed her head and arched her brows in eloquent disdain. "It couldn't have been easy, being married to a Westcott."

That set Cole's teeth on edge. Amazing, how she'd suc-

ceeded in arousing his defensiveness, his anger, his frustration—and on such short acquaintance, too. Other women had
gone to extreme lengths to engage even his shallowest emotions; he'd never allowed them access. Business associates
had also tried to push his buttons; he'd prided himself on
never reacting.

Why should he care what this woman, this business associate, tnis *McCrary*, thought of him or his family? He could
find another McCrary bride. His attorney had already collected names of a few other candidates although, admittedly,
their relationship to the original McCrary clan of Charleston
was distant. The court would have to accept them as descendants nonetheless.

He didn't really need Tess at all.

"Tell you what," he said, inexplicably loathe to let her out
of their agreement. "I'll leave it up to you to decide how
much my stepmothers should get. We'll write the amounts
into our prenuptial agreement before you leave this office today."

"Are you suggesting a compromise? I'm assuming that
you'll agree to an amount only if you retain the bulk of the estate. Your stepmothers would get—" Her scornful words
broke off when he aimed a remote control at the far wall and
panels slid open to reveal a large-screen TV.

"My assistant recorded a newscast this morning," he said.
"The media found the most outspoken of my father's ex-
wives. Or maybe I should say, she found *them*."

He played the taped interview for her. While Tess watched
his elegant blond stepmother express hope that the matter of
her late husband's will could be fairly settled—in her favor,
of course—Cole watched Tess. Would the truth make any difference to her way of thinking? Was she genuinely worried
about the welfare of these supposedly older women left in the
lurch, or did she oppose his inheriting the estate simply because he was a Westcott?

He read the surprise in Tess's face as she realized how

young and attractive the woman was. One year older than Cole, the interviewer pointed out. Diamonds flashed with her every move while she lounged in an opulent living room.

The surprise in Tess's gaze turned to dismay when the reporter asked, "According to your friends, you'd been intimately involved with his son Cole shortly before you married Harlan. Is that true?"

"We dated briefly," she hedged. Cole felt Tess's shocked gaze shift to him; he avoided looking at her. Why should it bother him, having her know about a meaningless affair that had ended the same night it had begun?

The reporter went on to paint a clear picture of Deirdre. She was Harlan Westcott's fourth wife. He'd given her over a million dollars in a divorce settlement, in accordance with their pre-nuptial agreement. She felt she deserved more.

The reporter mentioned facts about his father's other two ex-wives. Neither marriage had lasted an entire year. One woman went on to marry an eighty-year-old tycoon, and the other took the money from her divorce settlement and bought a brothel in Las Vegas.

"So, Tess... In your quest for fairness," Cole said, breaking the silence that had fallen after he'd turned off the television, "how much do you think my stepmothers should get from my father's estate?"

She turned a troubled gaze on him. "They didn't love him, did they? Any of them."

For the umpteenth time since he'd met her, Cole regarded Tess McCrary in astonishment. *Love him?* Had anybody *expected* them to? Had *anybody* perceived them as more than mere luxuries a very rich man could afford?

He remembered the first time his father had remarried, when Cole was eleven. He *had* expected from his stepmother if not love, then at least the show of warmth he'd seen between mothers and their children.

He'd almost forgotten about that disillusionment. "I don't suppose they did."

"Did he love any of them?"

Cole felt uncomfortable with her questions. Maybe because he'd never been sure of how his father had felt about anybody. "I don't know."

Something too much like sympathy filled her gaze.

Anger stirred in him. Since when did anyone have cause to pity Harlan Westcott? He'd led a full, happy life. Damn the woman. She had a way of harping on the most uncomfortable subjects.

"That's why he came to believe in the curse, wasn't it?" she theorized in an unexpectedly gentle tone. "Because he never found real love."

"Damn it all to hell, Tess, you don't know that any more than I do." But he did know it. She'd hit the nail on the head. "His wives may have provided exactly what he'd wanted, and visa versa."

"I don't see how." After a reflective silence, a cry of dismay escaped her. Cole raised his brows in question. She bit her lip and glanced away from him.

"What's wrong now?" he demanded, almost reluctant to ask.

"If I marry you, everyone will see *me* as the same kind of woman."

He squinted at her, trying his best to follow her convoluted logic. He wasn't sure understanding was humanly possible.

"Oh, I know I'm not as beautiful as one of your father's ex-wives," she amended with an impatient wave of her hand, "but all the same, people would see me as mercenary. Reporters have already asked whether we'll, um—" She cleared her throat uneasily. "—consummate the marriage."

He sensed the effort it cost her to maintain eye contact with him, and gazed at her in wonder. She, Tess of the Infamous BB Gun, found it hard to look him in the eye and talk about consummating their marriage. He found her shyness over the subject to be adorable. He found the innocence behind her shyness, behind her concern, downright irresistible.

He wanted her.

The realization hit him out of nowhere. Blind-sided him. Stunned him.

"If we allow them to believe that we *are* consummating the marriage," she went on, striving to make him understand, "the world will see me as the kind of woman who would sleep with a man for money."

"*Marry* a man for money," he corrected, aware that his voice was a little too gruff. *He wanted her.* "Women do it everyday, and nobody thinks less of them for it."

"Women sleep with men for money everyday, too. I don't want anyone thinking that *I* do." She lodged a hip against his desk and contemplated the problem.

And he contemplated the lushness of her mouth and the smooth luminosity of her skin. He wanted her.

"I'll have to set the media straight," she decided. "During your interview. I'll make it clear that this is strictly a business deal, and that we won't be sleeping together." She slanted him an anxious glance. "You'll back me up on that, won't you?"

He hesitated, hating to answer. "I'm sorry, but we can't do that."

"What?" Her expressive eyes widened. "Why not? Of course we can."

"Listen to me, Tess." He gave in to an urge and caught her by the shoulders—soft, firm, slender shoulders. "There's forty million dollars at stake. My father's ex-wives are going to try to have our marriage declared invalid. Their attorney will use any technicality he can find. That's why we can't announce to the world that we don't intend to live as husband and wife. The court might decide we're not really married."

"Are you saying that we have to let everyone think that you... That I..."

"...are married, in every sense of the word."

A blush heated her cheeks. "But everyone will know we're marrying to satisfy the will. And they're bound to realize you're paying me to do it. I can't stand the idea of having everyone think that I'm *sleeping* with you for financial reasons."

And he couldn't stand the idea that she might not sleep with him at all. "Then we'll have to convince them otherwise, won't we?" At her puzzled look, he clarified, "We'll make them believe we're in love."

"In love? Oh, come on. Who's going to believe that?"

Her scorn wasn't exactly flattering. But she had a point. Even under the best of circumstances, a woman like her would never really *fall in love* with a man like him. She belonged to that class of deeply honorable women, most of whom weren't model beautiful, famous or notably rich. Women who valued family, friends and personal integrity more than fortunes. He'd realized such women existed, in an almost mystical realm, as far he was concerned. He hadn't personally known of many, and none in his own generation.

Those women seemed to share an understanding that Westcott men lacked whatever it took to earn true devotion. Like his father and grandfather, Cole would never win a good woman's heart, which was why Fate had blessed them with wealth. A simple matter of compensation.

It hadn't been such a bad deal.

But now he wanted more by way of compensation. He wanted Tess McCrary. "I guess we'll just have to be convincing."

Tess stared at him, thoroughly unnerved by his suggestion. It seemed such a dangerous, foolhardy thing to do, pretending to be in love with Cole Westcott. She struggled to find her voice and hoped he wouldn't notice her breathlessness. "Don't you think they'll think it's a little too coincidental that your father's will demands you marry a McCrary and a McCrary suddenly falls in love with you?"

A smoky warmth smouldered in his gaze. "It could happen."

Tess was suddenly very afraid that it could.

3

"COME ON, TESS." With that smoky sensuality warming his gaze and roughening his voice, Cole released his hold on her shoulders, slid his hands in a lingering path down her arms and caught her hands in his. "Let's go meet our public." His slow, roguish smile only worsened her inner havoc. "Let's show them how much we've, uh, fallen in love."

Her sense of self-preservation urged her to snatch her hands away and run from him as fast as she could. But her practical side wouldn't allow it. He was right about the danger of ignoring the media. Better to spread the news he and she had manufactured than fuel the random gossip that might be brewing.

She supposed her cooperation in this interview told him clearly enough that she intended to go through with their deal. Though Tess hadn't exactly told Cole, she *had* made up her mind to help him claim his inheritance. She didn't want to see him lose his home and the historic properties he felt such surprising passion for. Had he manipulated her into taking his side? Had she fallen victim to the infamous Westcott charm?

He seemed to assume her acceptance as a natural turn of events. Did his assumption stem from his vast experience with women, or did he believe he'd bought her cooperation with his offer of two million dollars? Or...worse yet...did he somehow sense her bewildering response to him, which heated her blood and undermined her resolve whenever he gazed at her in a certain way?

She hadn't much time to reflect on those disturbing questions. Within moments they were entering the luxurious Magnolia Room; her hand was firmly encased in his larger, stronger one. Reporters and cameramen immediately jumped to attention, but didn't mob them, at least. A woman stepped forward and led them to the piazza where a camera crew posed them against a wrought iron railing. A breathtaking view of the harbor and the morning sky was the perfect backdrop.

When video cameras were strategically placed, and a brace of microphones erected before them, the interview began.

Tess had a hard time focusing on the questions, which were mercifully aimed at Cole. He had released her hand and slipped an arm around her shoulders. He slanted her frequent glances, all backlit with an alluring mix of warmth, humor and devilment. He called her "honey," as if they'd been a couple for quite some time.

"No," he was saying in calm response to a question, "you have the wrong impression. I'm not marrying Tess because of my father's will. We're in love."

Brows shot up. Mocking glances were exchanged. Tess inwardly cringed, wishing she could crawl beneath a carpet and tunnel her way to an exit. Why had Cole ever thought anyone would buy their "love" story? They would be portrayed to the world as liars and schemers.

"The truth is..." Cole continued, unfazed by the expressions of disbelief, "my father put the stipulation in his will because he knew how much I've always loved Tess McCrary."

Tess turned her head to gape at him. The man was simply too creative for comfort—and in an "evil genius" kind of way.

"I'm not saying my past relationship with Tess was ideal," he expounded. "Far from it. This McCrary woman can be damn stubborn when it comes to wanting things her way. And believe me...she wants *everything* her way."

She opened her mouth in protest. Even in this honey-sweet charade, he'd found a way to slam her. But two could play at *that* game. Let him finesse his way out *this*. With the image of Lacey LaBonne in mind, Tess smiled and retorted, "Leave it to a Westcott to think that fidelity is an unreasonable request."

He crooked a brow in clear discomfort. He *had* to remember Lacey's "gloryin' in the spotlight" less than an hour ago— ranting about the postponed trip to St. Lucia. "Aw, honey, we're not going to discuss *that* on camera, are we?"

"Not if you don't want to...honey." To their audience, she said, "See? I let him have his way now and then."

Their banter won a few grins. Tess began to relax. Maybe they *could* pull this off.

Overriding a chorus of questions—many concerning the role fidelity would play in their marriage—Cole went on with unperturbed self-assurance, "Tess and I might not see eye-to-eye about everything, but my father believed we'd never be happy without each other. He tried for months to persuade us to put aside our differences. The stipulation in his will was his final attempt to force our hands." His mouth curved in that wry smile Tess was coming to know. "I suppose Westcott men *can* be as stubborn as McCrary women." His gaze shifted to her—a warm, worshipful gaze. "Thank God for my father's stubbornness. He knew Tess wouldn't want to see me homeless. She can't find it in her heart to turn me down now."

She would have backed away in sheer self-defense if he hadn't been holding her pinned to his side, his muscular arm corralling her. My, oh my! The man was too good at lying— and not only with his words. Her very heart thumped out a warning. *Beware! Beware!*

The reporters, she realized, scribbled madly on their notepads. Cameras flashed from all angles. The excitement level had risen palpably. At least, Tess believed it had. Or maybe it was only her own chaotic response to this silver-tongued scoundrel....

"Tess," came the next question from the teeming mass of

reporters, "how did you feel when you learned about the stipulation in Harlan Westcott's will?"

"Surprised." She hoped they didn't ask her too many questions. She was still unreasonably shaken...and not nearly as good at lying as her alleged fiancé was.

"How long have you known Cole?"

She glanced at him uncertainly. When in doubt, she'd always believed in sticking as closely as possible to the truth. "We were young teenagers when we met."

"How did you meet?"

"His boat capsized in the river near my house. We met in the woods." A sense of irony provoked her to add, "I believe I had a strong impact on him, right from the start."

Acknowledgement sparked in his eyes, and she knew that he, too, was remembering that BB. "She really did get under my skin. Made a lasting impression."

The rogue!

"And you've been dating since then?" a reporter asked, clearly incredulous.

"Not continuously," Cole replied. "We went our separate ways for years. But, as they say, absence makes the heart grow fonder." He threw her off-balance with yet another meltingly tender stare. "When I saw her again, I knew she was the only woman for me. It just took me a while to convince *her* of that."

Amid murmurs of amusement—and the ridiculous pounding of Tess's heart—another reporter piped up, "Why no engagement ring, Tess?"

She stared at the reporter blankly. With a three-day engagement period, why would anyone expect an engagement ring? Of course, with the story Cole had just fabricated, no one knew that she'd basically met him for the first time two days ago, other than the day she'd shot him.

Cole didn't disappoint, though. "She hasn't picked a ring out yet. We have the choice narrowed down to twenty three."

More laughter rippled around them.

From the back of the room, someone called out, "What can you tell us about the curse your father added to his will?"

The abrupt change of subject jarred Tess.

"Curse?" Cole repeated. She felt him stiffen, but he smiled with his usual charm. "Just a private joke between my father and me."

"Is it true that the curse was placed on both families by a McCrary daughter in the nineteenth century when she was prevented from marrying a Westcott son?"

"I believe I did hear a version of the same tale."

"Excuse me, Mr. Westcott, Ms. McCrary," said the stocky reporter who had earlier introduced himself to Lacy La-Bonne. "I did a study of your family histories dating back to when that curse was written in 1825." Everyone fell silent. "Did either of you know that since that time, not one Westcott marriage or romantic relationship has lasted beyond a year, and not one McCrary family has remained together without losing a loved one to tragedy?"

The revelations stunned Tess. She'd known that her own branch of the family had suffered an excessive number of tragedies—deaths, injuries, disappearances. Her parents hadn't remained untouched; they'd lost a child to illness before Tess had been born. But she hadn't realized that tragedy had been stalking *every* family related to her, and for so many generations. She also hadn't been aware of the Westcotts' difficulties. No marriages had lasted beyond a year...*since 1825?*

Cole uttered a short laugh. "I've never paid much attention to superstition. As far as the Westcott family's poor performance in the marriage department goes, I've been told that it has more to do with character flaws than curses. Though, of course, I can't imagine what those character flaws could possibly be." He tipped a winsome, roguish smile at the cameras, and laughter from his audience lightened the mood.

Tess couldn't share in that laughter. If the reporter's facts were correct—and she intended to check them—both families had suffered for over a hundred and seventy years!

The curse means nothing, she told herself. *Nothing.*

"Ms. McCrary, how do you feel about the curse?" prodded Sam.

She forced a smile. "I think it's a fascinating bit of historical trivia. Stories handed down from generation to generation always interest me."

"So you don't believe the curse is responsible for your family's tragedies?"

"Of course not." But she felt as if she were lying.

"Isn't it true that you were engaged to Professor Phillip Mattingly last year, and that he disappeared without a trace while on an anthropological study?"

The air left her lungs, and she felt the warmth drain from her face. *Phillip.* They knew about Phillip. "Y-yes," she replied, her voice weak and unsteady, "but I'm sure his disappearance had nothing to do with—"

"What do you believe happened to him, ma'am?"

She stared in distress at the beady-eyed, ruddy-faced reporter. "I don't know." Anxiety and desolation swept over her. *Had the curse caused Phillip's disappearance?* Had he suffered—or was he suffering even now—simply because she'd loved him? Had she been wrong to form an emotional bond...to cast him in the role of her "loved one"?

Cole tightened his arm around her. "That's all the questions we'll have time for today. Thank you for coming. Berta will show you all to the door."

"Were you in love with Mattingly, Tess?"

"If he showed up tomorrow, would you still marry Cole?"

"If he's listening to this broadcast, is there anything you'd like to say to him?"

Each question stuck in her heart like a poison dart.

Cole drew her to him in a protective embrace; cradled her against his chest; sheltered her with both arms from the prying eyes and merciless cameras. His heart beat forcefully beneath her ear; his body heat engulfed her. "I said no more questions." Steel had replaced the velvet in his voice. "Bruno and Tyrone, can you please help our media friends gather their equipment and accompany them to the door?''

She heard the grumbles, the disappointed groans and, after a while, the terse urgings to "hurry it along, pal." She didn't lift her head or move as much as a muscle. She needed to calm herself, to gather her poise.

She hadn't been thinking about Phillip at all when she'd agreed to this interview. *If he's listening to this broadcast, is there anything you'd like to say to him?* She hadn't thought of that possibility. But if he were able to watch a television or read a newspaper, wouldn't he also be able to call her? If that were possible, he would do it. She knew Phillip enough to be sure of that.

No, something terrible must have happened to him.

Because of the curse?

An insidious voice within her whispered, *If the curse is real, more tragedies will happen until you marry a Westcott.* Her sister Kristen and her fiancé Josh would be marrying next month. They were so starry-eyed. So much in love. So deserving of a "happy ever after."

Nothing bad will happen to them. The curse isn't real.

And she *would* be marrying a Westcott, two days from now.

"Tess," Cole whispered into her hair, "are you okay?"

She drew in a deep breath and forced a calm she didn't feel. "Yes, I'm...I'm fine." Pulling from his embrace, she avoided meeting his gaze. Had she really hidden her face against his chest until everyone had left? "I, um, just hadn't expected them to know so much about my...my personal life." She turned away, needing to escape.

"Tess." He caught her arm, and reluctantly she turned back to face him. She wasn't sure what she expected to see in his eyes, but no levity remained. "This guy, Phillip. Do you..." he paused, looking hesitant and concerned. "Do you think you should tell me about him? I mean, is there anything I should know before we—"

"There's nothing you need to know about him." She hadn't

meant to sound so sharp, but she couldn't talk about Phillip now, especially not with Cole. She couldn't bear to have him make light of Phillip's disappearance or mock her in any way.

"You *are* going to marry me," he said softly, his gaze somber and watchful, "aren't you?"

"Yes." She averted her face by reaching for her purse on a nearby table. "I'll send you the signed prenuptial agreement this afternoon," she said, struggling to regain equal footing with him. She'd made such a fool of herself, clinging to him the way she had.

"Good. I'm headed out of town on business, but my assistant will be waiting for it."

She nodded without comment. Without meeting his gaze.

Cole suddenly wished he didn't have to leave town. The furor of the media and the vulnerability she'd shown had left him feeling edgy. Protective. He had no choice, though. The business couldn't be put off.

He watched her slip the strap of her purse over one slender shoulder, straighten her gray suit jacket—which exactly matched her eyes—and smooth her vivid auburn hair, though not a strand had escaped the elegant twist. "Tess," he called after her as she moved toward the door, "what's your ring size?"

He expected her to turn back to him with a question about their wedding rings, or some pithy comment, or at least the hint of a smile. She did not.

"Five and a half," she replied, not sparing him as much as a gaze. She then strode from the dining room in her high spiked heels and tailored suit, brisk and untouchable, armed with the cool aplomb of a seasoned executive.

Cole instructed a security guard to escort her to her car.

In something of a daze, then, he headed for his office. Her sudden switch from soft and vulnerable to Iron Maiden had his head in a spin. But the armour she'd drawn over herself didn't make him forget how she'd huddled in his arms, fighting off tears.

Her vulnerability had to do with Phillip Mattingly. Professor Phillip Mattingly. She'd been engaged to him, it seemed. He'd disappeared.

Were you in love with Mattingly, Tess? the reporters had asked her. *If he showed up tomorrow, would you marry Cole?* It hadn't taken a genius to see the pain on her face. It hadn't taken a psychic to feel her misery.

She still loved the guy.

Just another potential complication, Cole told himself. A possible inconvenience. But as long as she went through with the ceremony this Friday and lived at Westcott Hall for the next five months, it didn't matter how she felt about another man. *It didn't matter.*

Why the hell, then, did he feel as if he'd been sucker-punched in the gut?

THE FIRST WARNING of trouble was the Closed sign hanging on the door of the shop when Tess returned. Her mother wouldn't have closed if it hadn't been necessary. Foreboding rode heavily in Tess's chest as she unlocked the door and hurried inside. Had her father learned of her impending marriage and suffered another heart attack?

Before she reached the telephone, she found a note her mother had left near the cash register. *Meet me at the emergency room.*

Apprehension pulsed through her as she drove. She prayed the crisis was minor. If her deal with Cole had given her father a fatal heart attack, she'd never forgive herself.

"Tess, oh, Tess!" Her distraught mother rushed to her the moment she stepped into the emergency room of the busy urban hospital. The paleness of her face and the fear in her eyes sent Tess's heart plunging. "You were right. We should have told your father ourselves. A friend of his called him and asked about you and that Westcott boy. Kristen couldn't stop him from turning on the television and watching the news."

"Oh, no." Self-blame sliced through Tess. "I can't believe

he heard about the marriage that way. Did he have a heart attack? Is he—"

"He's in traction."

Tess blinked. "Traction?"

"But that's not the worst of it." Margaret drew Tess to a private corner of the emergency room and related in an urgent undertone, "Kristen said that after he watched the news, he got into his pickup truck and said he was going to straighten things out with Westcott. She couldn't stop him, so she called Josh. Josh found him at Westcott Hall."

Tess felt herself blanch. "Daddy went to Westcott Hall?" She knew how explosive his temper had been lately, and how much he hated the Westcotts. Had Cole returned home from his restaurant to find her father waiting for him? But no, Cole had said he was heading out of town. "So what happened, Mama?"

"Josh found him outside the gate of Westcott Hall, arguing with a security guard." Her mother's voice was tight with barely constrained tears. "He was demanding to see Cole, and the guard told him Cole was out of town. Ian didn't believe him, and said something derogatory about the Westcotts. You know how he always does. The guard said *he* was a Westcott—Cole's cousin—and ordered him off the property. Ian said he was on a public road, not private property, and he wasn't leaving. The guard threatened to have his truck towed for being illegally parked. Ian threatened to get his gun."

"Dear God. He didn't pull that old hunting rifle out of his truck, did he?"

"No, but Josh was afraid he would. So Josh went to the truck to get the rifle and hide it in his own car. But then the guard saw Josh with the rifle and drew his gun."

Tess gasped, afraid to even imagine the outcome.

"Ian lunged at him to stop him from shooting, and Josh jumped in to stop the fight. Before they knew it, the guard's gun went off. Then the cops pulled up with their sirens wailing. Your father couldn't stand up because his back went out. He'll probably be in traction for weeks. But the worst of it is—" Margaret's voice broke and her eyes filled with tears "—Josh was shot."

Horror washed through Tess. "Shot?"

"The bullet's in his hip. He's being prepped for surgery now. Kristen's with him."

Tess sat down, her legs suddenly weak. "Do the doctors think he'll be okay?"

"They're not sure." Margaret sat beside her, white-faced. "Even if the damage isn't permanent, he's in serious trouble. Both Josh and your father were arrested."

"Arrested?" Sick with anxiety, Tess closed her eyes, wishing she didn't have to hear any more. "What were they charged with?"

"That Westcott guard turned out to be an off-duty policeman. They were charged with assaulting an officer with a deadly weapon. They could be sent to prison."

As the horror of the situation crested over her, filling her with dread, a realization hit Tess. *It was happening.* Two more loved ones of the McCrarys would be sacrificed to tragedy.

"The rifle wasn't even loaded," her mother said with a sob. "He never keeps it loaded unless he's hunting. But with our luck, they'll be convicted anyway, both him and Josh. I just know it."

Tess knew it, too. She felt it in her bones. Her father and Josh would be sent to prison. Her father would probably die there. Her mother would pine away in grief. Josh would suffer through a living hell and be branded a convict—and possibly lose the use of his legs from the bullet wound. Kristen's heart would break.

Not one McCrary family has remained together without losing a loved one to tragedy...since 1825....

The curse, she realized, might not be to blame. As a rational, educated woman, she couldn't say that it was. But as a

McCrary daughter facing yet more devastating heartbreak, she couldn't say for certain that it wasn't.

Which meant that she had to do everything necessary to lift that godforsaken curse, just in case it was real.

At least Fate had been fair enough to give her the chance to fulfill the curse's demand. She'd be marrying "Westcott of Westcott Hall" in two days time. She would allow nothing, but nothing, to get in the way of those plans.

THE MEDIA ARDENTLY embraced the news that Tess McCrary's father and an accomplice had been arrested trying to force their way into Westcott Hall with a gun. The long-standing animosity between the Westcotts and the McCrarys was rehashed ad nauseum. Photos of her father and Josh appeared on newscasts throughout the day, along with snippets from the interview she and Cole had given that morning—mostly shots of Cole drawing her against his chest in a protective stance and glaring at the cameras.

Reporters, friends, mere acquaintances and complete strangers telephoned, e-mailed and attempted to visit. McCrary cousins and uncles left angry messages in support of her father and raging against "those damn Westcotts." A crowd gathered in the parking lot of her apartment complex until security chased them off.

Tess felt like a fox running from a pack of hounds. She was glad that Kristen and her mother were staying at the hospital for the night. At least they'd have their privacy guarded by hospital staff. They were both frantic with worry, as was Tess. The bullet had been removed from Josh's hip, but the surgeon said it could take days before he'd know if Josh had sustained lasting damage.

Her father, meanwhile, remained stretched out in traction. He refused to speak to anyone in his immediate family other than to mutter that they'd betrayed him.

Tess tried to break through his stubborn silence. "I understand why you're angry, Daddy. I'm sorry I didn't tell you about the marriage. But it's just a business deal, and we're getting millions of dollars for it...and McCrary Place." His profile remained mulish. "Now that you're in legal trouble, you'd better pretend you're happy about the marriage. The prosecutor will have a hard time convincing a jury that you assaulted the guard if they believe you were visiting Cole on a friendly basis."

His face mottled. His lips curled. His nostrils flared.

Her mother hurried Tess away from his bedside. As upsetting as his anger was, she supposed it was better that he wasn't speaking to her. No amount of his ranting would stop her from going through with this wedding.

Forcing herself to focus on necessary details, Tess sent the signed prenuptial agreement to Cole, then spent the rest of that afternoon posting bail to keep the police from transferring her father and Josh to jail. Her mother had to put up her home as collateral for the bond. Tess took out a loan with her own car as collateral to retain a defense attorney.

And through it all, she tried to get in touch with Cole via his secretary. He responded by leaving messages for her on her home phone—simple requests for *her* to call *him*. The number he'd left was constantly busy, probably with the same glut of calls she'd been experiencing. A chaotic, hit-and-miss game of phone tag ensued.

The game was complicated by the fact that she spent many hours that evening at the hospital with her mother and Kristin. Her father gave the hospital strict orders to put no calls through to his room, which prevented Cole from reaching Tess there. Josh remained in the Intensive Care Unit, where calls were not accepted.

By the time she returned home late that night, Tess settled for leaving a message on Cole's voice mail explaining what had happened—and that her father's gun hadn't been loaded—and asking if he'd intercede on their behalf. Maybe he could talk to his cousin, the security guard, and persuade him that Ian McCrary hadn't been assaulting him. *Hey, Cuz, remember that old McCrary cuss and the kid with the rifle who jumped you? They're really not so bad...*

Tess groaned out loud and stared miserably at the ceiling as she lay in bed.

The guard was probably like all the other Westcotts—a McCrary hater—and couldn't wait to put one behind bars. And if, by some miracle, Cole *did* get him to agree to have the charges dropped, her father just might turn around and sue the security guard for injuring him and Josh. Cole himself might be held liable, too, since the guard had been working for him. All facts considered, Cole and his cousin would be better protected by having Ian McCrary convicted.

What a mess.

It was a good thing they'd planned to marry in a civil ceremony—a quick signing of papers with no pomp or celebration to complicate matters. She could just imagine the problems that might arise if they invited family or even friends. With grim humor, she wondered what the etiquette books had to say about *that* situation. Should a note be included in the wedding invitations asking guests to please refrain from drawing weapons or engaging in fist-fights during the ceremony, or should a bouncer be situated between the bride's side of the room and the groom's?

No, emotions were running too high in her family to invite anyone to the wedding ceremony—and her father would see to it that those emotions ran even higher. Anyone who attended the ceremony would be branded a traitor for life. She imagined the same contentious emotions might be escalating in Cole's family.

For all Cole knew, her father really was out to get him. She wouldn't blame him if he changed his mind about marrying her. He could probably find another McCrary bride. He had that evil-genius thing going for him.

But would marriage to another McCrary woman—one who wasn't as closely connected to the original McCrary clan of Charleston—satisfy the curse?

Listen to yourself, Tess…rambling on about curses. How crazy it sounded. As much as she tried to talk some sense into herself, though, she couldn't ignore even the slightest possibility that the curse might be valid. Too much tragedy had stalked her family for too many generations. Too much heartbreak loomed in the future.

If Cole decided on another McCrary bride, he might satisfy the terms of his father's will, but not necessarily the curse. She couldn't allow him to change his mind about marrying her.

She also needed the money now more than ever. Medical and legal bills were accruing. How could she turn down money when two men's futures might depend on having plenty of it? *Three* men's futures. Phillip hadn't been found yet. With only a widowed mother on a fixed income and a younger brother in college, he had no one else to pay for the search efforts.

With these pressing financial needs in mind, she'd written "two million dollars" into the prenuptial contract. Cole had, after all, offered that amount. But now she felt guilty for having accepted so much, as if she'd succumbed to a bribe. She wondered if Cole thought of her acceptance in that light. Did he believe she'd set aside her reservations about the marriage because he'd established her price?

Burying her face in a pillow, she chastised herself for caring what he thought. As long as he went through with the ceremony on Friday, lived up to their agreement and fulfilled the terms of that curse, it didn't matter what he thought about her.

Even so, she fell asleep craving communication with him.

Early the next morning, the doorbell rang. She peeked out, expecting to see reporters or other unwanted visitors. To her surprise, a deliveryman stood there with a huge bouquet. Two dozen long-stem roses, and a small silvery gift-wrapped box.

She accepted the velvety red flowers, breathed in their cool, misty fragrance and waited until the deliveryman left before opening the card. *I'll do everything I can.* C.

A ridiculous sheen rose to her eyes. She wasn't even certain why. The drama of the past two days had obviously unhinged her. The man was only a business associate. A money-making vehicle. An element necessary in lifting the curse. A pleasure-seeking, shallow-hearted playboy.

Not an ally. Not a friend. Certainly not a lover.

Glad that she'd kept her perspective regarding him, she opened the gift-wrapped package. Inside a velvet-covered ring box sat a dazzling diamond engagement ring.

Size five-and-a-half. A perfect fit.

Business, she reminded herself with only a touch of desperation. All of this interaction with Cole Westcott was merely business.

She would not lose sight of that fact.

4

COLE CALLED HER later that afternoon, when she returned from work, the day before their wedding. She kept the phone call brief, to the point, focusing entirely on the problem her father had incited.

"I'm sorry, Tess. As long as my cousin Leo insists your father and Josh attacked him, the D.A. can and probably will press charges. I can't advise Leo to say that the whole thing was a misunderstanding. There's the matter of a bullet in Josh's hip. Any compromise on Leo's part could leave him open to lawsuits, and maybe Leo's being fired from the police force."

She appreciated his honesty. And she knew he spoke the truth—a compromise would open them to potential legal problems. As much as she wanted to, she couldn't swear that her father and Josh *wouldn't* sue Leo, and possibly Cole himself.

He repeated the reassurance he'd given earlier in his note. "I'll do what I can."

She thanked him, careful to keep her tone business-like. Though she uttered a bland acknowledgement that she *had* received the ring he'd sent, she did not thank him for it. She would consider it a prop necessary in their charade.

She didn't mention the roses at all. They'd affected her too deeply. And the warmth in his compellingly masculine voice stirred unwanted reactions within her. How would she ever make it through the next five months as his wife?

The only way to maintain her sanity was to discourage personal interaction of any kind.

On Friday, therefore, the day of her wedding, she dressed in a neat beige suit, twisted her hair into a no-nonsense chignon and slipped into a pair of sensible pumps. She refused to soften her appearance with flowers, pearls or any other adornment that might give Cole the idea that she considered this ceremony to be an actual wedding.

It was a business transaction. Nothing more.

She packed a light suitcase to take with her to Westcott Hall. Cole had made it clear that she was to "move in" to Westcott Hall directly after the ceremony. She understood the necessity of spending her nights there—to convince the court that they were living as husband and wife. But she would leave the majority of her possessions here, in the apartment she shared with Kristen. Her life wouldn't actually change much at all...except, of course, for her nights.

Her nights. Ridiculous, how the very thought flustered her. The marriage would be in name only, of course, and she'd have a private suite in Westcott Hall. She doubted that Cole himself would spend many evenings at home. She had no idea, then, why her blood rushed at the idea of sleeping under his roof. *Because it isn't natural for a McCrary to live at Westcott Hall.* Any McCrary would be nervous, venturing into that hostile territory.

She calmed herself by thinking about the wedding rather than the nights following it. The ceremony was set for late afternoon. Because of the media attention, Cole had changed its location from the courthouse to a small country chapel. Security arrangements would be simpler there, he believed. He was also sending a car for her.

She planned to spend her morning at the bridal shop. If reporters plagued her, she'd shut the doors and finish taking inventory. No sense in wasting a business day.

With her small suitcase in hand, she paused at the door of her apartment. The crowd of journalists and cameramen had doubled in size since yesterday. Holding her breath, she descended the steps and strode to her car. They shouted questions, followed her with video cameras and snapped photos.

A caravan of vehicles trailed her car through town.

It was then, as she parked in front of her parents' quaint, downtown shop, that she realized she could turn this media frenzy to some advantage. Her family was in the bridal clothing business, and she was about to be a bride. A widely televised bride, from the looks of it. Her parents could never afford to pay for such extensive exposure for the Belles & Brides Boutique.

Glad for the distraction the idea provided, Tess called her mother away from her father's bedside, where he continued to ignore family members. She also summoned Lianna, one of her dearest friends since elementary school, to help with her hair—and because she badly needed someone with Lianna's optimism to lend her moral support.

When her allies arrived, Tess chose a simple gown of rich ivory satin with an off-the-shoulder neckline, a soft basque waist and full, box-pleated skirt trimmed in delicate pearl appliques. Her mother, who specialized in alterations, took in a quick tuck at the waist to insure a perfect fit.

Lianna then worked her magic with scissors, a comb and a curling iron while she and Tess indulged in a heart-to-heart about the latest developments in their lives. Tess's part of the discussion centered around her dealings with the endlessly infuriating Cole Westcott. An hour flew by, and by the end of it, Lianna had caught Tess's hair up in a cluster of loose curls with a few tendrils trailing in seeming abandon. She finished by weaving a tiara of pearls and blossoms through the artful disarray.

Even Kristen helped with the preparations, tearing herself away from Josh's bedside long enough to bring Tess a pearl necklace and earrings from home.

By five o'clock, Tess stood in the dressing room of the shop and gazed with surprise into the mirrors surrounding her. She barely recognized herself. She'd been transformed from a plain-Jane businesswoman into...well, a fairly spectacular bride. Amazing what a gown, pearls and an abundance of lustrous curls could do for a girl.

When her amazement faded, another emotion welled up unexpectedly—a strong, almost painful wistfulness. She'd dreamt for so long of the day she would wear a gown like this, celebrating the wonder of a life-long commitment, and beginning her life anew as wife of the man she loved.

Today was not that day. Phillip would not be her groom, and though she refused to admit defeat, she had to realistically face the fact that she might never see him again. The sense of melancholy grew too overpowering, and she forcefully subdued it. She would not think about Phillip or the wedding that hadn't taken place last year. She would concentrate on the business at hand.

The business at hand. Her marriage to Cole Westcott.

Apprehension knotted her stomach. What would he think when he saw her? With his ego, he'd think she'd gone to extremes to impress him. Or worse, that she viewed this wedding as a real one; that it meant more to her than it should.

"Relax." Lianna slipped into the dressing room with an encouraging smile, her dark eyes warm and dreamy. "You look incredible. You'll knock his socks off."

Tess shot her friend a fond but exasperated glance. "If you're talking about Cole, I don't care about knocking his socks off...or any other part of his attire, for that matter. Haven't you been listening? This is business, Li. Just business. I'm going to speak to the press right outside the display window of the boutique, where the cameras will pick up the name of the shop."

"Yeah, yeah, good plan. But getting back to Cole and his, uh, *removable* attire..." Lianna's mouth curled in a naughty half-grin and she arched one tawny brow. "You've got to admit it's an intriguing idea. Even if he wasn't ridiculously rich, he's got those bedroom eyes, and that tight muscular build, and all that thick, silky hair that makes a woman just want to—"

"Lianna, *please*," Tess begged. She'd forgotten Lianna's tendency to drool over handsome men. "I'm well aware of what the guy looks like." *And sounds like. Smells like. Feels like....* "But there's nothing personal between us."

"You keep saying that, but I can't believe it. The two of you were so cute together on the newscast. And the way he stared at you...mmm...I don't know how you didn't just *melt*."

"I've already told you, he was putting on an act. We did that bit about being in love only because I didn't want everyone believing I was sleeping with him for the money. I barely know him. The marriage will be in name only, and this is strictly a business deal. Can't we just leave it at that?"

"Gosh, I hope not," Lianna muttered with a dejected shake of her light brown mop of spiral curls. "You'll have a great opportunity to get to know him."

"In case you're forgetting, I'm in love with someone else."

Lianna winced, bit her bottom lip, and studied Tess with troubled concern. "So you still think Phillip will come back?"

Tess drew in a pained breath and concentrated on straightening her pearls. She wouldn't think about Phillip now—not when she was dressed as a bride, and he wasn't her groom. They'd had so many plans for their wedding, their future. "I pray he will."

"How long are you going to put your life on hold," demanded Lianna, "hoping for this miracle? Phillip's been gone for over a year, with no word to anyone. And you haven't even dated. Get on with living, Tess. You're being thrown together in wedlock with this gorgeous hunk of manhood. Why not open your mind to the possibilities? I think you should pack one of those fabulous negligees you have here in the shop—the one in candlelight lace, I think—and wear it tonight. See where things lead."

Tess knew exactly where such insanity would lead—to an intolerable situation. She couldn't imagine anything more debasing than becoming one of Cole's many women, especially when she would have to live at his house for the next five months. An otherwise casual fling would be dragged out into awkwardness. Besides, she never had been capable of casual flings. She'd been with one man, and one man only. It would take more than a sexy, gorgeous, velvet-voiced millionaire to change that.

But oh...the thought of going to bed with him *did* make her heart pump harder. "Forget about the negligee," she told Lianna. "Cole has his women, and I...I have my memories of Phillip to keep me warm until he comes home."

Lianna opened her mouth to argue, but Tess's mother appeared at the door of the dressing room. "The limo is here," she announced with an air of excitement, despite the anxious shadows beneath her eyes. "And two big young fellas who look like bodyguards are waiting to escort you."

"Thanks, Mama." Tess's heart thumped in a maddening tattoo. She turned to Lianna and squeezed her hands. "And thanks for your help, too, Li. If this were my real wedding, you know that you and Kristen would be there at the altar with me."

"I can meet you at the chapel in a jiffy. You need someone at the altar with you. Won't take me but a minute to run home and change...."

"No." Tess shook her head emphatically. "The media won't be allowed inside the chapel grounds, so there's no need to carry on the pretense inside. This isn't a real wedding, and I don't want you or anyone else I love getting confused about that fact. Besides, you don't want to get on my father's bad side, do you? If you, Mama or Kristen attend the ceremony, you'll be branded as traitors for life."

Lianna assured her she could deal with her father's wrath—and that she wouldn't get confused about the nature of the marriage—but Tess prevailed. "Okay," Lianna acquiesced. "I'll be there in spirit, though...even if it's just to ogle your groom." With a rueful smile, she ushered Tess from the dressing room. "Oh, and don't worry about your suitcase. I'll give it to the bodyguards."

"Don't forget your flowers." Her mother handed her the fragrant bouquet of lavender cattleya orchids, pink roses, and white lilacs that a florist friend had sent. With a quivering lip, Margaret whispered, "Oh, honey, you look so beautiful. I only wish—"

"It's okay, Mama." She hugged her mother, then turned abruptly toward the exit, dismayed at the tightening in her own throat. This wasn't a real wedding. The fact that she was dressed as a bride, though, seemed to be confusing the issue—even in her own mind. This would never do!

Two strapping young men in suits and ties nodded politely and fell into place beside her. Summoning her poise and reclaiming her perspective, Tess breathed deeply, then stepped outside onto the city sidewalk, into the balmy May afternoon.

A roar of questions from the reporters assailed her, reminding her of her immediate purpose. She paused beside the display window, just beneath the shop's tastefully gilded sign. "I'd like to say that, contrary to rumors, my parents couldn't be more delighted that I'm marrying Cole Westcott. If it wasn't for my father's recent back injury, he'd be escorting me down the aisle today. As it is, he and my mother are sending me off with their best wishes, and my grandmother's wedding pearls—" she touched the antique strand at her throat "—and one of the finest gowns from their new spring collection here at Belles and Brides Boutique."

With a careful turn so the cameras could focus on the graceful folds of the satin gown swirling around her, she proceeded to the gleaming white stretch limo where a uniformed driver held open the rear door.

She hoped the limo wouldn't turn into a pumpkin. At least, not while the cameras were rolling.

SHE WAS LATE. Cole stood at the top of the chapel's stone stairway and gazed across the lawn at the oak-canopied driveway, resisting the urge to pace.

Inside the chapel waited the preacher and Cole's witnesses for the ceremony. He had chosen two well-respected political supporters of powerful South Carolina judges, just in case a question should be raised regarding the legality of this marriage. He'd seen no reason to choose family or friends, or to invite personal guests. This wasn't a social occasion, but a business transaction.

What was keeping Tess?

Had the media attention caused problems? He himself had been hassled, followed and photographed every time he'd stepped outside. And though he'd stationed guards at the gate of the chapel grounds, a few journalists had perched themselves along the wrought iron fence, their zoom lenses ready. He suspected a few may have jumped the fence and now lay in wait behind the bushes.

Cole paced across the chapel's porch, his eyes peeled for the limo's arrival. Maybe he should have gone to get Tess himself. He'd considered it, but his presence at her parents' business would have shown defiant disrespect for her father, like kicking a man when he was down. He'd called Ian McCrary at the hospital—the only civilized response to his visit—but McCrary was refusing all calls. Probably rethinking his strategy of attack.

Cole hoped not. The last thing they all needed was more hostility.

In hopes of avoiding future problems, he'd suspended his cousin Leo from his part-time job as security guard at Westcott Hall. Leo should have called Cole when McCrary showed up. He would have set up a meeting with him. Leo always had been touchy when it came to slights against the family, though. Cole hoped to find him another part-time job away from Westcott Hall, at least for as long as Tess would be living there. As troublesome as Leo was at times, he had a good heart—along with a new little family that required more money than his cop's salary provided. The stubborn son-of-a-gun refused to take a dime from Cole unless he worked for it. He hoped Leo hadn't landed them both in legal difficulties.

Cole wished he himself had been there to prevent the crisis. He wondered if Tess blamed him for her father's injury and arrest. They'd spoken briefly over the phone about the incident yesterday, and she'd assured him that her father's rifle hadn't been loaded. He hadn't been trying to gun him down.

Good to know. But another question had been hammering through him that couldn't be easily answered. Did Tess, like her father, view him as the enemy? Her cool tone of voice and abrupt conversation led him to suspect she might.

Cole glared at the vacant driveway. He didn't care how she viewed him, as long as she honored their bargain.

What if she'd changed her mind? He gritted his teeth and drove his hands into his pockets. Not too difficult a question, really. He'd choose another McCrary bride. All this publicity had flushed out a whole slew of candidates. He'd received mail and phone calls from McCrary women around the country—and McCaslins, McClintocks and McDaniels, too. Some were willing to marry him on *any* terms. Some sent photos, videotapes, declarations of love...even perfumed panties. A few applicants actually seemed like reasonable, level-headed possibilities.

He glanced at his watch and cursed. Tess had better show up. If she didn't, he'd go and get her, even if he had to barge into a stronghold full of armed McCrarys and bodily carry her out.

Had her family talked her out of marrying him?

Another possibility gripped Cole then with a sickening lurch. Had the news broadcast brought her long-lost fiancé home to her?

No. She would have called. Tess McCrary, with her haughty manner and prim business suit and tender-hearted scruples regarding the welfare of women she'd never even seen...she would have done the honorable thing and called him. Tess McCrary, with her changeable gray eyes that scolded and challenged and reached deep inside him with the damnedest allure....

It made no sense, her hold on him. She wasn't a traffic-stopping beauty. Some men might not even find her particularly attractive. But then, those men hadn't looked close enough. They hadn't prodded at her armour, teased her out of her poise, stoked her inner fire until she glowed, flashed, sizzled. Beckoned. Yes, beckoned.

Five more minutes. That's all he'd give her.

A glimmer of white flashed through the thicket of live oaks and palmetto trees. The limousine soon glided around a curve into full view. Was she in it? The tinted windows prevented him from knowing.

The long, sleek vehicle pulled to a stop. To Cole's frustration, reporters rushed from behind bushes and trees to swarm the limo. The driver climbed out and strode to the back door, where a cluster of jostling photographers blocked Cole's view. Tyrone and Bruno appeared, only their heads and shoulders visible over the teeming crowd.

She'd obviously come, or his employees wouldn't be hovering near the back of the limo. Security guards converged from all corners of the property, forcing the journalists back, creating an opening in the crowd. Tyrone and Bruno moved to either side of the walkway as the driver opened the rear door.

A woman slowly disembarked from the limousine. *A bride.* A traditionally gowned, tiara-wearing, bouquet-carrying bride!

Cole stared in astonishment for the briefest moment before rational thought kicked in. It wasn't her. It wasn't Tess.

Anger and disappointment surged through him. What was this—a decoy for the media? A lame idea for a joke? A McCrary plot to piss him off? Someone had sent a woman of Tess's approximate height and build, with the same vibrant color of hair and creamy complexion, but dressed in a way that Tess would never consider dressing. She'd be wearing a touch-me-not, kick-butt business suit...probably in gun-metal gray.

The imposter lifted her face toward the chapel, and wide, luminescent gray eyes connected with Cole's. Familiarity jolted the very breath out of him.

Tess.

He couldn't have been more stunned if a bullet had struck him.

A rosy hue crept into her cheeks and she shifted her gaze away from his to focus on the path ahead of her. With regal grace, then, she proceeded up the stone walkway and ascended the long, wide, chapel stairway.

Cole stared in utter stupefaction.

She was beautiful. Not merely attractive, or alluring. *Goddamn beautiful.*

And it wasn't just the rich ivory satin, the gleam of pearls, the elegance of the exotic flowers trembling in her hands. It wasn't even the beauty inherent in every bride.

It was the first time he'd seen her hair not confined by a frazzled braid or a pragmatic twist, but curling in a lush, shining mass of fiery auburn. It was the first time he'd seen her long, slender throat and shapely shoulders bare. The first time he'd seen the full roundness of her breasts, the sweet, narrow curve of her waist, all so clearly delineated by the soft, sleek-fitting satin.

Goddamn beautiful.

She drew closer. A rushing sound pulsed in his ears; his mouth went dry. The provocative scent he'd come to think of as hers and the fragrance of blossoms immersed him. She'd reached the top of the stairway and halted, her gown gently rustling, the breeze riffling shiny tendrils about her neck and face. Though she stood beside him, her gaze remained fixed on some distant point.

He couldn't, for the life of him, stop staring.

Slowly, with clear hesitation, she glanced up at him. "I guess that I...uh..." her voice sounded low and unusually breathless "...I'm a little late."

He angled his head to study her closer; to drink in the incredible beauty she'd somehow kept hidden from him. The hint of shyness in her eyes, the hushed quality of her voice, only entranced him further. "Are you?"

"I believe so. Sorry if I've kept you waiting." Her mouth, which had always captivated him, always warmed his blood, now glimmered with a wildly sensual sheen. "So...are you ready?"

"Ready?"

"To go inside," she said in a near whisper, casting a surreptitious glance in the direction from which she'd come.

Only then did he realize that journalists watched and cameras flashed from a short distance beyond the stairway. Only then did he remember where he was, why he'd come, and the fact that a preacher and two witnesses awaited them inside the chapel.

She was here. His McCrary bride. He would marry her. In the eyes of the world, she would belong to him.

A sharp, hot pleasure expanded within him. He crooked his elbow and offered her his arm. Graciously she took it. Together they strolled toward the entrance of the chapel. Two uniformed guards swung open the heavy wooden doors, which then closed slowly behind them.

"You're late," Cole told her, trying to keep his eyes off of her for civility's sake...and failing miserably.

She slanted him an odd glance, as if he'd said something unreasonable. "I thought you hadn't noticed."

"What gave you that idea?"

Curiously enough, a slight smile lit her eyes. He had to stop then, just inside the small, private vestibule, to fully immerse himself in that smile. He had no idea what had prompted it. He also had no idea what had prompted her to dress as a bride. A genuine, honest-to-God bride. As if they'd be saying their vows in front of family and friends. As if those vows would mean something. As if she would, in truth, be his.

He suddenly needed to know what she'd been thinking when she'd slipped into that gown. Inspecting the elegant ivory satin with deceptive leisure, he murmured, "Nice dress." He then fixed his gaze pointedly on hers. "Why are you wearing it?"

Self-consciousness flickered across her face, and she lifted one bare, satin-edged shoulder in a suggestion of a shrug. "Business purposes. With all this publicity, I thought my parents' bridal shop might benefit from—"

"Try again." He wasn't about to let her off the hook with such a simple, sensible explanation—not when his imagination had supplied so many more interesting motives. "The truth this time."

Her delicate auburn brows wove together in puzzlement. "You don't believe me? Think about it. With all those television cameras rolling, I—"

"I think you and I both know you had an ulterior motive."

She parted her lips in outraged innocence. "*What* ulterior motive?"

"You'll never admit it," he predicted, pressing closer, as the afternoon sun streamed through the vestibule's leaded windows and bathed the room in a golden glow, "but you're a tease, Tess McCary."

"A tease!" After a wide-eyed stare, she squared her jaw, and a low but unmistakable fire lit in her eyes. "I have no idea what you're talking about, but I figured you'd think this gown had something to do with you. You must be the most egotistical man alive."

Cole couldn't help thrilling to her fire. He wanted to feel her heat at closer range. He wanted to pull her against him, smooth his hands over her naked shoulders. Inhale the scent of her skin, her hair. Taste her mouth. Oh, yes...he *needed* to taste her mouth.

"You're deliberately teasing me," he charged in a voice soft and gruff, "by dressing like a bride when you have no intention of giving me a wedding night."

Her blush burned as warmly as the indignation in her glare. Oh, he'd rattled her composure but good this time. Which was only fair. She'd damn near shattered his.

While she searched for words to slay him, he tipped her chin up and distracted her by gazing deeper into her gorgeous gray eyes. "Or..." he whispered, his lips a mere breath away from hers now, "have you changed your mind about that?"

Tess stared at him with her pulse beating wildly in her throat. How could she think, how could she speak, when he saturated her senses with his nearness? Though he wore an exquisitely tailored suit of rich sage-gray that must have cost more than her gown, and his dark, gleaming hair had been freshly cut, his jaw smoothly shaven, she felt a savage male heat emanating from his strong, lean body...a heat that too easily aroused a savagely sensual response within her.

Had she changed her mind about "not giving him a wedding night?"

Good heavens...*had* she?

"N-no," she managed to reply. "Of course I haven't."

"Then take fair warning, ma'am." His husky, southern-soft whisper and heated green gaze warmed her like the finest brandy. "I intend to change your mind."

Her heart raced. Wicked anticipation flared in her stomach. Before she had a chance to douse it, the vestibule's inner doors swung open.

A gray-haired minister in flowing golden robes halted in clear surprise. "Oh, there you are," he said to Tess with a smile. "I was worried you weren't going to make it." He included Cole in his gaze. "I believe your witnesses are growing impatient. Shall we begin the ceremony?"

Feeling as if they'd been caught in some carnal act, Tess murmured in embarrassed consent. Could the preacher tell that he'd interrupted a blazingly sensual moment? And since when did she, Tess McCrary, indulge in blazingly sensual moments with Cole Westcott? Worst of all—why should the knowledge that he wanted to make love to her thrill the very breath out of her?

With an annoyingly poised nod to the preacher, Cole returned her hand to its earlier place on his arm and urged her into a smooth stride behind the preacher. Trying to ignore the warm, muscled hardness she felt beneath the fine wool of his suit, Tess kept her head high and her gaze staunchly away from Cole as they marched down the aisle between gleaming wooden pews.

In an attempt to calm her jangled nerves, she breathed in the scent of ancient wood and stone, burning candles and freshly cut flowers. Even if lovemaking never entered the picture—which it definitely wouldn't!—she was *marrying* Cole Westcott. Marrying him! Though she knew the pragmatic purpose behind it, the concept still awed her. She'd never been a wife before. And she'd certainly never had a husband.

Don't romanticize it, Tess. This marriage is nothing more than a technicality. Part of a business plan. Cole wouldn't really be her husband, but a business partner. Her pulse continued to clamor, anyway.

Candles glowed amid flowers on altars at the front and sides of the chapel. Two distinguished, middle-aged gentlemen in three-piece suits rose from a front pew. With cordial greetings for her and a few congenial words to Cole, the men accompanied them to the chapel's podium.

The preacher donned a pair of glasses and opened a book to a ribbon-marked page. "Ahh, here we are," he murmured, lifting a fatherly gaze to them. "Are you ready to begin?"

Tess gripped her bouquet in a stranglehold, but nodded.

"One question, Reverend." Cole's deep, calm voice echoed in the small but cavernous chapel. "Is that part still in the ceremony about 'you may now kiss the bride'?"

The preacher's bushy brows jutted above his glasses. "Yes, of course."

Cole turned to Tess with a pleased air that garnered smiles from everyone. Everyone, that was, except Tess. The disturbing heat still lingered too potently in his stare. "Good."

The sensuality he'd provoked earlier now stirred and glowed within her like embers. She considered asking for that part of the ceremony to be skipped, but the preacher had begun his solemn intonation, and the two witnesses were eyeing her and Cole with discreet but palpable interest.

She wasn't sure who these men were. Unless she wanted word to spread that she was marrying Cole only for the money—an image she didn't want to project—she couldn't very well refuse to kiss him.

And if she were being perfectly honest with herself, she would have to admit that an overpowering curiosity had taken hold of her—a compelling urge to experience Cole's kiss. Just once. A brief, innocent taste. When would she ever find a safer, more appropriate time than now?

The preacher droned on about love and commitment—concepts she refused to think about too deeply, since her "vows" would be a lie before man and God. Growing more uncomfortable as the preacher edged toward those vows, she glanced at Cole from the corner of her eye.

He continued to peer at her with a subtle, understated intensity. She soon became mesmerized by that intensity...enmeshed in the most unwise fantasies...helplessly drawn to him....

"I, Cole, take you, Tess," he was pledging solemnly, "to be my wife. To stand beside you and with you always. To love you and live with you, through good times and bad, through sickness and in health, for richer or poorer...."

A startling swell of longing tightened her throat, and when it came time for her to repeat after the preacher, she struggled to force the words out. These promises were lies. Beautiful, beautiful lies. As she said them, she wished fervently that someday she would say them again, and mean them. When, where and with whom, she couldn't imagine.

But that wasn't quite true, she realized with a crazy kick of her heart. At the moment, she could imagine only Cole. The pomp and ceremony were obviously affecting her in alarming ways. Why hadn't she pictured Phillip? Disconcerted because she hadn't, she concentrated fiercely on the ceremony, shoving all perplexities to the back of her heart until later.

The preacher, meanwhile, spoke about the wedding ring as a symbol of unending love. Cole reached into his pocket and brought out a band of brilliant, interlocking diamonds that flashed and sparkled with incredible fire. The magnificence of the ring astounded her. He'd gone to such expense—hundreds of thousands of dollars, most likely. And all for a charade.

He took her left hand in his, and with sureness and grace, slipped the exquisite diamond band onto her finger, beside the engagement ring. "With this ring, I thee wed."

The softly uttered words and the solemn way he watched her as he said them almost undid her. She could imagine how he would search for the perfect ring, the most exquisite he could find, if the time ever came when he really meant that statement. And the ring would be a message to his bride— one that told her of how he valued the pledge between them. Tess wasn't sure how she knew that about him—Cole West-cott, the footloose playboy, breaker of foolish hearts. But somehow she *did* know he was capable of great sincerity, and that he wasn't beyond spending a fortune to show it.

She wasn't crazy enough to believe he felt that way about *her*, of course. He didn't. But the idea that he might someday be emotionally vulnerable to one special woman filled her with a tenderness that nearly moved her to tears.

No, she wasn't that woman, but the ring *was* the most exquisite she'd ever seen. His assistant had probably chosen it. Not that it mattered. She'd be giving it back to Cole, along with the engagement ring, when they parted ways.

The preacher moved on to Tess's part of the ring exchange,

and with a surge of embarrassment, she realized that she hadn't given a thought to a ring for Cole. Cole pressed something into her palm. A man's plain gold band. She met his gaze with gratitude and apology. A ridiculous reaction. This was *his* deal—a business transaction to save his inheritance. Of course he hadn't expected her to buy him a ring.

She had to get a grip on her careening emotions.

Resting his large hand across her palm, Tess slid the gold band onto his long, sturdy finger. But the ring wouldn't move past the last knuckle. He covered her hand with his free one and helped her slide the ring into place. The contact, the joined effort, the symbolism of the ring itself, filled her with an unexpected sense of intimacy.

Before she could collect herself, the preacher looked up from the book and pronounced them husband and wife. "Now, Mr. Westcott, you may kiss your bride."

Tess's breath lodged in her throat. Her pulse sped up. She braced herself.

But Cole didn't immediately kiss her. He wasn't that merciful. He plucked the bouquet from her hands and tossed it aside. Then he gathered her to him with a firm but caressing hold on her shoulders—her bare, suddenly sensitive shoulders—and his gaze meandered across her hair and her face as if he meant to visually absorb her. By the time he reached her eyes, his stare had grown smoky and intense, and she'd become vibrantly aware of the throb at his temple, the rush of his pulse, the flexed muscle in his jaw.

And the intoxicating heat radiating from his very skin.

His gaze descended to her mouth. He smoothed his warm, virile hand up the sensitive curve of her neck, cupped her nape and lowered his dark, ruggedly beautiful face to hers.

And he kissed her. A soft, lush, intricate kiss. A slow, voluptuous tasting. Languid warmth spread through her, like ripples in a pond, travelling to the outer reaches. To secret, yearning places. She drew him in with mindless need, sliding her arms around his neck to bring him closer. His body molded to hers, and his hand coursed down to the small of her back and splayed there, holding her captive against muscled hardness. Making her want…and want…

The kiss slanted for deeper access. An almost inaudible groan rose in him, along with a wildness. She welcomed the wildness. Fed it. He fought to subdue it, tangling his fingers in her hair and forcing the kiss to a ruthless close. His mouth broke from hers abruptly, as if they'd been fighting rather than kissing, and their loud, labored breaths echoed like gasps in the silence of the chapel.

He didn't immediately pull away from their embrace, but kept her close, his jaw pressed to her temple, their heartbeats pounding. Slowly, then, when she'd begun to feel that she could stand on her own, he lifted his face from hers. Withdrew from her arms.

Feeling the loss keenly, she opened her eyes…a slow, dazed lifting of her lashes. Sensuality continued to simmer within her. She felt dizzy. Hot. Disoriented. *Needful*.

Never had she been kissed like that! Never had she felt such an empowering rush of desire. She sought out his gaze in awe. If she should see cocky male satisfaction, or even pleased amusement, she would consider it his due. But as her eyes found his, she detected no trace of ego or masculine posturing.

Only hunger. Raw, sensual hunger.

For her.

Which only rekindled her heat.

"Let's go home," he breathed.

Yes. Oh, yes. Home.

But then masculine voices intruded—the witnesses, murmuring congratulations. Their words sounded oddly stilted, yet edged with amusement. The preacher's face had reddened, and he busied himself with his book.

Comprehension dawned gradually in Tess. Had they made a spectacle of themselves? In *church?*

While Cole turned away to respond to a well-wisher, Tess

smiled blindly at another, and a vague fear settled over her heart. Cole was much more dangerous than she'd suspected. She hadn't stepped foot out of the chapel yet, and she'd already been halfway seduced. With a single kiss!

In a haze of anxiety, desire and confusion, she accepted the bouquet somebody handed her and allowed the preacher to guide her to a side table, where she signed her name to the marriage certificate.

Cole signed his name, paid the preacher, then turned to Tess. The mere connection of their gazes stirred her profoundly. "There's a limo out back," he murmured, his voice itself a caress. "We can escape the crowd."

Before she could think clearly enough to form an alternate plan, he slipped an arm around her waist and swept her along a side corridor, holding her close to him, immersing her in his scent, his nearness.

The panic she'd tried to suppress broke to the surface. "Cole, wait." She tried to slow their forward movement. "I can't...I won't...I mean, I have to..."

But Bruno and Tyrone had stepped out of the shadows, claiming his attention without slowing his pace. "The press is still out front by the other limo, boss," reported one of them in a gruff undertone. "I put her suitcase in the trunk, Mr. Westcott," rumbled the other.

Tess soon found herself in a fragrant flower garden where a pearl-gray limousine awaited. A uniformed driver swung open the rear door, and Cole hustled Tess inside, rescuing the folds of her gown from being caught in the door; arranging them around her with capable hands. He then settled in beside her, and the limo sped off through the chapel's back gardens, into the encroaching golden-pink twilight of a spring evening.

Tess reluctantly rested against a soft, fragrant leather seat in a luxurious chamber with plush gray carpeting, smoked-glass tables, romantic saxophone music and champagne chilling on ice.

Cole skimmed his hand along the top of her shoulders. "Tess," he whispered. "I thought we'd never be alone."

"Cole," she choked out, her skin tingling from his touch. If she didn't stop this madness, she'd be lost. Stiffly she held herself apart from him, gaining his immediate attention. "Would you mind dropping me off at my parents' shop? I...um...left my car there."

He narrowed his eyes on hers and offered slowly, "I'll send someone for your car."

"No, I have things to do this evening." She swallowed, unnerved by his stunned, silent, forceful disapproval. "I'll meet you at Westcott Hall later."

He withdrew his arm from around her and edged forward to study her more intently. "What's wrong, Tess?"

"Wrong? Nothing. I just—"

"The kiss," he deduced with disquieting perceptiveness. "It scared you."

"Scared me?" She forced a scoffing laugh. "No, of course not. I...I..." The determination in his eyes stopped her from evading the issue. A bluff seemed particularly unwise. "Maybe a little."

"Why?"

"It was a very good kiss," she admitted in a half whisper.

"It was an incredible kiss," he corrected. His gaze traversed her face again with a thoroughness that liquefied her spine. "I want another."

Sensuality curled through her. "I don't think it would be wise. Kissing like that—" she shook her head, her gaze shifting beneath his "—may lead to *involvement*."

He angled his face into intimate alignment with hers. "You think so?"

"It might," she theorized. Humor laced his heated gaze, and her heart turned over. The rogue! She wanted to give him a hardy shove. She wanted to kiss him. She wanted to incite him to wildness again.... "Involvement would be a mistake," she insisted over the rapid staccato of her heart. "We have to live in the same house for months. Things would get awkward."

"Things would get hot."

Temptation pulsed within her. "I agreed to a marriage in name only."

"This has nothing to do with our agreement, or any other obligation. It has to do with you and me..." he wrapped his finger in one of the curls beside her face "...and that kiss that almost embarrassed us in front of the preacher."

"Almost?"

A smile touched his mouth. "If I hadn't stopped it when I did...yes, ma'am, we would have embarrassed ourselves."

Oh, how true! Mortification swamped her at the thought.

"As it was, we only embarrassed the preacher. Then again," his voice lowered to a sultry murmur, "his flush might have been from all that heat we were throwing off." His gaze boldly carressed her mouth. "Why shouldn't we get 'involved,' Tess? We *are* married." He released the tendril of her hair and gently skimmed his fingers down her cheek. "You *are* my wife." He curved his palm along her jaw and brushed his thumb across her lips, stunning her with a rush of keen sensation. "And this is our wedding night."

Desire washed through her at his touch, at the longing in his gruff whisper, and she closed her eyes beneath the sensual onslaught. She'd never wanted a man as she wanted him—with this heart-stopping, breathless intensity. Not even Phillip. How could that be? She'd *loved* Phillip. But she *wanted* Cole. And Phillip was gone, maybe forever....

"I thought you understood," she whispered, struggling to lift her lashes beyond half-mast, but affected too strongly by the stroke of his thumb across her mouth, "that there was someone else."

The stroking of his thumb stopped. She opened her eyes in unreasonable disappointment. He looked none too happy. He didn't withdraw his palm from where it cradled her jaw, though. Nor did he retreat from their intimate nearness. "I'm willing to overlook that."

A spurt of amused annoyance helped clear her mind of the drugging sensuality, and she pulled away from him. He wanted to take her to bed, and was "willing to overlook" the fact that she was in love with another man. If that wasn't classic Cole Westcott, she didn't know what was. "Big of you."

"*I* think so. What other husband would—"

"But you're not really my—"

"What the hell?" He lurched forward and peered beyond her, through a side window, his attention snagged.

Tess realized that the limousine had pulled past the stately front gate of Westcott Hall and was winding its way between enormous trees toward a columned, plantation-style mansion. "What's wrong?"

Cole nodded toward a butter-yellow Lincoln Continental parked in the circular drive. "That's my attorney's car. What's he doing here?"

The limo glided to a halt near the grand front stairway of Westcott Hall, and a lanky, silver-haired man in a white shirt, suit trousers, a red bow tie and suspenders climbed from the Lincoln, a pipe clenched in his teeth. As Cole and Tess alighted from the limo, he sauntered toward them. "We've got problems, Cole," he drawled in an aristocratic, southern voice.

"Do they involve my father?" Tess asked anxiously.

"No, ma'am. At least, not to my knowledge." He shifted his gaze back to Cole. "But a potentially serious situation *has* arisen that may require a slight change in strategy."

Cole frowned with barely contained annoyance. "Can't we talk strategy tomorrow, Henry? In case you haven't noticed—" he glanced pointedly at Tess's gown "—this happens to be our wedding night."

Tess blushed and averted her gaze.

"Er, yes," acquiesced Henry. "That's exactly the *potentially serious* problem I've come to discuss."

Cole stared at the old family retainer in frustration. He didn't want to hear about problems this evening, no matter how potentially serious. And he damn sure didn't want to discuss a change in legal strategy, especially if it concerned his deal with Tess.

Because regardless of what complications had arisen, she *was* his bride, and he was going to take her upstairs and make love to her all night long. *All* night long.

That was one vow he intended to keep.

5

"WHAT DO YOU mean, the curse wasn't translated right?"

Cole's explosive question reverberated through the closed library door. Tess, who waited in the adjoining room while Cole conferred with Henry, resisted the urge to press her ear against that door. Instead, she sat in the armchair closest to it and strained to hear the attorney's explanation.

She couldn't catch another word. Her curiosity surged, along with anxiety. *Had* the curse been translated incorrectly? It was possible. The curse had probably been written in Cole's family bible the same as it had in hers—in Gaelic. Someone had printed an interpretation beside it. Tess had assumed it was accurate. Maybe it wasn't.

It was vital for her to know. The safety and happiness of all her loved ones might depend on her satisfying that curse. What were its demands? Did they include a marriage between "the Westcott of Westcott Hall" and a "daughter of his McCrary neighbor"? If so, what could the difference be?

Unable to sit still, Tess paced across the elegant, spacious drawing room. A *drawing room*, Cole had called it, for Heaven's sake. She'd never known anyone with an honest-to-goodness "drawing room." With its twenty-foot ceilings, elaborately carved trimwork and exquisite antique furnishings, it looked more like a museum than a home.

With her wedding dress sweeping around her like an antebellum gown, she paced past a glossy grand piano, velvet loveseats and brocade armchairs, venturing as near to the library door as her honor would allow. She wouldn't listen through keyholes. She *wouldn't*.

Just as she considered changing her mind, the door opened and the men walked out, looking grim. "Think about it, Cole," Henry was saying. "It's not too late to change plans."

A shifting of Cole's jaw and a darkening of his eyes gave Tess the idea that he disagreed. He had discarded his suit jacket, she noticed, and removed his tie. The open top button of his white silk shirt allowed for an alluring glimpse of his strong, bronzed throat and a few dark, curling wisps of chest hair. His shoulders seemed even wider than before; his chest more powerful; his waist more tapered. He looked ready for an evening of relaxation—at home, *with her.* Her stomach warmed. "Thanks for the information, Henry," he uttered, sounding more perturbed than grateful.

Henry lifted a hand in acknowledgement, nodded to Tess, returned his pipe to his teeth and strode from the room. Cole then turned his gaze to Tess—a long, hesitant gaze.

She couldn't curb her curiosity a moment longer. "What did Henry say?"

Letting out a harsh breath, Cole plowed the fingers of both hands through his hair in frustration and paced away from her. He clearly wasn't looking forward to sharing the news. Her anxiety deepened. How bad could it be?

He halted with his back to her, his fists resting on his hips as he presumably stared at an oil painting of Queen Victoria. "I'm sure you remember our discussion about Deirdre and my other two stepmothers. If I fail to satisfy the conditions in my father's will, they'll inherit his entire estate."

"Yes, of course I remember."

"My father's only stipulation is that I fulfill every term of the curse that he'd photocopied from an old family bible. Henry and I took the interpretation at face value, assuming that all I'd have to do, basically, is marry a McCrary. But Deirdre's attorney had the curse translated into its literal meaning. When Henry found out about his tactic, he also took the curse to an expert in the Gaelic language."

"And?"

Slowly Cole turned to face her, that odd hesitancy still in his gaze. "The curse's demands are a bit more...complex...than we first thought."

"Complex? How so?"

He studied her with a measuring look, as if trying to judge the wisdom of telling her. "Let's talk about it after dinner. My housekeeper set a table for us on the back terrace."

His evasion of her question elevated her anxiety, robbing her of appetite. "We can talk about it *over* dinner," she amended, unwilling to be held off until the end of the meal.

"After," he insisted. "I'd rather not ruin Mrs. Johannsen's wedding day feast. She's been preparing for it all week. I haven't seen her this excited over any event since my graduation from college. It would kill her if we didn't savor every bite."

Tess didn't have the heart to argue with that. In fact, she respected him for caring about his housekeeper's feelings. But her stomach tightened in concern over the information he would withhold until after dinner. The interpretation of that curse must be disturbing, indeed, if he believed it would ruin their meal.

Cole held out his hand to her. She hesitated to take it. The thought of holding his hand seemed too intimate. She hadn't forgotten the tumultuous heat he'd started with his touch in the limo, or his sultry whisper about making love to her tonight. She had to keep her wits sharp unless she wanted to end up in his bed.

Did she? Frazzled by her answer, she quickly altered that question to: Should she?

For an instant, she had to search her mind for her reasons against it. *Because you're not in love with him, and he's not in love with you. Sex would only lead to complications.* Oh, and then there was Phillip. The man she loved. The man who had dropped out of her life with a suddenness that left her reeling.

She was so tired of the gap he'd left behind. She yearned for something to fill that gap; something warm, positive and exciting. But she feared that making love to Cole would only bring her more emptiness in the long run—a different but no less painful form of abandonment. She wasn't ready to risk that.

Instead of accepting Cole's hand, she took his arm, as she had in church. With a rueful quirk of his mouth, he folded his arm into proper alignment and escorted her down the wide, central hall to the back terrace.

Even that slight, casual contact with him flustered her—the feel of warm, hard muscle beneath the silk of his shirt; the power exuded by his tall, solid body. His very nearness heightened her senses. The mild evening air as they stepped outside seemed especially fragrant with magnolia, jasmine and the brackish scent of the river. The sound of crickets and frogs rang through the rustling trees with a particularly melodious lilt. The spring breeze ruffled her hair and the satin of her gown; caressed the bare skin of her shoulders and throat with a gentle, almost sensual, touch.

She was too vulnerable to him, even when he was behaving himself.

The moment they reached the table set for two on the wide back terrace, she withdrew her hand from his arm and distanced herself from him. Mrs. Johannsen, the short, rounded, motherly housekeeper, set steaming plates of food on the table and beamed at Tess in welcome. Cole pulled a chair out for Tess. She sank down into the seat and smoothed her wedding gown around her. The table had been set with snowy-white linen, fresh flowers, glowing candles, delicate gold-trimmed china and fine crystal goblets. She felt as if she were in a world-class restaurant rather than a private home.

Not surprisingly, the food was excellent: Carolina-style okra gumbo; sautéed lump crab cakes with lemon herb sauce; pan-fried quail; fresh shrimp, scallops, clams and corn in tomato saffron broth. Despite her lack of appetite, Tess set out to do justice to Mrs. Johannsen's Lowcountry feast.

Cole ate slowly and with clear appreciation, which somehow endeared him all the more to Tess, seeing how Mrs. Johannsen glowed with satisfaction. Neither Cole nor Tess spoke much. She caught him a number of times staring at her in that disturbingly measuring way, as if he were trying to read her mind or see into her soul. Perhaps he was wrestling with some decision regarding her.

She remembered Henry saying, "It isn't too late to change plans." Had he meant their marriage? Had he advised Cole to end it *now*? Was Cole considering it? A confusing rush of emotion spilled through her at the possibility that he might— anxiety over the curse's resolution, yes, but also disappointment of a dangerously personal nature.

Perhaps her wedding night dilemma would be a moot point. Maybe he'd send her home.

She set down her napkin beside her plate and eyed him in determination. She had to have answers to her questions immediately. "What does the curse really say, Cole? *Does* it demand that you marry 'the daughter of your McCrary neighbor'?"

He drank from his water glass, touched his mouth with his napkin and tossed it down beside his plate. He then raised his gaze to her in that hesitant yet appraising way again. "Yes, it does."

Her relief was tempered only by her wariness of what *had* changed. "Then how does the new translation differ from the old?"

"It goes into more detail."

"Such as?"

Mrs. Johannsen chose that moment to bustle outside with two delicate brandy snifters of an after-dinner liqueur, preventing Cole from answering. She then cleared away the dishes, forcing Tess to hold back her questions and murmur her appreciation of the sweet, strong, mocha-flavored liqueur. Cole thanked Mrs. Johannsen for the splendid meal— which Tess seconded—then sent her home.

Tess waited until the housekeeper had left before demanding, "What details?"

Cole settled his broad shoulders back in his chair and absently swirled the liqueur around in the snifter. Despite the nonchalance of his pose, she detected tension in his face. "For one thing, I have to provide my McCrary bride with 'a safe, comfortable home.'"

"A safe, comfortable home," she repeated. "That sounds reasonable. What else?"

"It also specifies that I must 'forsake all others, keeping only unto her.' My McCrary bride, that is." His gaze entwined with hers. "You."

Tess stared at him in dumbfounded surprise. That had been the last thing she'd expected. No wonder he'd believed that talking about it would ruin his meal. As she pondered the implications of his forced faithfulness, worry churned within her. She would have no control over that issue. He might find ways to be more discreet about his trysts with other women rather than actually "forsaking all others." But the curse wouldn't be lifted unless he really complied.

Lacey LaBonne and other beauties flashed before her mind's eye. Was Cole Westcott *capable* of resisting temptation when she herself did not intend to take their place in his bed? Almost afraid to hear the curse's other demands, she asked, "What else?"

"This stipulation goes hand-in-hand with the last one...at least to my way of thinking." Bracing an elbow on the table, he leaned in close to her. "The curse decrees that I take you into my bed," he relayed in a gruff whisper, "and plant my seed within you."

A gasp stuck in her throat. "You're lying."

Without breaking their gaze, he reached inside his shirt pocket, drew out a square of paper and tossed it to her. "Read it yourself."

She opened the folded page with trembling hands. It was a

letter from Henry detailing his reasons for taking the curse to a translator and his subsequent findings.

You, Westcott of Westcott Hall, must wed the daughter of your McCrary neighbor, take her into your bed and plant your seed within her. You must provide for her a safe and comfortable home. You must forsake all others and keep only unto her. If you fail to do this, your family shall reap only loneliness and heartbreak.

Tess glanced up blindly from the letter, feeling stunned and shaken.

"Whoever printed the original translation must have considered all that to be a natural part of marriage and didn't see the need to outline those details." A slight smile bent one corner of his mouth. "Your great-great-grandmother herself must have known better. She worded the curse to prevent some scheming Westcott boy from doing just what we'd planned to do—ease out of the conditions on a technicality."

Tess couldn't utter as much as a word. She was trapped. Trapped!

"Now, my sweet McCrary bride..." he drawled on a wry note, "you might be thinking that no one will know if we satisfy those conditions or not. But Henry mentioned that the opposition is laying the groundwork to challenge my right of inheritance. There's no way of knowing what the court will require in the way of, uh, *proof.*"

"Proof?" she whispered, staring at him.

"Proof that I'm fulfilling every condition of the curse. Deirdre will probably have me followed in hopes of catching me in an extramarital affair. I wouldn't put it past her or her attorney—or the media, for that matter—to tap our phones or plant listening devices wherever they can in hopes of discovering...whatever."

"But that's illegal. They couldn't use anything they'd discovered that way in court."

"No, but with inside knowledge, they could come up with specific questions to ask us under oath and call witnesses to corroborate our answers. In any case, the court itself will probably require us to testify that I *have* complied with every condition of the curse. They may call others to testify, too. Our family members. Visitors. Household staff."

The color had drained from Tess's face until Cole felt sure she'd either faint dead away or bolt from the house with her wedding gown streaming behind her like Hollywood's version of a runaway bride. She did neither, though, but simply sat there, her big gray eyes as round and luminous as full moons.

He knew, of course, she wouldn't agree to go to bed with him to fulfill the terms of the will. She'd made it clear that she wasn't the kind of woman to trade sex for money, even in the guise of wedded bliss. What's more, he'd already committed himself to paying her two million dollars and the deed to McCrary Place after five months of marriage, the only stipulation being that she live with him during that time.

When he'd made the deal, he'd thought that the marriage itself and their cohabiting for five months would guarantee his inheritance. That no longer held true. If he didn't inherit his father's estate, that two-million-dollar obligation would clean him out of his own private funds and assets.

Henry had advised him to call off his deal with Tess McCrary. To send her home tonight and dissolve their marriage Monday morning. He could then choose another McCrary bride—one whose family didn't harbor a grudge against the Westcotts; one who didn't need for the world to believe they were in love before she married him. One who would consider herself lucky to go to bed with him. He would offer a much smaller settlement, contingent upon his inheriting his father's estate.

"There's too much animosity between your families, Cole," Henry had insisted. "She might double-cross you. She might stay married to you for five months, then testify that you didn't fulfill the conditions of the curse. She'd walk away with two million dollars, your stepmothers would inherit your father's estate, and you'd be left broke."

It was definitely a possibility. But Cole wasn't ready to give up on Tess McCrary quite yet. Because no matter how much her family despised the Westcotts or how desperate her father's situation might become, Cole believed that Tess would tell the truth under oath. She was just that kind of person.

He would have to play it straight. He'd have to provide for her a safe and comfortable home. Forsake all others and "keep only unto her." Take her into his bed. Plant his seed within her. His blood warmed and his body hardened at the very thought. Yes, he would *have* to do all of those things, and if he did, she would not deny it in court. Not if he knew Tess McCrary.

Did he know her?

Would she come to his bed; would she make love to him? Renewed determination rushed like lava through his veins. Yes, she would. He would make damn sure of it. He'd have to stoke the sizzling sensuality that sparked and smoked between them. No chore there. He almost smiled at the thought.

She would never relent on the basis of any monetary inducement.

But she *would* have to play by his rules to some degree, or risk that he would follow Henry's advice and dissolve their marriage before she could make any claim whatsoever on his bank account. Despite her scruples, she did need money in the worst way. She couldn't possibly shrug off that two million dollars...could she? She would also lose McCrary Place. He couldn't deed the property over to her unless he inherited his father's estate. She wouldn't want to give up her ancestral home...would she?

She would give it up, though, along with the money, if he demanded that she make love to him as part of the deal. He wouldn't make that mistake. But he *would* play his cards to win the stakes he was after. And those stakes were her—Tess McCrary Westcott, in his bed.

And claiming his inheritance, of course.

"Understand, Tess, that I can't pay you that two million dollars if I don't inherit my father's estate." A bluff, but just barely. "I also can't give you McCrary Place if I don't inherit it. Which means that neither one of us can take the chance that some member of our household staff or God knows who else might testify that we're not—" he hesitated, and finished in the gentlest tone possible "—sharing a bedroom."

He believed that a slight flush of color had risen into her face, but in the flickering candlelight and the mellow glow of the moon, he couldn't be sure. She didn't respond in any other way to his suggestion. "I know I promised you a private suite," he added, "but circumstances have changed."

"Yes," she murmured, barely audible, "they have."

"We need for the world to think that we sleep together, Tess. But just because we'd share a bedroom wouldn't mean we'd actually have to...do anything...that you're...against." Though he felt the reassurance needed to be voiced, he swore she wouldn't be against his lovemaking for long. Their kiss in the chapel still simmered in his blood—and somewhere in hers, too, he sincerely believed. How could anything that hot cool off so quickly? It would have to take days. Maybe weeks. Or months. "I'm not asking you to sacrifice your principles, or...sell yourself for the money, or..."

"Let's walk," she said, cutting off his rambling explanation and rising to her feet. The ivory gown billowing around her, the blossoms and pearls woven through her hair, reminded him of the ceremony that had bound them together into one legal entity. Legally speaking, she was his. "I need to walk."

He stood and extended his hand. He wondered if she'd take it. She hadn't before.

After only the briefest hesitation, she accepted his hand. A small measure of victory flushed through him, warming him; making him savor all the more the feel of her delicate but responsive hand. He led her down the terrace steps and along a bricked pathway into the formal gardens. The profusion of flowers and greenery, the gleaming river, the star-brilliant sky...beauty he'd experienced countless times was magically enhanced by the subtle scent of her; the warmth she inspired in him; the incredible loveliness of her face, her lustrous hair, her naked shoulders. Her body.

He wanted to pull her into his arms and kiss the hesitation right out of her. He had no doubt that he could. In a place as unlikely as a chapel, with three pious onlookers, she'd succumbed entirely to his kiss and ambushed him with her own. He wanted to feel that stunning heat again. Soon. *Now.*

He stopped beside a fragrant trellis of roses and took firm possession of her shoulders; peered into her eyes; filled himself with her beauty. "Tess, I—"

"Henry wants you to find another McCrary woman, doesn't he?"

Her perceptiveness, as well as the abrupt departure from his own line of thought, surprised him into momentary silence. "Yes."

"He's afraid that I'll stop you in some way from inheriting."

"That's true."

"I won't betray you."

He believed her. And he wanted her. So much he ached with it. "But what if we're called to testify? Would you be willing to lie under oath that you slept with me, as my wife, in every sense of the word?"

"I won't lie." No surprise there. "But I won't *have* to." Her gaze shone with vibrant sincerity.

His pulse leaped. What did she mean? Was he jumping to conclusions, reading too much into her words? But what other possible meaning could she have than—

"I'll share your room," she expounded in slow, halting words. "I'll sleep in your bed." His heart slammed to a near standstill. "And I *will* make love to you."

A sleek, potent heat filled him; a hot exhilaration. His astonishment was just as strong, though. He hadn't expected an immediate surrender. In the limo, she'd been holding him off and swearing she loved another man.

A glut of emotions hit Cole, so strong and unfamiliar that he almost let her go. If she loved another man, why had she decided to sleep with *him*? He'd told her he would overlook her emotional attachment to Phillip—and by God, he would—but why had she gone from refusing to hold his hand to agreeing to give him her body?

For the money? Because she didn't want to lose two million dollars and McCrary Place if he should decide to find another bride?

No. He didn't believe it. He might not have known her for long, but he knew her better than that. At least, he *thought* he did.

With his chest bound painfully tight by some invisible chain, he held her arms and searched her face by the hazy light of the moon. He didn't want to ask her; didn't want to risk having her change her mind. But the question burned in him. "Why, Tess? Why are you willing to sleep with me now when you wouldn't even kiss me in the limo or hold my hand before dinner?"

"I...I'd rather not say."

"Not say?" How did she manage to continually surprise him? If she was willing to sleep with him for the money, surely she could bring herself to utter a few flattering words to explain her change of heart. But she hadn't agreed because of the money. And he intended to make her admit it. "Is it because you're afraid I'll follow Henry's advice and find another McCrary bride?"

"I suppose it is."

"And you're going to sleep with me so you can honestly testify under oath that I've fulfilled the conditions of the curse."

"Yes."

"Because you want the money and McCrary Place."

Her lips tightened and her gaze glimmered with secrets. "Of course."

He wouldn't let her get away with hiding her real motive from him. "Then I must admit," he murmured in a honeyed tone as he ran his hands up her arms and allowed his gaze to travel suggestively, "that I'm looking forward to finding out just what kind of lovin' two million dollars can buy."

She flinched as if he'd raised a hand to her, making him regret the comment. He braced himself for a torrent of curses or at least one good "go to hell." But she remained white-lipped and silent.

Which only angered him more. "I'm not going to back out of our deal, Tess. If you honor your end of our bargain by living here for five months, I'll give you the money and McCrary Place. You don't have to sleep with me for it. In fact, I'd prefer that you didn't." And he realized that he meant it. As much as he wanted her, he didn't want to buy her. He turned to walk away.

"Cole."

He glanced back, expecting to see relief in her gaze, or maybe even gratitude.

Oddly enough, he saw something like alarm. "Why do you have to be so exasperating?" she cried. "You were pretty darn confident in your seductive powers before. Why not now? Why can't you just assume that your manly charms have overcome my common sense?"

If he wasn't so frustrated with her, he might have laughed. *Overcome her common sense.* Was that her idea of a compliment? He caught her gently beneath the chin to prevent her from escaping his scrutiny. "If you want me to believe that you're suddenly willing to fall into my bed because I'm irresistible, then tell me so."

Her expression grew troubled, then softened in the most bewildering way, and she did something that astounded him. She reached up and caressed his face with a gentle, lingering hand. "I can't tell you that." Her touch, her tenderness, filled him with a powerful yearning. "It wouldn't be fair. Even worse than a woman who sleeps with a man for money is one who cons her way into his life with pretty lies. I'll admit that you're...well...attractive." Her color flared and her gaze grew inexplicably shy. "And that your kiss in the chapel made me...forget myself," she confessed in a whisper. She lowered her hand from his face, and he immediately missed her touch. "But that's not the reason I've changed my mind about going to bed with you."

He was very close to shaking her—or kissing her senseless, carrying her upstairs and forgetting about "why." For some insane reason, though, he couldn't bring himself to do that. "Tell me."

She closed her eyes and lifted her face to the starry sky, as if beseeching heaven for strength. She then peeked out from beneath the long, thick lashes of one squinting eye, as if trying to judge the wisdom of telling him. "The curse."

He watched her in silence, waiting for more of the explanation. When nothing followed, he frowned. "What about the curse?"

"I believe it's possible...just *possible*, mind you...that, um...it could be valid."

"Valid?"

She spread out her hands imploringly. "Don't you see, Cole? Your family hasn't had a marriage last beyond a year and mine has suffered tragedies in every family circle *since 1825*, when the curse was written. And now my father and future brother-in-law are in terrible trouble, and my mother and sister are facing devastating heartbreak. Can't you see that some dark power might be at work here?"

"You actually *believe* in the curse?"

"I'm not sure if I do or not, but why take the chance that it might be real? If it is, you and I have the means to lift it."

"By marrying, and following all the terms set out in the curse. By...making love."

"Yes."

She had, somehow, managed to do it again. His insides tangled into knots so tight, he could barely breathe, and he wasn't even sure why. Incredulity swamped him to think she believed in the curse, no matter how tentative that belief might be. And though he was glad that the money hadn't been her motivation—damn glad—the idea that she was willing to make love to him to repeal the curse made him feel equally used.

If that wasn't bad enough, she'd practically scorned his "manly charms," as she'd put it. Manly charms. Ha! Charms, manly or otherwise, had nothing to do with the explosive sexual chemistry that had nearly detonated in the chapel over a simple kiss. Or the heat that flared between them every time they touched, or stared at each other for too long, or came within touching distance.

Unreasonable anger flooded him. He knew it to be unreasonable. After all, he'd married her only to satisfy a will. He was using her as blatantly as she was using him. His anger mixed with equally unreasonable desire. Why should he want her so damn much? He'd had his pick of beautiful women since he was a teenager, and as long as he inherited the Westcott fortune, he always would.

That thought didn't help one damn bit.

The anger, the desire, the need to affect her as strongly as she affected him, funneled into a powerful drive. He would take her up on her noble offer, this woman willing to sacrifice herself for the sake of her family. He'd make sure that she couldn't testify in court that he hadn't "taken her into his bed and planted his seed within her."

Oh, he'd do that, all right. And he'd do it well. He'd make

love to her like she'd never been loved before. He'd drive it all from her mind—the curse, the will, and her blasted fiancé. The guy she probably wished she'd married today.

"You understand, then," she was saying, her eyes wide and earnest, "why I was so concerned that you might choose another McCrary bride. If you did, she might not be a descendant of the original McCrary clan of Charleston, and the curse might not be lifted."

"We sure can't risk that," he agreed.

"No, we can't. No matter what we might personally *want* to do, we have to comply with the curse."

"It's our duty."

"Yes, it is. Including the 'forsaking all others' part."

He compressed his lips, drew in a loud, deep breath and exhaled slowly through his nostrils. In a tone of hard-edged determination, he said, "If I must, I must."

Tess eyed him in doubt. He sounded sincere enough, but she wondered if he truly understood the gravity of the situation. "Including Lacey LaBonne."

He reached for her, his eyes darker, warmer, more intense, as he drew her closer. "You'll have to help me through it."

Warmth stirred within her at his sudden nearness; his intensity. She worried, though, that he wasn't focusing on the big picture quite the way she was. "You do realize the seriousness of this...quest...don't you?"

"Oh, yes, ma'am." His husky, drawled response warmed her blood. "We'd better not waste another minute." He skimmed his hands over the curve of her cheeks, his fingers fanning and caressing as he tilted her face to his. Her heart tripped into a faster, heavier beat. "Who knows what kind of trouble might be brewing among our kinfolk, even now?"

"That's true." She couldn't ignore that alarming possibility. "It may be working against us until we actually..."

"...satisfy the demands." His heated gaze lured her away from her worry; drugged her with a splendid rush of sensuality. "Every last demand, Tess," he whispered. He closed his eyes and swept his mouth across hers—a long, slow, feather-soft conquest.

Heat seared through her, along with explicitly sexual longing. The force of that longing frightened her. It would be so easy to forget her worries, forget the reason behind their love-making, and lose herself in the heat. *Lose herself.*

She couldn't allow that. Couldn't give up her control or forget her purpose, even for a moment. She had to fortify herself against the seductive pleasure. Carry out her duty without forfeiting anything important.

She jerked away from his embrace before he could deepen the kiss. "Okay, then." Her voice quavered, and she could barely force herself to meet his frowning, questioning stare. "The original terms of our agreement are still in force, and we will...work together to...meet the demands of both your father's will and the curse."

He muttered in vague, impatient agreement and reached for her again.

She backed away, winding her fists in the fabric of her billowing satin gown. "You might be right about the curse stirring up trouble. I'm going to call home to be sure that no new problems have cropped up, and to see how my father and brother-in-law are doing. And then I'll need to get my suitcase. I only packed one. I didn't have time to pack another. And I'd really like a hot bath, and some time alone to—" She realized she was rambling and forced her words to a halt. "Why don't we set a time that's convenient to both of our schedules?"

He frowned at her, his gaze searching hers in the most unsettling way. "Tonight." His tone, his stare, left no room for negotiation.

Distrustful of her voice, she nodded.

"Upstairs," he said, like a gunfighter naming the site of a duel. "The hallway to your right. Last bedroom."

Drawing in a shaky breath, she nodded, wrenched her gaze away from his dark, determined face and hurried toward the house. She didn't exactly run. She wouldn't allow herself to run.

"Your suitcase should already be there," he called out. "And so is a phone. I'll be up in an hour. One hour, Tess."

One hour. He would meet her then in his bedroom. To "take her into his bed" and "plant his seed within her." She wasn't sure her trembling legs would carry her all the way to the house, let alone up a flight of stairs.

As she neared the terrace, she couldn't help one quick glance behind her. He remained where she'd left him—a tall, broad-shouldered silhouette in the moonlit garden.

She didn't allow herself to regret breaking away from his kiss. This was business, not pleasure. She'd do what was required. Nothing extra. Nothing too unnecessarily personal. Nothing too...stirring.

She hoped he'd gotten the message.

6

OTHER THAN A BRIEF PHONE CALL to her mother that assured her no new developments or disasters had occurred, Tess spent the hour preparing herself for the night ahead of her. She'd always considered herself a strong, solidly grounded woman, yet faced with the prospect of making love to Cole, she felt vulnerable.

Which was crazy. He could take no more than she offered. Possession of her body did not necessarily mean possession of her heart and soul. *Did it?*

Of course not.

He kept to his word and stayed away, but she felt his presence anyway as she undressed in his immense bedroom, stepping out of her bridal gown and petticoats; laying them carefully across an armchair. The elegant décor of the room in soothing shades of blue, muted burgundy and pearl gray ensconced her in an aura of luxury—a feeling the man himself also inspired in her, with his thick, dark, sun-gilded hair and heart-stirring smile; his easy strength and quick intelligence. His incredibly potent kiss. *Luxury.*

But that kind of luxury had no place in her world. And she had no permanent place in *his* world. She couldn't forget those facts. She would approach their encounter tonight in the most impersonal way possible. She *would have sex with him* in the most impersonal way possible.

How would she ever manage that? She would *have* to.

Heat flushed through her just thinking about it, and she forced her attention to her surroundings. Expensive contemporary furnishings, fabrics and draperies, plush carpeting and classical works of art shared space with unique treasures he'd probably collected in his travels. Where had he gone, what had he done, in his travels? Who had he taken with him? Women, probably.

She wasn't one of his women. She couldn't bear to be one of them.

He had no personal photographs anywhere in sight. Other than a jar of coins and small tray of cuff links, he had no personal clutter on his dressers or desk. No clues to his inner person. Faint traces of his scent lingered in the air, though, evoking images of his face, memories of his touch. His bed, she noticed, was larger than king-size and plush with a downy comforter and a mound of burgundy satin pillows. A sensuous bed.

Her heart rushed, and she turned away from the evocative sight. She'd be sharing that bed with him tonight...*and every night for the next five months.* But the curse hadn't specified how many times the "planting of the seed" had to be done. One time should suffice. They would slip beneath the bedcovers and...well, just *do it.* Get it over with. Plant the seed and move on.

The term "plant" had caused her a few moments of acute anxiety when she'd first had time to mull it over. "Planting," to her way of thinking, usually involved a seed taking root. In this case, did it imply *conception?* Would the wearing of a condom interfere with the curse's demand to "plant his seed within her"? She intended to follow the terms of the curse implicitly, but the possibility of pregnancy added a whole extra dimension that would require *much* more thought.

Holding her panic firmly in check, she found a leatherbound Webster's Dictionary on his desk and looked up the word "plant." To her great relief, she discovered that the third definition would fit their purpose. *Plant: To place firmly or forcibly; such as "planted a hard blow on his chin."* According to this definition, Cole could *plant* his seed within her, and the condom wouldn't interfere. Thank God!

And when the deed was done, she would stay on her side of the bed and he'd stay on his. They could pile those pillows between them and barely realize the other person was there at all.

Yes, that could work.

Forcing a calm she didn't feel, she escaped from the bedroom to the adjoining bathroom, where she removed the pearl-and-blossom tiara from her hair, washed her face and brushed her teeth. On the other side of the porcelain sink sat his razor, shaving mug, toothbrush and other masculine sundries.

She felt as if she were trespassing on his inner sanctum. The feeling was uncomfortable. Intimidating. Provocative. She wanted to open closets and drawers; search out secrets; know him in a deeper, truer way. She would never invade a person's privacy, though. Especially not Cole's. She was already venturing too far into his personal space...and he into hers.

He would "plant his seed within her." Firmly, forcibly, place it there.

A prickly anticipation rushed over her, and she busied herself with a steamy soak in the Jacuzzi tub to help calm her nerves. Afterward, she unpinned her hair from its upsweep and spent some soothing time brushing the wavy mass to a high sheen.

She rarely wore her hair free like this, except to bed. No amount of brushing kept it civilized for long. Phillip had suggested she cut it for efficiency's sake. At the time, she'd been working as the financial aid director of the university where he taught, and their schedules had left her little time for styling it. Although she'd always considered her long hair to be one of her few physical attributes that might be considered a plus, she *had* planned to have it cut. But then Phillip had disappeared, her father had had the heart attack and she'd been forced to quit her job at the university to run the bridal shop. The time she spent on her hair no longer seemed to matter.

She wouldn't think of those long-ago days she'd spent with

Phillip now...or the fact that she would soon be sleeping with another man. *Making love* to another man. Thrusting aside a confusing tangle of emotions, she searched the overnight bag for her nightgown and robe.

She found instead the candlelight-lace negligee that Lianna had urged her to wear. Her devious friend had obviously switched it with the demure night apparel Tess had packed. Making a mental note to kill Lianna, she rifled through her suitcase in a frenzied attempt to find something—anything—to wear other than the negligee. Sheer, sexy lace would set exactly the wrong tone.

Unfortunately, she had packed only for one night, reluctant to tote too much unwieldy luggage through the crowd of reporters and to the wedding ceremony itself. She found only the slacks and sweater she would wear to work in the morning.

Tess ground her teeth in annoyance. If only she were staying in a private room, her friend's mischief wouldn't matter. But she was staying here, in Cole's bedroom. With Cole. She would *not* wear a negligee.

A knock at the bedroom door startled her. "Tess?"

Her pulse spiked at the deep, sexy rumble of his voice. "Yeah?"

"May I come in?"

"Oh...um, yes." She would have to ask to borrow a shirt, or maybe pajamas. But she couldn't answer the door in a towel! That, too, would set the wrong mood.

She heard the door handle turn and catch. "The door's locked."

Of course it was. She hadn't entirely trusted him to keep out. Glad for the few minutes' reprieve her distrust had won her, she tugged the bath towel off of her, flung it onto a towel rack and hurried to the armchair in the bedroom where the wedding gown lay. "Oh, I'm sorry. I forgot that I'd locked the door. Didn't want any of your household staff to walk in on me. I'll be right there."

As she talked, she stepped into her wedding gown—minus the petticoats and underwear—and fumbled with the back buttons. She wasn't able to reach the very top ones. She paused for a moment in a desperate attempt to calm the rioting of her heart, then strode across the room and opened the door.

Cole stood with his shoulder against the jamb, a champagne bottle in one hand and two stemmed glasses in the other. A lock of his dark hair had fallen across his forehead, and the vertical groove beside his mouth had deepened, though the only smile she saw was in his eyes. "Your hour's up."

So was her temperature and her pulse, and her heart, which had risen into her throat at the sight of him.

He strolled past her into the bedroom, his powerful presence proclaiming it as his domain; proclaiming ownership of all within. *Calm down, Tess. He can't take more of you than you're willing to give.* He wore a black-trimmed, jade green robe that emphasized the vivid green of his eyes and the sweep of his thick dark brows and lashes. The soft sheen of the fabric somehow accentuated the ruggedness of his face and the muscular build of his body. A warrior in silk.

He's not a warrior, and you're not his conquest—or his enemy. Then what was she to him? Not one of his lovers. Not really his wife, since their vows had been lies. What could she ever hope to be to him?

He set the champagne bottle and glasses on a table, then reached for a wall switch and dimmed the lights to a golden glow. Barely sparing her a glance, he sauntered with easy masculine grace to his bed and flicked back the covers. He then opened a drawer beside the bed and tossed a small package onto the nightstand. Condoms.

Did he think he would need more than one? She couldn't imagine *that*. But then she *did* imagine that, and her blood stirred.

She wondered if he wore anything beneath his robe. Dark,

silky curls glimmered across a bare expanse of his chest. His tautly corded legs and suntanned feet were also bare. She suspected he wore nothing at all beneath the loosely sashed silk. The idea of all that raw male power barely sheathed aroused a tingling heat beneath her skin...and a wicked sensuality deeper within her. She wanted to run her hand up his bare thigh and feel his muscles clench.

She had to hold that sensuality in check.

He turned his attention to her then, like a thousand-watt spotlight, heating the very air between them. After a long, silent stare, he ambled around her in a close half circle, his gaze never leaving her—a male animal circling his intended mate. She caught the faint scent of soap and a citrusy, woodland fragrance that reminded her of orange groves, summertime lemonade, fragrant forest glens. But beneath the lightness of the aftershave lurked a vitally male redolence that brought to mind their frenzied, heated kiss in the chapel.

She wouldn't think about that kiss now, or the way she'd nearly come undone in his arms.

"You're still wearing your gown," he observed, coming to a halt before her.

"I forgot to pack my night clothes." Nervously she raked a long, stubborn auburn lock back from her face. His eyes followed the movement, then drifted over her unruly hair. Did he think she was foolish or vain for wearing it so long? Would he find her more attractive if she had cut it? She didn't think so. She sensed approval in his silent regard. Warm, sensual approval that made her want to feel his hands sifting through her hair. "Do you have a shirt or pajamas I can borrow?"

His gaze left her hair and descended in a slow perusal of the rest of her. She realized then that the bodice of her off-the-shoulder gown gaped open a little too much because of the unfastened top buttons in the back, and the skirt clung to her hips and legs rather wickedly because of the missing petticoats. She was also barefoot. And bare-legged. In fact, entirely naked beneath the thin ivory satin.

She supposed she should feel self-conscious. She didn't. A naughty, wanton compulsion coursed through her. Despite her better intentions, she wanted to entice him.

She couldn't give in to the impulse! She knew what lay beneath his calm nonchalance. Fire. Sexual fire. *Play and you'll get burned.*

A noticeable heat now simmered in his eyes, and huskiness softened his voice. "You don't need a shirt or pajamas. And I'm glad you're wearing the gown. I've thought all day about how I'd like to take it off of you."

Erotic warmth pulsed through her at that prospect. "Actually, I...I'm glad you brought that up." She squared her jaw in a show of strength to counteract the weakness of her knees and the disturbingly throaty quality of her voice. "I *won't* need help taking off the gown, and I *will* need a shirt or pajamas. I'd rather that we don't take off any more clothing than absolutely necessary to...um..." a flush climbed into her face and a breathlessness overtook her "...get the job done."

Incredulity flickered in his stare.

She went on in a nervous rush, "We're here to fulfill specific demands of the will and the curse, and that's what we'll do. That's *all* we'll do. This is serious business. *Not...*" her voice wavered only slightly "...pleasure."

His brows gathered like storm clouds, and she braced herself for a clap of thunder or jagged fork of lightning. But he turned with his usual nonchalance to the bottle of champagne, pried the previously popped cork out with his thumbs and filled both glasses with the pale, frothy liquid.

"A toast." He handed her a glass. "To...*serious business.*"

He'd even made the word "business" sound sensual. Unnerved, she clinked her glass with his and indulged in a fizzy, fortifying swallow of the cool, fragrant champagne. Regardless of how she tried to look at the situation, the prospect of their intimate involvement shook her.

He drank to the toast, lowered his glass and watched her.

"Make no mistake, ma'am," he drawled. "I always try to mix business with pleasure."

Her fingers reflexively tightened around the smooth, cool champagne glass, and she fought the urge to press it against her overly heated face or between her breasts. "I'm not saying that this...business of ours...should be *un*pleasurable, but—" Her words caught in her throat as he slid a hand around her waist and drew her to him. "Wh-what are you doing?"

"Sitting." He sank into an armchair and stationed her on his lap; or, more specifically, on his thigh. He'd whisked the skirt of her gown out from behind her before pulling her down, and it billowed around her as she descended. Which left only the silk of his robe separating his sinewy thigh from her naked bottom. His warmth and hardness sent heat shimmering along her every nerve. "Sitting *is* allowed during a business transaction," he murmured, his breath a hot torrent against her jaw, "isn't it?"

"I...I suppose so." She couldn't think clearly enough to resume her discussion of the point she'd been trying to make. His hand had splayed below the small of her back. The other cradled her hip. Heat radiated through the ivory satin from his touch. And his handsome, virile face hovered near hers, generating chaos within her.

"You're not wearing anything underneath," he whispered in a strangled tone of discovery, "are you?"

"No."

A muscle flexed in his jaw, and his hands tightened on her. Her heart nearly beat its way out of her chest. Slowly he removed the champagne glass from her hands and set it aside while his gaze touched her face, her hair, her throat...her breasts, barely contained within the gaping bodice of her gown. Her nipples hardened against the satin just from his visual exploration.

When he met her eyes again, she nearly melted from the force of his heat. "I want you, Tess. And business has nothing to do with it."

Desire spiked so sharply through her that she reached for him in panic, catching his strong, clean-shaven jaw between her hands. "Cole, listen, please," she implored. "What we're doing tonight *is* just business, and that's the way it has to be. I don't want things to get too...personal...between us."

He shut his eyes with a pained frown, turned his face and pressed a lingering kiss into the sensitive core of her palm. "Why?" The long, drawn-out word rushed hotly across the moist place where he'd kissed her, sending spirals of heat to her stomach.

"Because I've only known you a week." A good enough reason, but not the important one. How could she possibly tell him that he affected her too deeply? "*Less* than a week."

"It doesn't feel that way, Tess." His stare blazed and bandied with hers, pressing for deeper intimacy. For entrance to her soul. "It feels like I've known you all my life."

Her throat tightened with both fear and desire. She couldn't doubt his sincerity. She felt the same—as if she knew him in a profoundly fundamental way that had nothing to do with chronological time. And though she hadn't intended to share anything too personal with him, she heard herself pouring out a very basic truth. "I've never been intimate with anyone I wasn't in love with."

Something deep within the forest of his eyes darkened, as if a cloud had eclipsed the sun, and she felt tension steal over him. With a frown and a groan, he shifted her deeper into his arms and kissed her—a hot, probing, possessive kiss that stunned her with its intensity. He lodged her against the cushioned arm of the wingback chair and prolonged the intercourse of their mouths until her blood ran hot and her arms came around his broad, taut shoulders. "Then fall in love with me," he uttered against her mouth. "Fall in love with me, Tess."

She knew she should pull away from him—*run* away from him—but his seductive heat lured her into another kiss. "I can't do that," she breathed at the first opportunity. "I can't... *Ohhh!*"

He'd abandoned her mouth for her throat, lavishing hot, humid kisses down the side and back up again. Exquisite sensations distracted her, aroused her, but she had to make sure he understood the limitations. "Only what's necessary. We won't do anything that's not absolutely, positively—"

The decree ended on a little groan as he swirled his tongue down to the shadows within her gaping bodice. His mouth crossed the upper swells of her breasts in light, tingling passes that focused her attention entirely on him.

Her nipples soon begged for the heated glide of his tongue, but he withheld that from her, refusing to dip any lower. His hand, meanwhile, coursed across the satin of her gown, around the curve of her hip and upward, inciting a riot of sensation everywhere he touched. Her body moved beneath his hand in helpless response. He stopped short of her breast. A maddening thing to do.

He distracted her from that flagrant neglect, though, with the hot, sensuous glide of his mouth down the slope of a breast. She held her breath and bit her lip in keen anticipation as he grew nearer to the rigid peak. Nearer, yes, but not touching. Not...quite...touching! His forceful, increasingly ragged breaths steamed into her bodice, sensitizing her all the more.

And then his thumb strummed over one satin-covered nipple, and his tongue dipped inside the satin to lash across the other aching crest. Shards of pleasure pierced her. She gasped, moaned and closed her eyes to savor the surprise.

Pleasure heated and expanded as his fingers fanned across her breast and caught the tightened bud between them, working it into a sharply reactive point beneath the satin. His tongue coaxed the other into exquisite hardness, and pleasure compounded into need. Heat gathered and pulsed low in her womb and between her legs, driving her hips into motion.

Play the
"LAS VEGAS"
GAME
GET 3 FREE GIFTS!
FREE GIFTS!
FREE GIFTS!
FREE GIFTS!
TURN THE PAGE TO PLAY!
Details inside!

Play the

"LAS VEGAS" Game

and get

3 FREE GIFTS!

FREE GIFTS!

FREE GIFTS!

1. Pull back all 3 tabs on the card at right. Then check the claim chart to see what we have for you — 2 FREE BOOKS and a gift — ALL YOURS! A[...] FREE!

2. Send back this card and you'll receive brand-new Harlequin Temptation novels. These books have a cover price of $3.99 each in the U.S. and $4.50 each in Canada, but they are yours to keep absolutely free.

3. There's no catch. You're under no obligation to buy anything. We char[...] nothing — ZERO — for your first shipment. And you don't have to ma[...] any minimum number of purchases — not even one!

4. The fact is thousands of readers enjoy receiving books by mail from the Harlequin Reader Service®. They like the convenience of home delivery[...] they like getting the best new novels BEFORE they're available in stores[...] and they love our discount prices!

5. We hope that after receiving your free books you'll want to remain a subscriber. But the choice is yours — to continue or cancel, any time a[...] all! So why not take us up on our invitation, with no risk of any kind. You'll be glad you did!

Visit us online at
www.eHarlequin.com

FREE!
No Obligation to Buy!
No Purchase Necessary!

Play the
"LAS VEGAS" Game

PEEL BACK HERE ▶
PEEL BACK HERE ▶
PEEL BACK HERE ▶

YES! I have pulled back the 3 tabs. Please send me all the free Harlequin Temptation® books and the gift for which I qualify. I understand that I am under no obligation to purchase any books, as explained on the back and opposite page.

342 HDL C23P   **142 HDL C2YW**

NAME   (PLEASE PRINT CLEARLY)

ADDRESS

APT.#   CITY

STATE/PROV.   ZIP/POSTAL CODE

Offer limited to one per household and not valid to current Harlequin Temptation® subscribers.
All orders subject to approval.

7 7 7   **GET 2 FREE BOOKS & A FREE MYSTERY GIFT!**

🍀 🍀 🍀   **GET 2 FREE BOOKS!**

🍒 🍒 🍒   **GET 1 FREE BOOK!**

🔔 🔔 🔔   **TRY AGAIN!**

(H-T-05/00)

She needed more than he was giving. She needed to feel his hands and mouth on her everywhere. *Every*where.

As if she'd cried that need aloud, he lifted his dark, warrior face and peered at her, his gaze hot, his color high. "Feel free to stop me, Tess," he invited in a hoarse whisper, "from doing anything that isn't absolutely, positively necessary."

She hissed in a breath and ground her teeth and sank her fingers into the smooth brawn of his shoulders—not because of what he'd said, but in an effort to tame the fire that threatened her control. "Okay," she whispered. "Okay."

But even as she said it, her hands drove up into his hair, tangled at his nape and forced his face back down to her breasts as she writhed against him in silent demand. He expelled a loud, harsh breath and took what she was offering. Gone was the teasing; the slow, light touches. He pushed the gown down enough to liberate her breasts, and with his face contorted in fierce concentration, he savaged her.

Oh, but in the most blood-stirring way.

He suckled and circled and drew each mound into his mouth until her body bowed up into a hard arch. He ran his hands down that arch, groping every curve, and when he reached the tangle of her skirt, he thrust his hand beneath it.

He stroked her thighs in long, hard, provocative caresses. She trembled and gasped and parted her legs, giving him freer access to the tender insides of her thighs. He groaned her name, slid out from the armchair to his knees and shoved her skirt above her hips, his gaze smoldering. And then his fingers surged into hot, needful places...gliding, delving. Pumping to the rhythm she remembered from his kisses.

Her blood caught fire, and she *became* the rhythm—wild, sinuous undulation. He pushed deeper. Harder. And his mouth was there, along with his thrusting fingers. Pure, vibrant sensations radiated through to her very core. She didn't know exactly *what* he was doing, or *how* he was doing it, but he wasn't "planting his seed." He wasn't following directions.

She didn't stop him, though. Wouldn't *think* of stopping him. Because whatever he was doing, it was very, *very* necessary. The importance grew with every deep, rhythmic slide of his fingers, every swirl of his mouth, until the need and the pleasure escalated into the hardest, longest, most blinding climax of her life.

Intermittent waves of torrid contractions left her trembling. Panting. Feverish and dazed. Acutely sensitive to every touch—the fall of satin against her legs as he dropped her skirt into place; the shift of his body as he reached for her; the slide of his hands on her bare shoulders and back; the stir of his breath against her hair.

Fear rose within her, stronger than before. Never had she been so utterly possessed by sexual passion. Never had she climaxed with such stunning force. But worst of all, even knowing that he'd deliberately seduced her away from her better judgement, *she still wanted him.* No good could come from it. He wasn't hers, and never would be, but his potent lovemaking might make her forget that. Though the pain of losing Phillip had indelibly scarred her, she had the feeling that Cole could do much worse. She had to rally her defenses against him.

But when he hoarsely whispered her name and turned her face toward his, she didn't resist his kiss. *Couldn't* resist it. Her body had been too well primed for loving, and now she craved the feel of him. She expected a sweet and tender kiss to soothe her after that explosive climax.

Sweet and tender didn't enter into it. He led her directly into a hot, explicit mating of mouths, ruthlessly fanning her banked fire. "I want you naked now," he rasped with tangible hunger. "I have to feel you against me." He pulled her to her feet and unfastened the buttons of her gown, drawing her into another voracious kiss.

She knew she had to take control. Pleasure this keen had to be addictive, like the hot, virile flavor of his mouth and the smooth tautness of his muscles beneath his open robe. He pushed the gown down past her hips until it slithered to the floor. She shoved his robe from his shoulders and savored the crush of her breasts against his chest.

But instead of losing herself in the rhythm of his driving tongue, she veered away to kiss his jaw, neck and chest, concentrating on her goal rather than the erotic taste of his skin. She *would* take control. He'd be "planting his seed" before he even knew it. And then the deed would be done, the games would be over and he could never lay siege to her again.

He swept his hands down her naked back, cupped her buttocks and lifted her against him, forcing her legs to wrap around his hips. His erection strained between their bodies and against her feminine softness as he carried her to the bed. Pleasure wended through her, but so did dismay.

She hadn't been expecting his size and hardness. She'd already been overwhelmed by his sexual appeal before she'd known about his physical advantage. She'd clung to the hope that if she avoided his kisses and minimized foreplay, the intercourse itself would only mildly arouse her. She'd been hoping she could mentally distance herself.

Now that he held her naked against his hot, sinewy body on the way to his bed, serious doubts attacked her. There could be no dallying! No long, heated session. It was up to her to hurry things along. Get the damn seed planted. Put this night behind her.

Not easy with him kissing her throat as if he might devour her...and rocking his hardness in maddening motions against the most intimate part of her. No, indeed, not easy at all.

And then they were falling onto the bed, his mouth at her breast while his hand sought the throbbing heat between her legs. Out of sheer desperation, she grabbed his wrist and stopped him. "Cole," she panted, "we need a condom. I...I think you should put one on now."

"Not yet."

"Yes, now."

Dazed and panting with need, Cole raised himself on a

forearm and stared down at her. He knew that if he were thinking straight, he wouldn't be surprised by her insistence. He'd never made love without a condom, and the heat they'd stoked between them already burned hotter than any love-making he'd ever known. Maybe she was right. Maybe if he didn't put one on now, he'd lose all sense and make love to her without it.

Oh, he wanted to. He wanted to drive himself deep into her with no barrier between them. The very thought sent a fiery surge of desire through him, threatening his self-control. He'd damn sure better put the condom on now.

But the way she'd stiffened beneath him and caught his wrist still bothered him. Was the condom the only reason she'd stopped him?

I've never been intimate with anyone I wasn't in love with, she'd told him.

He nearly groaned when he remembered his answer. *Then fall in love with me, Tess.* Why the hell had he said it? She'd been hesitant to get sexually involved with him from the start, but he'd sensed even more uneasiness after his thoughtless response. Until, of course, he'd distracted her with his mouth and his hands and deep, hot kisses that had left his insides burning for her.

Fall in love with me, Tess. Did she think he'd been mocking her, or shrugging aside her morals? He'd said it without thinking—a gut reaction to her hesitation. And to the fact that she was in his arms only because of some damn curse...and to the thought that she'd given herself, body and soul, to another man, but never would to him. Women didn't really fall in love with Westcott men. That was a documented historical fact. He'd come to accept it.

But he wanted her.

That wanting drove all other considerations from his mind. *Would* she make love to him? Could he survive this night—or the next five months of nights—if she didn't?

Rolling away from her and onto his knees to reach across

the bed, he grabbed a condom from the nightstand. As he sat back on his heels and ripped open the foil packet, she surprised him by looming up behind him, pressing her lush, hard-tipped breasts against his back and running her hands around his ribcage in light caresses. Heat suffused him, and his hands fumbled with the condom.

"Hurry," she murmured. She then feathered kisses along his shoulder and ran her fingers in teasing circles across his chest, rousing his nipples to hardness.

He hurried. His heart hammered, his blood rushed. *She wanted him.* Her hands swept in scintillating paths from his chest to his abdomen, and her lightly kneading fingers splayed down to his groin. His arousal pulsed to an aching hardness. *She wanted him!*

Before he had the condom rolled all the way down his erection, he felt her weight shift on the bed. The warm press of her body left his back and glanced along his arm, and she shifted onto her knees to face him, her long, elegant legs folded beneath her slightly splayed thighs.

The sight of her took his breath away. Her luxuriant hair shimmered around her like a waterfall of fire, cascading down her shapely shoulders and around her high, full breasts. Teasing tendrils fanned and curled near her cinnamon-dark nipples. She was slender, yet pleasingly curved. Soft, yet strong and toned. Dewy-skinned. Supple. And *oh* so tight and hot.

He wanted her.

And it seemed she wanted him. Tense with need, he raised his gaze to meet her eyes. To search them. Read them. Glory in her heat.

But she wasn't meeting his gaze. She glanced at his hair, his chin, his nose, his eyebrows. But didn't meet his eyes. "Let's do it *now*," she whispered. And she raked her fingertips slowly up his thighs.

His blood surged in a dizzying rush. He had no problem with *now*. Smoothing the condom into place, he rose on his

knees and pulled her against him, taking her mouth in a rol-
licking, sumptuous kiss.

Her body fused with his. His hands flowed over voluptuous curves and into moist, hot valleys. She broke away from
the kiss with a breathy cry. "No!" He blinked to focus
through a sensual haze, but before he could make sense of her
protest, she added, "You've done enough. It's *my* turn now."

And she slid a hand around his straining erection and
nested its tip between her thighs, beneath the auburn curls of
her femininity.

"Tess," he groaned, catching at her hips in helpless reflex
as she began to undulate. In all his imaginings since he'd met
her, he hadn't expected such aggression. She never failed to
surprise him, though. Or to enflame him.

His hardness probed into silky wet heat, forcing a loud ex-
pulsion of breath from him. She gasped at that initial penetra-
tion, stunned into momentary stillness. Then her eyes closed
and her hips resumed their sinuous revolutions. Slowly,
slowly, she drew him in.

Lightly, rhythmically, he thrust up into her.

A long, deep groan rolled from her throat, and her fingers
bit into his shoulders. "No!" she cried, her eyes still tightly
closed. "Don't...don't move."

"What?" he breathed, too caught up in currents of molten
sensation to clearly understand. Had she told him *not to
move*? She had to be kidding! Grinding his teeth, he filled his
hands with her firm, flexing buttocks and gyrated harder,
driving himself further up into the heaven of her tightness.

Her face began to glisten. A pulse beat wildly in her throat.
"Please," she begged, her silvery eyes flashing open. "This
would be so much easier if you'd just...let...me...*do*...it!"

And she shoved at his shoulders, catching him off-guard,
knocking him off balance. He tumbled on an awkward angle,
his tight grip on her bottom bringing her with him and preventing their bodies from disjoining, though just barely. Her
hair spilled over him in a fragrant, silky rush, and his arms

corralled her. Panting for air, reeling with bewilderment and frustration, he rolled onto his back and trapped her against his chest. "What are you doing, Tess?"

Evading his gaze, she pushed up and fought free of his arms. Apprehension sluiced through him. Something was wrong. Very wrong. Squaring her jaw, she tossed her hair behind one shoulder, straddled his hips and maneuvered him deeper into her.

Acute pleasure jolted from his loins, bringing his shoulders up off the bed. Too stunned to utter more than a guttural groan, he fell back and watched her in a hot-blooded daze. She braced her hands on her thighs, shut her eyes and circled her hips in sleek, powerful gyrations. Sharp pangs of sensation assailed him. Her internal muscles clenched him, stroked him.

The pleasure rose too quickly; the intensity grew too great for him to last long. But he didn't want it to end this way. He wanted to prolong their coupling. Draw her into it. Share it.

It occurred to him then that she *wasn't* sharing it. At least, not in the way he craved. She'd forced him deep into her body, but she'd also shut him out—avoiding his gaze; fending off his touches; withholding her kiss.

The clear, simple truth hit him. She was doing only what was necessary. Planting the seed. *Taking care of business.*

Teetering at the edge of an earth-shattering climax, he grabbed her hips and stopped her. Her eyes flew open. She looked dazed, wild and seductive...and very near climax herself. It didn't help him to know that. Struggling to stave off his own imminent release, he ground his teeth, pulled her down into his arms and rolled with her.

She fought to escape his hold, but writhed against him all the while, pushing him closer to a completion he didn't want. He tried to withdraw from her intimate heat, but she squeezed her inner muscles around him and clamped her hands around his buttocks to hold him fast. She clearly didn't want to be in his arms...yet she intended to keep their bodies intimately joined.

To finish the job.

He couldn't let her get away with it.

"Tess." He wrestled her down, trapped her beneath him and pinned her forearms beside her head, exerting force with his torso and thighs to subdue the movement of her body. "Tess, *don't do this.*"

With a gasp and a sob, she suddenly arrested into utter stillness.

Their frantic breathing rasped loud and harsh. Their hearts thundered. He buried his face in the silky, tangled mass of her hair and called on every ounce of his willpower to stave off his climax. He wouldn't move, wouldn't even try to pull out of her, until he'd quelled the raging pressure in his loins.

The moment spun out in panting, simmering silence.

As the immediate threat subsided, he lifted his head, needing badly to connect with her. Needing to understand. Her flushed, glistening face radiated with an intensity that mystified him, but at least she *was* meeting his eyes. He urgently probed her gaze for answers.

And she probed his, searching...searching...as if he'd surprised and bewildered her as much as she had him.

But the need was still too strong to allow for clarity. The heat was banked, yet still too potent. And he was still achingly hard and throbbing within her.

Their silent communication seethed.

He flexed his grip on her hands beside her head, twining his fingers with hers, greedily absorbing the feel of her beneath him and the compelling heat of her stare.

And then he cocked his pelvis and rocked...ever so slightly...within her. Her body clenched, her breath hitched, her fingers tightened spasmodically around his. And her gaze consumed him.

Sweat beaded on his face at the effort of his restraint as he rolled his hips in an infinitely subtle thrusting. Torrential pleasure flooded him. He watched it—*felt* it—course through her, the same molten rivers of sensation. But desire radiated from somewhere deeper than the pleasure, and he gritted his teeth, wanting everything she was withholding.

Releasing her hands, he trapped her face between his palms and plied her with a scouring gaze. "Kiss me, Tess," he implored in a desperate whisper, his thumbs sweeping in compulsive arcs beside her mouth. "It's necessary. So damn necessary."

Her gaze darkened with renewed turbulence, as if some inner battle raged. He felt her resistance. *Knew* that she'd refuse. And the pain of her abandonment squeezed him breathless.

But while he struggled to deal with the pain, the warmest, sweetest vulnerability broke through in her stare. And though she looked like she might cry, her hands wended up his back, her arms slid around his shoulders and she gave herself over to a kiss—a moving, sharing, electrifying kiss that stoked his need hotter than anything ever had in his life.

Then they made love. Heart to heart, muscle against muscle, they undulated together in a slow, erotic dance. The essence of poetry, of song. And when the need and the pleasure built to an overwhelming force, the detonation ripped through both of them with awe-inspiring power.

Tess felt as if she'd been reborn.

She knew then, as she lay gasping against his slick, quaking body, that she'd been wrong in all of her earlier self-assurances. He *had* taken more—much, much more—than she'd ever intended to give.

7

TESS WOKE UP in bed alone. She also woke up too late. On a Saturday morning, yet. The bridal shop's busiest day. At least, in a theoretical sense. They hadn't seen much action in the last few months, but that only made every business hour more vital. She should have opened the store an hour ago.

She showered and dressed in a mad rush, then scrambled down the elegant grand staircase of Westcott Hall in hopes of finding her car. Cole had promised he'd have someone drop it by the house last night. He'd kept his word. Her modest old sedan sat in the circular drive, looking ridiculously out of place at the Westcott mansion.

She felt just as ridiculously out of place. What was a good little McCrary girl doing here, anyway?

Regrouping after an evening of torrid sex with Cole Westcott. Her heart turned over at the thought. She'd been putty in his hands. *Hot* putty. At least she *had* managed to pry herself from his embrace once he'd fallen asleep. She'd huddled on her side of the bed for the rest of the night, rehashing the details of her surrender.

And it *had* been a surrender. Unconditional. Her intentions to stay mentally detached and to keep things impersonal had gone up in a blaze. By the time he'd "planted his seed within her," their lovemaking had become extraordinarily personal. Or rather, it had felt that way to her. And she'd started believing that he was kissing her and making love to her with a passion that meant something more than mere sex.

Not good. Delusions like those could only lead her to emotional disaster. As she drove down the tree-canopied highway toward town, she firmly reminded herself that words whispered in the heat of sexual arousal couldn't be taken as signs of anything deeper. *Fall in love with me, Tess,* he'd said. *Kiss me. It's so damn necessary.*

Oh, he was good. His urgent whispers, his soul-stealing gazes. If she hadn't believed his reputation as a dangerous lady's man, she certainly did now. How could any woman resist giving him everything he wanted once he set his mind to seduction? Then again, she supposed there weren't too many women who would even think of resisting. He had to have legions of eager lovers.

That thought disturbed her way too much. Another bad sign. Their marriage was a business arrangement. She shouldn't care at all about his other women.

Dismay jolted through her. His *other* women? Had she really thought of them as *his other women?* That would mean that she considered herself one of them. And she didn't! She had married him, yes, and made love to him...but that didn't mean she was personally *involved* with him.

God, Tess. How much more involved could you be? Squeezing the steering wheel until her fingers hurt, she assured herself that legal and sexual involvement did not necessarily mean emotional involvement. And wasn't that her biggest reservation concerning Cole—her fear of becoming too emotionally attached to him?

She'd obviously been without a man for too long. The thirteen months she'd spent alone had left her too vulnerable.

Slowing her speed as she approached city streets, she wondered if Cole had been affected at all by their lovemaking, or if he took passionate nights of sex pretty much for granted. She couldn't help noticing that he'd left this morning without waking her. No long, hot, early morning kisses. No blazing caresses. No wild acts of passion.

At least she could be thankful for *that.* Very thankful.

But...hadn't he *wanted* to make love to her this morning? Had he grown bored with her already?

Motoring slowly past her parents' boutique, she found no open parking space and had to walk two city blocks from her car. When she reached the shop, she gaped in surprise. Not only was it already open, but the place bustled with activity—women rifling through dresses on the racks, trying on veils and tiaras, debating over styles. Both her mother and Kristen were there, thoroughly engrossed in helping customers.

"Hey, look. It's her," someone remarked. Everyone glanced toward the doorway where Tess stood, and whispers rustled like crinoline petticoats.

"Oh, Tess, thank goodness you're here." Her mother broke away from a cluster of women who were debating over bridesmaid dresses. "Are you okay, honey?" she whispered, clearly worried. "Did he expect you to—" With a sharp glance at a woman standing nearby who watched and listened with blatant interest, she murmured, "We'll talk later. Will you help these ladies choose a style while I tend to Mrs. Capelli? She's here to pick up her daughter's gown."

"Excuse me." A bubbly young redhead pushed past Margaret to beam at Tess. "Do you have any more gowns like the one you wore yesterday? When I saw it on the newscast, I knew I *had* to have one just like it. It was gorgeous!"

A hubbub of enthusiastic agreement broke out around her. One matronly woman noticed her wedding ring and grabbed her hand for a closer look. A chorus of "oohs" and "ahhhs" sounded. Comments flowed about her dress, her hair, her flowers, the limo, the chapel...the groom....

"And when you walked up those chapel stairs, I got chill bumps from the way he watched you." "If he isn't just to *die* for..." "What are you doing at work today, girl? If he was my new husband, I'd be honeymoonin'."

New husband. Legally speaking, he was. Only she and he knew differently.

Forcing a smile, she joked, murmured thanks for the compliments and sold an astounding number of dresses. At the first lull, her mother and sister wilted into chairs on either side of Tess, stunned by the response to the prime-time television broadcast.

"I decided to open the store this morning," Margaret said, "since your father's still in the hospital, and there's not much for me to do. I barely had the place open before I was swamped. Then Kristen dropped by to tell me the news about Josh, and when she saw how busy I was, she stayed."

"The news?" Tess turned to Kristen in surprise. "About Josh?"

Her sister's lovely blue eyes lit with a smile, and she explained, "Late last night, Josh started to feel tingles in his leg. This morning, he responded to reflex tests. The doctor said those are excellent signs that he might recover all feeling and use of his leg."

"Kris, that's great." Tess squeezed her hand. "I'm praying that he does."

"Pray that he beats those criminal charges, too. I can't stand to think of him being sent to—" She broke off, bit her lip with a sudden welling in her eyes.

Tess's heart bled for her. "We'll beat those assault charges, Kris. It was just a misunderstanding, and we'll make the court see that."

"That reminds me," Margaret said. "A lawyer called your father all the way from New York. He offered to represent him and Josh in the criminal action for next to nothing. We think he's after the publicity. Wouldn't it be great, not having to pay?"

Tension percolated through Tess at that news and she wasn't even sure why. "What's this attorney's name, Mama?"

"Let's see. Hmmm." She screwed up her face, then shook her head. "I can't recall at the moment. But your father was very pleased. It seems like our luck may have started changing for the better."

Luck? The luck of the McCrarys was starting to change for the better? The thought brought to mind the curse and all its implications. Could their turn of luck be due to the fact that she and Cole were complying with its terms? She pushed that notion away, reluctant to get her hopes up; to believe it could be so simple.

"What about you, honey?" Margaret eyed Tess with concern. "Did everything go okay yesterday? We hardly talked at all when you called last night. You sounded so preoccupied."

"Preoccupied?" Of course she'd been preoccupied, with Cole on his way up to *plant his seed within her.* "I was just tired, I guess."

"This morning when you were late, I was worried. You're never late."

"I'm sorry you were worried, Mama. I overslept. I had a hard time getting to sleep last night, so..." Warmth rushed to her face. "N-not a *hard* time, really. Being in a strange bed, I... Well, the bed wasn't *strange.* But—"

She was saved from her floundering by another gust of business. Chattering customers gradually filled the shop and kept all three of them busy for a while.

When the pace again slowed and only a few customers remained, the telephone behind the counter rang and Kristen answered. "Oh, hello, Mr. Westcott." Tess, who stood directly across the counter from her, stiffened in surprise. Kristen pointedly met her gaze. "I guess you're right," she admitted cautiously into the receiver. "*Cole,* then."

Tess noticed that her sister's usually friendly tone held a cool note of reserve. She supposed she understood. Her family had always considered him the enemy, but even more so now, in light of their opposing legal interests. Oddly enough, though, Kristen's coolness toward Cole bothered Tess. It hadn't been his fault that the crisis had happened. His cousin's, maybe, but not his.

Caution lurked in Kristen's eyes as she politely responded to something Cole had said. "They're both doing a little better, thanks. But we won't know for a while how much damage has been done." After another moment, her golden eyebrows rose. "Oh, thank you. That's...very nice." In a warmer tone, she murmured, "Yes, I'll get her."

Covering the mouthpiece as she handed the phone to Tess, she whispered, "It's him. Cole." As if everyone in the store wasn't already aware of that. Customers had broken off in their conversations the moment she'd said "Mr. Westcott." Kristen knit her brows and added in a confidential undertone that Tess hoped only she could hear, "He says he'll do everything he can to help us with Daddy and Josh's situation."

A warm, gratified feeling radiated through Tess to know he'd reassured her sister. He was a fundamentally kind, caring man, and she had no doubt he meant what he'd said. She knew he didn't want to see her family harmed.

That thought stopped her cold. *She knew he didn't want to see her family harmed.* When had she come to that conclusion? He was a Westcott...one of the very ones who had helped drive her father to ruin. Yet, she *did* trust him.

A little more of her world had somehow ceased to make sense.

"Tess?" prompted Kristen, holding the phone out to her with a concerned frown.

Taking the phone from her sister with a ridiculous thud of her heart, she turned her back to the watchful eyes, which included Kristen's and her mother's. "Hello?"

"Hi."

The very sound of his sexy baritone set her pulse to leaping. "Hi."

"I haven't stopped thinking about you all day."

Reaction sizzled through her, as sharply as if he'd pulled her into his arms. Conscious of her audience, she cast a quick look around. Everyone turned politely away, but the shop remained suspiciously quiet.

"Hold for a moment, please." Striving for a business-like air, Tess returned the receiver to Kristen. "Would you please hit the hold button and hang this up? I'll take it in the bedroom." Mortification struck her as she realized what she'd said. "I...I meant the *office!* I'll take the call in the *office.*" Her face burned as she strode to the back of the store, pretending not to notice the customers' smirks and knowing glances.

How could she have made such a humiliating slip? It was all *his* fault for throwing her off-balance. After locking the office door, she snatched up the phone. "I can't believe you're calling me at work and saying things like that."

"Things like what? That I haven't stopped thinking about you all day? It's true. And uncomfortable as hell, believe *me.*" She heard the wry note in his voice, and imagined how his eyes looked right now, brimming with that fine, dry humor. "I was called away too early this morning. Pipes broke at one of my waterfront restaurants and flooded the place. The manager quit, the chef threatened suicide, and the governor is supposed to be holding a fund-raiser there tonight. Otherwise," his voice lowered into a gruff, teasing murmur, "I'd have knocked the phone off the hook at home and we'd still be there, you and I, in my big ole' bed...doing all sorts of *necessary* things."

She leaned weakly against the desk, overcome by a flux of heat, indignation and reluctant amusement. Worst of all, pure feminine gratification. He *had* wanted her this morning. And he wanted her now. "I think that's assuming quite a lot."

"I think we need a honeymoon."

She pressed a hand to her heart. Every thundering beat shook her.

"What about it, Tess? A few weeks. Somewhere we can be alone."

"You can't be serious."

"I've never been more serious."

She bit her lip and looked up at the ceiling. What was she doing, letting him rile her into a state of starry-eyed arousal? And over the phone, yet. "Cole, about what happened between us last night..."

"Our wedding night happened last night."

She almost groaned. She liked the way he saw things, and didn't want to argue. She liked the way he made her feel, and didn't want the feeling to end. "But we both know that we aren't—"

"I'll tell you what I know, Tess. For the rest of my life, when I think of *my bride*, I'll remember last night. And I'll get hot and hard for wanting you."

An awesome heat washed through her. An irresistible heat. *The rest of his life.* She knew it wasn't true. He'd used it as a figure of speech. Poetic exaggeration. And though he'd called her *"my bride,"* she hadn't really been his bride. Their vows had been a mockery. Someday he *would* marry, she felt sure. And Tess McCrary would be long forgotten. Rightfully so.

But his hoarse whisper had set her ablaze with dangerous yearning. He was a threat. A terrible threat. She couldn't take anything he said or did too seriously.

"Choose a place," he urged. "Anywhere. And we'll lose ourselves there."

Oh, yes. She would indeed lose herself. In the steadiest voice possible, she replied, "You do understand, Cole, that the seed has already been planted. There's no need for a...replanting."

Abject silence answered her. She believed she'd stunned him.

Rising on weakened legs from her perch at the edge of the desk, she murmured, "I've got to get back to work."

"There *is* a need, Tess. We proved that last night."

"I'm too busy to talk now." Her whisper shook. "I'll see you—" At *home*, she'd been about to say. But the word seemed too intimate.

"At home," he finished for her. "I'll see you at home, Tess. For dinner." As she struggled with the realization that he understood her too well, he added, "And bring the rest of your clothes, along with anything else that would make you feel that you live here. Do you need help moving anything? I'll meet you at your apartment, if you want. I can send a moving crew and truck tomorrow for the bigger pieces."

"No, I won't be moving furniture. I won't be staying all *that* long."

Tense silence stretched between them across the phone line.

"Maybe not. But while you're with me, I want my home to be *your* home."

She couldn't allow herself to start thinking that way. She didn't try to explain, though. He wouldn't understand. Or he might understand too well. "Thank you." She hung up the phone before he could say another word. He had a way of rousing her emotions even when he was simply being nice.

The rest of the afternoon passed in a daze for her. Though she tried to keep her mind on her work, Cole never left her thoughts. And every time she glanced at the clock, it was to see how much longer she had until she'd be with him again.

That realization alone shook her up. Worse, though, was the knowledge that he wouldn't let her have the last word about their lovemaking. She knew him well enough to be sure of that.

With a disturbing sense of self-discovery, she realized that the challenge of squaring off with him over *that* particular issue stirred her. And her growing tension had less to do with apprehension than with anticipation. Breathless, bone-deep anticipation.

To be with him again. To spend another night in his bed, regardless of what they did there.

Trying to ruthlessly squelch that anticipation, she dropped by her apartment after work and took her time packing another suitcase. She wouldn't hurry or glance at her watch or wonder if he was waiting for her. And she wouldn't be caught without adequate clothing again, no matter what situation arose. As she tossed in the last few pairs of shorts and tops, her gaze lit on the framed photograph of Phillip on her dresser.

Emotions assaulted her—guilt that she had betrayed him with another man; anger that he had left her and never returned; longing for the simplicity of their relationship. But strongest of all was confusion. Why had her lovemaking with Cole wrenched her very soul from its moorings, when she'd never felt anything close to that with Phillip?

Thinking back, she tried to remember the specifics and couldn't. Their physical relations had always been pleasant, though. Loving. Considerate. She'd believed herself to be satisfied. What accounted for the strikingly vital difference?

Passion. There'd been no real passion with Phillip.

Perhaps she wasn't being fair, comparing Phillip to Cole in that way. While Phillip had been the attractive, golden-haired professor that had set feminine hearts aflutter on campus, he'd also been an everyday kind of guy who became preoccupied with his work and, during his off-time, with the university's sports, world news, classic cars and, always but always, anthropology. Which, although annoying at times, had also been endearing. He was a steady, hardworking man who would make a wonderful partner throughout life. So what if passionate lovemaking wasn't his strong suit?

Cole, on the other hand, was a fantasy lover come true. Sinfully handsome, hard-bodied, quick-witted, he possessed the uncanny ability to appeal to the female of the species on every conceivable level—his looks, his voice, his touch. His humor. His ability to say and do the exact right things to light fires in a woman's blood. He focused with such thrilling intensity on a woman that she felt incredibly desirable. And his kisses made her believe in her heart of hearts that he was falling in love with her.

Tess closed her eyes against the heated pang inspired by that thought.

Like the blaze of a shooting star, though, Cole's awesome magic couldn't last a lifetime, or even years. By his very definition—fantasy lover—he belonged not to one woman, but to every woman. She couldn't allow herself to believe differently.

Taking the photo of Phillip from her dresser, she resolutely packed it along with her clothes. She wouldn't flaunt the photo in front of Cole, or display it in his house. She respected him more than that. But she *would* keep it with her, tucked away in her belongings for occasional glances. Whenever she felt too drawn to Cole, too overcome by his appeal, a glance at Philip's face would remind her of the important difference between them. Even if Phillip never returned, she couldn't fall into the trap of expecting Cole to play the role that Phillip would have filled so admirably.

She also retrieved the old family bible from her desk and made a copy of the curse with the scanner she'd bought during her years as financial aid director. It had occurred to her earlier today that if the translation had been written incorrectly in Cole's bible, hers could also be wrong. Did the McCrary family's curse mention any specifics she wasn't aware of? Just to make sure she was covering all her bases, she would have a translator look at the original Gaelic version as soon as possible.

Determined to keep her thoughts on practical matters such as this, she drove to Westcott Hall. When she arrived and discovered nobody home except Mrs. Johannsen, she told herself she was glad. She used the time to unpack her suitcase and arrange her clothes into the dresser and closet space that Mrs. Johannsen indicated as hers, upon express orders from Mr. Westcott.

"Oh, by the way. He wanted me to tell you that he's running late," Mrs. Johannsen remembered. "Something about having a drink with the governor before a fund-raiser."

Good, Tess told herself. More free time alone. Weren't things going swimmingly?

"He said for you to go ahead and eat. I'll bring up a tray for you, and then I'll be going home."

Tess murmured her thanks, ignoring her hope that he

wouldn't be *too* late. When she'd finished her unpacking, she dined on the chicken casserole, salad and home-baked bread Mrs. Johannsen had delivered.

She then went down to Cole's library, where she found Henry's name on the speed dial of the telephone. To her surprise, Henry himself answered her call rather than a recorded greeting. She asked for the name of the translator he'd used and explained her reason for wanting it.

"I hope you understand, Ms. McCrary, that the curse in *your* family bible has nothing to do with the terms of Harlan Westcott's will." The suspicion in his genteel, southern voice surprised her. She could almost hear the gears grinding as he tried to figure out the ulterior motive behind the request.

"My reason for wanting the curse translated has nothing to do with the will, either, Henry."

The reassurance didn't seem to particularly appease him, but after a moment of doubt-heavy silence, he sighed. "You probably know the translator I used, anyway. She teaches at the university where you worked." Reluctantly he gave her the name.

Tess couldn't believe she hadn't thought of Professor Kathleen O'Brian on her own. Although they hadn't been close, they'd had many friends in common, and she'd known of Kathleen's expertise in many languages. She called her immediately, and Kathleen urged her to fax her the curse right away. She promised to have it back to her by some time this evening—much sooner than Tess had expected.

As she finished sending the information on Cole's fax machine, the library door swung open. A tall, hulking man with a buzz cut, jutting jaw and military bearing lumbered in and regarded her in surprise. "Oh, sorry, ma'am. I heard a noise, and thought Cole might be in here."

"I don't believe he's home yet."

His wiry ginger brows puckered. "Hey, aren't you Tess McCrary?"

The hostile, suspicious tone of the question tipped her off, and she recognized him from the news broadcasts. Setting her paperwork aside, she slowly rounded Cole's desk. "Oh, I know who *you* are. Cole's cousin. Leo. The one who beat up my father."

Leo's wide-jawed face flushed red. "I didn't beat him up. The old coot jumped me. And his accomplice came at me with a rifle."

She rolled her eyes, which clearly angered him.

"Now *you* tell *me* what you're doing nosing around in Cole's private library," he demanded, his mighty shoulders squaring. "He keeps his personal paperwork in that desk. Does he know you're in here?"

She clenched her teeth and glared. Cole did *not* know, of course. She hadn't had a chance to tell him what she was doing. How humiliated she would be if Leo turned her in and Cole accused her of snooping! "That's none of your business, Officer Westcott."

"Nothing Cole keeps in here is any of *your* business, Ms. McCrary."

"Her name," came a voice from the doorway, "is Mrs. Westcott."

Both Tess and Leo turned to Cole in surprise. Her heart gave a crazy kick at the sight of him; at the sound of his voice. But most of all, at the name and the way he'd said it. She hadn't given it a thought until now. *Mrs. Westcott.*

"Mrs. *Cole* Westcott," Cole specified, advancing into the library with a steely gaze fixed on Leo. "My wife." He then slid his arm around her waist, drew her against him and melted every thought from her mind with a long, hot, possessive stare. "My wife," he repeated in a gruff whisper that steamed against her face.

She knew he was making a statement to *her* as well as to Leo. That statement thrilled her. Made her want to be everything he claimed...and more.

"Aww, geez, Cole," Leo grumbled. "Don't get carried away with this marriage stuff. How was I supposed to know if you wanted her in here or not? You've always been touchy about letting anyone in your library."

Cole shifted his gaze away from his heated communion with Tess to level another warning stare at Leo, which set him back a step. "Understand this, Leo. This is now *her* library. And her house. If she wants to kick your butt out of here, you're out." Cole then glanced at Tess. "Do you want him out?"

The temptation was strong to banish him from the house—more for the harm he'd done her father and Josh than for the rudeness he'd shown her. Yet, in all good conscience, she couldn't do it. He was Cole's family. She couldn't take that lightly. And he *had* been looking out for Cole's best interests. With almost painful reluctance, she shook her head.

"You have the right, Tess. Never doubt it. If anyone, *anyone*, makes you uncomfortable, you can make them leave. And I'll back you up, all the way."

She swallowed against a sudden tightness in her throat. His sharing of his power and his home, his trust in her judgement and respect for her feelings, all touched her deeply.

Averting her gaze from Cole to stop him from seeing how much he had touched her, she glanced at Leo, who looked shaken, sullen and embarrassed. "I...I may have been partially to blame for Leo's hostility," she admitted, wishing her conscience didn't compel her to do so. Surprise flickered over Leo's face. "I might have provoked him."

"Imagine that," murmured Cole.

"She said I beat up her old man."

"You did," charged Tess, her passion engaged again.

"I did not." Steam virtually rose from Leo's reddened ears. "In fact, I was trying to stop him from hurting himself or someone else."

"Oh, I'll bet." She swung her braid back over her shoulder, rested a fist on one cocked hip and narrowed her eyes. "Is that why you drew the gun?"

"I drew the gun *before* he jumped me...when the other guy came out with the rifle."

"Well, if *that* wasn't brilliant! Couldn't you tell that he—"

"Hold it." Cole held up his hands and frowned, silencing them both. Though he couldn't deny gleaning a certain thrill from watching his slim little redheaded bride in her tight faded jeans get all fired up and go toe-to-toe with a mountain of mean brawn, he figured he'd better put an end to the confrontation before Leo said something that Cole would make him regret. "If you two want to discuss this matter, we'll do it some other time. It's getting late, and I'm tired."

"Late?" Leo scoffed. "It's not even nine. And on a Saturday, yet."

For having been a newlywed himself not too long ago, Leo was amazingly obtuse. Choosing to ignore that dim-witted observation, Cole said, "I'm assuming you're here about tomorrow. Have you brought over all of your supplies and found everything you'll need?"

He nodded, his resentment still palpable.

"Tess, your shop's closed on Sunday, right?" She nodded, and gladness seeped through Cole. He'd keep her in bed late tomorrow. "Good. Leo, let's change our engagement to lunch instead of brunch. We'll expect you around one-thirty." With a glance at Tess, he said, "Mrs. Johannsen is off on Sundays, so Leo's going to take up the slack. He plans to dazzle us with his culinary art."

Tess blinked, as if she hadn't quite understood.

Leo also blinked. "You mean, *she's* going to try the dishes, too?"

"Of course."

"*He's* going to actually *cook*?" Tess's incredulous question provoked another scowl from Leo. She turned in concern to Cole. "Are you sure it's safe?"

Leo's granite jaw jerked back and forth, and Cole heard teeth grinding. "Let's do this taste test some other time, Cole.

When we're alone. I don't want your opinion swayed by outside influences."

That was just the kind of comment he wouldn't tolerate—one that seethed with disrespect for Tess's role in his household. In his life. He was having a hard enough time defining that role even to himself without interference from anyone else. The word "wife" appealed to him immensely, though. And the idea of sharing his home with her, if only for a while, touched a resonant chord deep within him. He wouldn't have her slighted. "If you're referring to *my wife* as an outside influence—"

"Okay, okay," cried Tess, grabbing his arm to stop his angry advance on Leo. "Enough of this squabbling. By one-thirty tomorrow, Leo, you'd better be in that kitchen, or wherever it is you cook. I won't say a word, not one word, about your 'dishes' unless you ask for my opinion."

Leo glowered at her, clenching and unclenching his hands, then looked to Cole for guidance—as if he'd never dealt with a force quite like Tess before and hadn't the vaguest idea of how to handle it.

Cole couldn't help empathizing. Letting go of some of his anger, he nodded at his cousin in encouragement. Muttering that he'd be back at one-thirty tomorrow, Leo strode out of the library.

After they heard the front door slam, Tess stared in the direction he'd taken. A silent moment ticked by before she asked faintly, "He cooks?"

"He says he does." The relief of finding himself alone with her washed away the rest of Cole's anger. He'd been waiting all day to touch her. Hold her. He ran his hands up her arms, bare and smooth beneath her short-sleeved gold blouse. "He wants me to let him cook at a restaurant I opened on Shem Creek."

"But isn't he a cop, and a part-time security guard?"

"He's a cop, but they've got him on desk duty, and he hates

it. He's looking for some other line of work. He also needs more money because of his baby boom."

"Baby boom?"

"His wife gave birth to triplets two months ago. All boys."

"Triplets!" Tess gaped at him. "I hadn't pictured Leo as a father." After another moment of reflection, she asked, "How long has he been married?"

"Almost a year."

"A *year?*" Her eyes lit with an unexpected excitement. "That's wonderful. He's a Westcott. Don't you see, Cole? He's proving that the curse isn't real!"

Cole bit his cheek, hating to burst her bubble. "Actually, his wife left him last week, because of the incident with your father. She feels Leo is too hot-headed to be a cop, and is afraid that he'll be sued, and doesn't think he can support the family any other way. She's divorcing him."

"Oh. I'm sorry." Genuine distress shone in her gaze.

Cole wanted to kiss her. But he knew that her interest in Leo was too keen at the moment for her to be easily distracted. Determined to get it over with, he explained, "He won't take money from me that he doesn't earn. Unfortunately, I felt I had to suspend him from his guard duty after his fight with your father."

"I didn't know you did that." She clearly held mixed feelings regarding the issue. "But Leo's a Westcott. Why isn't he rich?"

Cole held back a rueful grin. At least he could always count on her for plain speaking. "His father lost his money gambling. Leo himself made matters worse with a few bad choices."

She nodded sympathetically.

He drank in the sight of her, sifting his fingers through the fiery tendrils beside her face, savoring the silky texture of her hair. He wanted to free the thick, shining mass from the maddening braid. Thrust his hands into it. Kiss her breathless.

He sensed tension stealing into her body as their gazes

locked. "Cole, about me being here in your library. I'm sorry if I wasn't supposed to be. I only came to find a phone number and use your fax machine. I—"

He shushed her with a finger against her lips. "You don't owe me an explanation for being in the library. I meant what I said. This is your home for as long as you stay." Slowly he brushed his finger across the lush, smooth curves of her mouth, his gaze avidly following. "You can do whatever you like."

Her eyelids fluttered in sensual reaction to the stroke of his finger, and hunger for her surged through him. He lowered his mouth to hers, swept his tongue along the same path his finger had taken, then delved into a deep, hot, stroking kiss. He molded her body to his and reveled in the taste, the feel, the heat of her.

He didn't think he could ever get enough. Their lovemaking last night had shaken him with such force that he hadn't been able to think of much else. He had no idea where the intensity came from, or where it would lead, but he wanted to go wherever it took him. Again and again.

And he wouldn't listen to her nonsense about there being no need to "re-plant the seed." Before he finished with her tonight, she wouldn't deny the need—the one that burned between them. "Come to bed with me, Tess," he urged.

"Oh, Cole..." With a regretful groan, she brushed his hair tenderly back from his face. "You've been so sweet and kind."

Sweet and kind, hell! He didn't want her thinking of him as sweet and kind...but as hot, hard and necessary.

"Offering to share your home, standing behind me even when I'm rude to your cousin. Calling me your wife. But our marriage isn't real. We didn't mean any of our vows. And if we keep carrying on the way we did last night, I...I might start losing sight of where the pretense ends and reality begins."

Pretense? Reality? He *was* hot and hard. She *did* want him.

Their lovemaking *was* necessary. There was no pretense about it. He didn't see much of a problem.

Tilting her face for easier access, he kissed and nipped his way along her jaw, licking its tender underside, stopping beside her ear only long enough to whisper, "Reality's whatever we make it." He then continued down the warm, fragrant curve of her neck, eliciting breathless moans from her.

He intended to make their reality the very best he could.

The telephone rang. He ignored it. His hands had found her breasts, warm and round, confined behind the cotton of her blouse and the stiff lace of her bra. He rubbed his palms over her nipples until they strained through the barriers, and a cry rolled in her throat. It all had to come off—the blouse, the bra. The jeans. Everything. He needed to feel her, skin to skin. Mouth to skin.

The fax machine clicked on as he reached to unbutton her blouse.

With an urgent gasp, she covered his hands and squeezed, preventing all movement. "I'm sorry, Cole." Her whisper was unsteady, her skin flushed. He knew her blood burned with a need as hot as his. "But I meant what I said. The seed has been 'planted' as well as it's ever going to be. That requirement has been fulfilled. Sex with you over the next five months wouldn't be good for either of us."

"It *would* be good, Tess, and you know it."

"That's not what I meant, and *you* know it."

He enfolded her hands into a warm, tight clasp between their thudding hearts and gazed compellingly into her eyes. "You really think we can live together, sleep together, and not—"

"I think we're going to *have* to." Pulling her hands away with a regretful yet determined look, she turned toward the fax machine. "This will probably be for me, from the translator."

He stared at her in acute frustration, trying to think of what to say, what to do, to make her see reason. He imagined her in his bed, lying beside him, and didn't know how he'd ever make it through even one full night without reaching for her. He couldn't do it. He *wouldn't* do it.

"I sent the translator the curse from *my* family bible," she was saying, watching as the transmission hummed and the paper slowly emerged. "I thought we'd better see exactly what it says, just in case there's something more than we already know."

Cole swallowed a groan. She was thinking about that damn curse again. Maybe *this* was the torture that the McCrary witch had planned back in 1825—to distract his sweet, hot McCrary bride with mumbo jumbo until he slowly but surely lost his mind.

Tess withdrew the printed page from the fax machine and silently read it. An odd, troubled look flitted over her face. She glanced rather furtively up at him, then skimmed the page again.

Curiosity filled him. "What does it say?"

She met his gaze, looking shaken. "Nothing. I mean, nothing more than yours said. Same old stuff." Abruptly she folded the paper, not once, not even twice, but many times, into a small, thick square.

"Let me see the translation."

"Why?" She held the square of paper behind her and backed away from him, piquing his curiosity more. "I told you, it's the same as yours. Except instead of 'safe, comfortable home,' it says I have to provide you with a *warm*, comfortable home.'"

"Shouldn't be too hard. We do 'warm' *so* well." He advanced a stealthy step, making no quick moves that might warn her of his intention to pounce. And he did intend to pounce. "Does it say you have to forsake all others and keep only unto me?"

"No, it doesn't mention that." She backed away another few steps.

"*No?* That's not fair. Leave it to a McCrary woman to stack the deck against me." He advanced a little closer. "What does it say about planting the seed?"

"Oh, it's definitely in favor."

And just before he made his move, she took off running.

8

TESS REACHED THE BEDROOM a half step before Cole—just in time to shut the door in his face and turn the lock.

"Tess, open up."

"I will. When I'm ready." Her heart raced from the exertion of her mad dash. Although he'd chased her every step of the way, she had the feeling he'd allowed her to outrun him—as long as she was headed for the bedroom. Devious man. He obviously hadn't been expecting a door to be slammed in his face.

"What's in that translation you don't want me to see?" he demanded.

"I don't know what you're talking about." She backed away from the door, opened her hand and unfolded the sweat-dampened square of paper.

"Come on, Tess. You hid the printout behind your back and tore out of the library like a scalded dog. Now you've locked me out of my own bedroom."

"A girl needs a little time to herself now and then." *To find a place to hide inconveniently worded curses and such.*

He shook the door handle. A tactically brilliant move. "Tess!"

She took the time to read the wording again, just in case something had escaped her. *You, McCrary of Charleston, must relinquish your daughter in marriage to Westcott of Westcott Hall. She must share his home and his bed.*

No surprise there. The curse in Cole's bible had basically required the same. *She must keep for him a warm and comfortable home.* Couldn't object to warm and comfortable.

The next line, though, had almost caused her to swallow her tongue. *She must strive with body and heart to satisfy his manly needs.*

Manly needs! No, she certainly couldn't let Cole set eyes on *that.* She knew exactly what he'd do. He'd carry on and on about his "manly needs." He'd turn her into his sex slave! Or rather, he would if he could.

"If you open the door, I'll let you keep your secret. I'll forget all about it."

"I'll bet you have your fingers crossed."

"Open this damn door!" He banged hard enough to rattle the solid, glossy oak panel on its hinges.

She pursed her lips in reflection. She'd come so far in fulfilling the demands of the curse—marrying Westcott of Westcott Hall. Sharing his home and his bed. Planting the seed within her. And things did seem to be looking up for her family. She wasn't about to lose ground now.

Satisfy his manly needs. With body and heart, no less.

"Don't make me get ruthless, Tess."

"I'm scared, Cole. Real scared."

He muttered a soft, fervent string of obscenities.

She'd really be in a pickle, she supposed, if she hadn't experienced a major, life-changing realization. When she'd read the words, "...strive to satisfy his manly needs," she should have been dismayed. Anxious. Possibly even horrified.

She hadn't been. She'd been glad. Her heart had lifted with sudden lightness. Her duty to her family and all future generations of McCrarys became clear—she had to keep making love to Cole Westcott. The matter was simply beyond her control.

The curse had absolved her of all guilt. Doubts and hesitation became irrelevant. She'd been handed the perfect excuse to indulge freely in her deepest, wildest urges with a man most women only dreamt about.

That was when the realization had hit her. Why did Tess McCrary need an excuse to do anything? She'd been afraid to act on her desires, and she'd felt guilty for betraying Phillip—after waiting faithfully for a year. How pudding-hearted was *that?*

No more. Her gladness at the curse's translation had opened her eyes. Yes, she was laying her heart on the line by making love to Cole. Every time they touched, every time they kissed, her need for him grew a little stronger. But such was the nature of any worthwhile sexual relationship, wasn't it?

She would take full advantage of these next five months. When the time came for them to part, she would walk away a stronger, more experienced woman. If her heart broke a little, so be it. Until then, she'd "strive to satisfy his manly needs," all right...but *without* his knowing about the curse's demand. No sense in needlessly tipping the balance of power in his favor.

Now that she'd aroused his curiosity about the translation, though, she'd have to pacify him in some way. Inspiration struck. She would type up an edited version of the translation as soon as possible. In the meantime, she'd just have to keep him distracted.

Speaking of which...

She frowned at the door. It was awfully quiet out there. Sensing an impending siege, she looked around for a place to hide the translation. She considered playing it safe and ripping it into shreds, but the professor had scrawled a fairly long personal note at the bottom which Tess hadn't read beyond the first line.

The sound of a key grating in the lock hurried her. Opening one of her dresser drawers, she shoved the note beneath clothing, shut the drawer and whirled around just as the door swung open.

Cole strode in and tossed a key onto a dresser. His gaze bore into hers as he stalked closer, every line of his powerful body a threat. "One last chance, Tess," he warned in the lowest, meanest drawl she'd ever heard—worthy of any movie villain. "I'm going to let you give me that little square of paper you were hiding. And if you fail to make the best of this final opportunity—" Mischief and mayhem glinted in his gaze as it inched down her body with clear sexual intent. "—you lose your right to object to a total body search."

Her blood warmed and pumped in a vitally sensual rhythm.

He pressed closer, teasing her with his salty, musky male scent. "Where's the translation, Tess?"

She lifted an obstinate brow. "*What* translation?"

Surprise flickered in his dark green gaze, as if he hadn't expected such a blatant challenge. And then he lunged, like a football player, catching her low around the hips. She shrieked as her feet left the floor. Hoisting her over his shoulder, he gripped the backs of her thighs and carried her across the room.

With her rump in the air, her head hanging down against his back and her blood rushing to her face, she locked one arm around his lean torso and slid her hand down his back, beneath the waistband of his khakis, to the taut, hot musculature beneath his briefs...and pinched him. Lightly. Repeatedly. Everywhere she could reach.

He arched and cursed at the shock of the attack, and with a few long strides, slung her onto the bed, where he fell across her and wrestled her into a hold *quite* ruthlessly. "You're just making it harder on yourself," he warned with uneven breaths, trapping her arms at her sides, wedging a knee between her legs.

She nudged her thigh against his hot, pulsating arousal, which strained behind his zipper. "Ohhh..." she breathed in a husky, appreciative murmur from deep in her throat "...do you think so?"

His gaze, sharp and hot and only mildly amused, delved deep into hers. "Oh, yeah, I think so." And as he spoke, he ran his hand over her breasts until heat coursed in wicked currents throughout her. "No sense putting up a fight. You've waived your right to object. Now I've got to conduct a thorough search," he whispered, "to find all your secret places."

She arched her back, thrusting her breasts into prominence, wanting to lure his caressing hand beneath her blouse. "Should I tell you if you're getting warm?" His palm scraped across a hardened nipple and she sucked in a breath. Faintly, then, "Or...hot?"

His hand left her breasts, coursed down to her tight jeans, around her hips and each mound of her bottom, leaving nowhere untouched. "There's no 'if' about it."

And though his golden-dark face loomed close above hers, he didn't kiss her. He just watched her eyes with a smoldering gaze as his questing hand ignited fires in her blood. Her body purled beneath his touch. He stroked her thighs, then up, up, along the inner seam of her jeans...to the valley between her legs. His fingertips raked. His knuckles pressed. The flat of his hand set a rhythm. Slower, harder...

She groaned, clutched at him, closed her eyes. "W-will this be..." she could barely force the whisper from her throat "...a *strip* search?"

"If necessary."

Oh, it was.

COLE WOKE UP in bed alone. And late. Past nine. On Sunday morning, yet. The one day that neither he nor Tess would be hurrying off to work, and he could keep her to himself.

At the sound of water running and the sight of the closed bathroom door, he relaxed against the pillows. She hadn't gone anywhere. Anticipation pulsed through him. They had hours before Leo would arrive. And hours after Leo left. Life was good. *Very* good.

He frowned at that reflection. Maybe *too* good.

As he thought back to the incredible night he'd just spent, an inkling of doubt wormed its way into his contentment. Something had come over Tess. What, he wasn't sure. He'd recognized the difference in her the moment she'd lifted that arrogant auburn brow and murmured, *"What translation?"* She'd then astonished him for the rest of the night with rowdy, teasing, provocative lovemaking.

She'd been open and free. Game for everything. Insatiable. Profoundly beautiful. So damn exciting. His mind still buzzed with visual images of her. His body still hummed from the erotic play of her hands and mouth, and the explosive force of his climaxes. And though there wasn't much about sex that he hadn't experienced many times over the course of his life, she'd taken him places he'd never been. He still didn't understand how. They hadn't done anything kinky, or even very original. But it had all felt new.

Apprehension curled through him. What had caused the change in her? The first time they'd made love, she'd been reluctant. Cautious. Reserved. Until, of course, he'd pushed her beyond rational thought. The next day, her caution had returned. *"The seed's already been planted."* But last night, she'd taunted him into lovemaking and held nothing back, meeting him with passion and pleasure equal to his own.

She'd always turned him on, even when she'd been at her most reluctant, with her inner fire blazing beyond her control. But now...

Her laughter, her unpredictability, her sheer sensuality, turned lovemaking into an adventure. The tenderness in her touches, the longing in her gaze even after they'd climaxed, turned it into something mystical. And holding her as she slept had been a pleasure too keen for words.

His apprehension grew. What exactly had fueled the passion behind her kisses, her lovemaking? He needed to know.

The remarkable change in her had occurred shortly after she'd read that new translation. Could something in it possibly account for such an astounding change? He didn't see how. But he had to find out what it said. He felt as if some vital part of him could be permanently lost if he continued living with her, making love to her, without clearly understanding her. The danger seemed pressing.

With a cautious glance at the closed bathroom door, he shrugged into his robe and ventured to her dresser. When he'd burst into the room last night, he'd heard a drawer sliding shut. She'd been standing right about *here*.

Cole opened a drawer. Her underwear drawer. Of course. A classic hiding place. Dismissing the twinge of guilt he felt at invading her privacy, he sifted through the silky panties and bras and discovered nothing hidden among them. He opened another drawer, and another, feeling his way through each. He hit the jackpot on the third one and found the paper beneath a neat stack of T-shirts.

It took him only seconds to read the translation. It wasn't but a few lines of type, but he stood staring at the words for a good long while. *She must strive with body and heart to satisfy his manly needs.*

Satisfy...his...manly...needs.

Cole wasn't sure if he wanted to laugh or break something. Both, actually. He understood now why she hadn't wanted him to see this. Because it gave him the upper hand. He could, in theory, name his "needs" at any time, and she would have to strive—*with body and heart*—to meet them. *If* she really believed in the curse and felt compelled to comply with its terms.

She obviously did. She'd gone to bed with him the first time for that very reason. She'd even insisted on doing only what was necessary to comply with the curse's demands. Had that been her motivation this time, too?

No. He swore it hadn't. She'd been so lighthearted. Passionate. Earnest. She'd made love to him *with emotion.* Deep emotion. With body and heart.

He clenched his teeth and drew in a deep, steadying breath through his nostrils. He no longer felt in the least bit like laughing. Before she'd seen this translation, she hadn't intended to make love to him again. Moments after reading it, she'd engaged him in the best sex he'd ever had. She'd more than "satisfied his manly needs."

Coincidence? He'd have to be a pie-eyed optimist to be-lieve that.

He took another deep breath, intent on calming his flaring emotions. Why should he feel so angry, so shaken? Even though she'd hidden this demand of the curse from him, she'd never lied. Never tried to disguise the ulterior motives behind their lovemaking, even when he'd wanted her to.

Why the hell did she believe so deeply in that damn curse, anyway? She didn't seem especially superstitious about any other matter. He hadn't seen her throwing salt over her shoulder or dodging black cats or avoiding cracks in side-walks.

Noticing the handwriting scrawled across the bottom of the page, Cole paused in the act of returning the note to the drawer. It was a personal note from the translator. A profes-sor at the university where she'd once worked. A casual greeting. A few lines about mutual friends. At the end, the professor had written, *Any news of Phillip? He's always in my thoughts and prayers.*

Phillip. Incredibly enough, Cole had almost forgotten about Tess's missing fiancé. She hadn't mentioned him since their limousine ride home from the chapel, when she'd told him she wouldn't go to bed with him on their wedding night because she was in love with someone else. She'd changed her mind only when she'd learned of the curse's demand to "plant his seed within her." And now she was "satisfying his manly needs" for the same reason. Her desire to lift that curse seemed to outweigh all other considerations.

Bothered by that, Cole lifted the clothing from the drawer to return the page to its hiding place. Another item came into view then at the very bottom of the drawer.

A photograph. Not just a snapshot that she'd casually tossed in, but a large, framed portrait. The kind that should be sitting on her dresser or living room mantle. A blond, blue-eyed guy that women would probably consider attractive gazed out with a pensive, studious look. Cole knew immediately who he had to be. Phillip.

He felt as if the wind had been knocked out of him.

She hadn't moved any furniture, knickknacks or family photos into his house—nothing to personalize a space for herself. She'd brought things like clothes, purses, shoes, paperwork for the business. Only the items she considered necessary for her day-to-day life.

She'd included this photo of Phillip. She hadn't set it on her dresser, which would have made Cole believe she'd brought it to make a statement. She kept it in a drawer.

He understood photos in drawers. When he'd been a boy, he'd found a picture of his mother. He'd never known her. She'd died before he was a year old. His father hadn't displayed pictures of her because she'd left him—left both of them—for another man. So Cole had kept her photo in his dresser. And when he'd been feeling particularly alone, particularly unloved, he brought it out. He barely remembered his thoughts about her back then, but he remembered his feelings. He had longed for her. Devoutly. With every fiber of his being.

Did Tess feel the same intensity of longing for this man? Did she bring the photo out when she was alone? Was she that much in love with him?

But if she was, why would she allow something as nonsensical as a curse to force her into another man's bed?

Slowly an answer occurred to him. He let the stack of T-shirts settle back into place over the photo and the translation, then quietly shut the drawer. Puzzle pieces fell into place, and he didn't like the picture they made.

A reporter had asked her once if she believed the curse had caused her fiancé's disappearance. She'd denied it, but Cole had seen the anguished look in her eyes. He'd held her while she'd struggled to compose herself. He should have known then. He should have realized that she believed the curse had caused Phillip's disappearance. Did she think that if she complied with all its demands, he might come back?

Cole balled his fists and stared blankly at a far wall. Had she married him, made love to him, to bring Phillip home? Was that the passion he'd felt in her kisses—the passionate belief in a cause? Or, worse yet, the passion she'd felt for Phillip?

He sat down on the bed in a heartsick daze. *You're jumping to conclusions. You know none of that as fact.* But for once, the loose ends all fit neatly together.

The bathroom door opened, and Tess peeked out. "Oh, you're up." She wore only a towel, and her amazing wealth of auburn hair cascaded freely about her slender figure. "Good morning," she greeted with a small but warm smile.

"Good morning."

"I'm filling the tub. I noticed that it's, uh..." her gaze took on the same sultry, playful light he remembered from last night "...big enough for two."

He couldn't bring himself to reply. She was so damn beautiful it hurt to look at her. And the welcome in her smile seemed so damn sincere. How could she gaze at him like that if she was pining after another man?

"I was thinking what a shame it would be to waste all that *hot*, *wet* steam on just me." She let the door swing open further and posed against the jamb. The peach-colored bath towel barely came to the top of her thighs. Her incredibly long, bare, curvaceous legs reminded him of how he'd kissed his way up them. How they'd felt, wrapped around his shoulders...and later, around his waist....

"Of course, if I've already *worn you out*," she purred, "I wouldn't want to push you into physical exhaustion or anything."

He narrowed his gaze on hers. She knew how to taunt. She surely did. And she knew how to get him hard, even when he didn't want to be.

"Cole?" A little frown entered her eyes, as if his stillness and silence had finally registered.

But what could he ever hope to gain with stillness and silence? Regardless of how she felt about him—or *didn't* feel about him—she'd committed herself to living with him. And sleeping with him. And though she hadn't admitted it, to "satisfying his manly needs." For the next five months.

Five months. He would have her for at least that long.

He suddenly knew what he had to do in that span of time. He had to make her stop living in the past. He had to make her see that she was too young, too passionate, to mourn for a man who would probably never come back. He'd been gone for over thirteen months. A man didn't stay away that long while a woman like Tess waited for him—not if he was alive. At the very least, he would have called her. He had to have met with a fatal accident or foul play—a tragedy that Cole wished on no one.

But Tess couldn't stop living because of that tragedy. It was time for her to get on with her life. He had to woo her away from Phillip's memory. How the hell to do that? How could he know what she loved so damn much about him; what he'd given her that no one else seemed able to give? No, he wouldn't play that game. He couldn't be Phillip, and wouldn't try to be. But he *could* make love to her. He could take her places, and buy her things, and make her laugh.

And make love to her.

"Cole, is something wrong?" Her concern eased some of the tightness in his chest. Nothing would convince him that she didn't care about him, at least a little.

"Yeah, something's wrong." He slowly rose to his feet, allowing his gaze to roam the sweet, beckoning curves of her body. "That towel's all wrong for you." He ambled closer, his need to touch her growing into an ache. "I was thinking how much better you'd look—" He slid his hands around her hips. "—wearing only soap suds."

Sensuous color flooded her skin. Her eyes grew smoky

gray. "I guess that depends," she whispered, sliding her hands beneath his robe, "on where you put them."

His resolve—along with other things—hardened. He'd make the best of his time with her. He'd banish Phillip from her mind, her heart. He'd fill her so completely, she'd only have room for him.

LATER THAT MORNING, Cole pondered the nature of his "manly needs." It seemed that the more she satisfied them, the stronger they got.

Not that he minded.

They'd made lavish use of soap suds, pounding jets and warm wash cloths. They'd sloshed at least half of the water out of the deep garden tub. He'd damn near drowned himself, and she'd ended up with a mouthful of soap. By the time they got out, they were holding each other up, weak with laughter, and their fingers were wrinkled beyond the prune stage.

But they *had* made the most mind-blowing love.

They then slipped into bathrobes and lounged on the second-floor piazza with coffee and light pastries, talking about nothing important. Embarrassing things they'd done, crazy things they'd seen. Friends they'd had growing up. Her cats. His dogs.

And when she teased him about his Doberman named Cupcake—the price of promising his youngest goddaughter she could name him—Cole pulled Tess down onto a cushioned chaise lounge and silenced her with long, lush kisses. How could he want her again so soon? How could he not?

He'd promised her a tour of the house and grounds, though, and she wouldn't settle for a postponement. Gracious though he was in defeat, he couldn't help murmuring, "A man does have his needs, you know."

She shot him a quick, stunned glance. The innocence of his expression apparently relieved her of suspicion. Just to be sure, he distracted her with historical anecdotes about the paintings in the corridor outside his bedroom. They whiled away the next couple hours on a tour of Westcott Hall similar to the one the historical society sponsored every fall, except spiced with inside stories of the family's scandals and peccadilloes. Her laughter, wry observations and overall fascination made time fly by.

They barely made it back from the plantation's carefully restored outbuildings and the riverside gardens in time for Leo's culinary audition.

"Do you think Leo can really cook?" Tess asked as they trudged in through the back door.

Cole's gaze flickered to her in surprise. She sounded worried. "I have no idea."

"It must be hard for you, trying to do what's right for your restaurants *and* help out a relative in need."

"Yeah, I guess it can get touchy."

"Maybe you can hire him as a bartender, or a waiter." After a moment, she added, "Oh, I meant if the cooking doesn't...you know...turn out."

"Leo can't tend bar or wait tables. He's not comfortable talking to people or handling money." Dismayed by his cousin's situation, Cole shook his head. "Too many employees depend on the success of the restaurants to take chances with the chef."

"But think of Leo's babies." As they neared the kitchen, the sound of utensils and pots clanging alerted them to Leo's presence. "Three of them."

There was no doubting her concern.

Cole fought the urge to kiss her. It wouldn't be fair to Leo to show up late. And if he kissed her now, they *would* be late. They might even miss the taste test altogether.

"COME IN, sit down," Leo called out in his usual gruff, impatient voice the moment they sauntered into the kitchen. He wore jeans, a camouflage T-shirt with short sleeves that exposed his marine corps tattoo and a white chef's apron. Kettles and skillets steamed on the stove, scenting the air with onions, garlic and delicious aromas.

Cole and Tess sat on stools at the central work island, which Cole had added to the old-fashioned kitchen to please Mrs. Johannsen.

"I've figured out how to prove to you that my dishes are far superior to the ones served in your restaurants," Leo announced. "No offense, Cole, but facts are facts." He set three small plates of salad in front of him. "Try these salads, then write down the one you like best." He handed him a pen and paper. "Starting from your left, this is A, B and C. I'll write down the letter of mine, just so there's no question of foul play."

"What about Tess? Where's her salads, pen and paper?"

Leo cast an awkward glance at her. "I'll set lunch out for both of you after you're finished with the test. She already agreed not to give an opinion."

"She promised not to say a word about your cooking," corrected Cole. "That doesn't mean she can't vote." Leo frowned and Tess assured Cole that she'd rather watch. "I'd like to know her opinion," Cole insisted. "It can't influence mine if we're writing our choices without discussing them."

"But she might deliberately choose one that she doesn't really—" He broke off as Tess whipped around to stare at him, open-mouthed, clearly indignant that he would doubt her integrity. At least, out loud.

Cole, too, stared at him, but with eyes narrowed in warning.

Leo obviously got the message. Compressing his lips, he strode to his work area and returned a few minutes later with three salads, a pen and paper for Tess. "No discussing your choices," he told her with a threatening glare.

"I already promised I wouldn't." She glared right back at him.

Cole held back a smirk. He probably should have warned

Leo not to mess with Tess, unless he was willing to risk ending up with a BB in some part of his anatomy.

Hoping that Leo's cooking would be at least edible, Cole tried the first salad and believed he recognized the house dressing from the Bay Street Inn. He speared a forkful of the second.

But the look of intense concentration on Tess's face distracted him. She gave ample time to each salad, then wrote down her choice, turned the paper over and covered it with her hand. To prevent his cheating off her paper, Cole supposed.

"You ain't eating, Cole," Leo prompted in a gruff, impatient singsong.

Realizing Leo was right, Cole finished sampling the other salads. He had to admit, he couldn't identify which *hadn't* come from his restaurants. Dutifully he wrote the letter of the one he'd liked best.

"Okay." Leo looked nervous. "Let's see which one you chose, Cole."

Cole revealed his choice, and a grin spread over Leo's face. With a flourish, he showed his letter, which matched Cole's. "I thought you'd like that dressing." He then glanced at Tess, his pleasure suddenly shadowed by unease. "Uhhh, what about you? Which one did you pick?"

She flipped her paper over with a happy smile.

Leo blinked and flushed with pleasure. "I *told* you it was good. See there?" he said to Cole. "Even *she* liked it." Only someone who knew Leo well would recognize the surprise in the glance he gave her. Cole suspected that surprise had more to do with her smile than with her selection.

Beaming with renewed confidence, Leo said, "Let's try the she-crab soup."

Cole wasted no time. He tried all three bowls and wrote down his preference. Tess, on the other hand, sampled with intense concentration.

He noticed that when she moved on to the last bowl, Leo's

face grew taut and expectant. He could have rigged a neon sign above the bowl that flashed "Leo's," for all his subtlety.

Tess glanced at him, dipped her spoon into the bowl and judiciously tried the creamy she-crab soup. Cole watched in avid interest. *This should be good.*

Her eyes grew wide. "Mmm." She took another spoonful, savored it, and closed her eyes. "Mmmm!"

Cole bit back a smile. So much for not voicing her opinion—or attempting to influence his. And he had no doubt she intended to do just that. She'd obviously made up her mind that Leo should have the job.

Leo didn't seem bothered by the fact that she wasn't playing strictly by the rules. He nearly floated off the floor in delight at her reaction. Tess set down her spoon, grabbed her paper and scribbled her choice. Graciously Leo proclaimed, "I think we should let the lady show her answer first."

Grandly she revealed her choice. Leo whipped his paper around, and they gazed at each other in clear satisfaction.

"If you want to…you know…*say* something, you can," Leo granted.

"Oh, Leo! This has to be the best she-crab soup I've ever tasted. These others are good, but this—" She spread out her hands to showcase the favored cup of soup. "—*this* is heaven. What gives it that…that flavor, that richness?"

Cole swore he'd never seen Leo so damn happy—except maybe, *maybe*, when Helen had accepted his marriage proposal, or when his boys were born.

"It's my secret ingredient. I'll take that secret to my grave. But it's the way you handle the cream sauce that makes the difference, too. Some chefs think that you have to—"

"Uhhh, excuse me," cut in Cole, too amused to keep quiet, "but are you at all interested in *my* selection?"

Leo glanced at him as if he'd forgotten he was there. "Oh, yeah. Sure." With a worried frown, he invited, "Let's see which one you chose."

Cole showed him, and Leo's smile returned, full force.

As they sampled the rest of the dishes, Leo watched every expression that flitted across Tess's face. Unfailingly she chose his dish. No surprise there. His expressive anticipation left no doubt which one was his.

Amazingly enough, though, Cole himself had chosen Leo's dishes every time, too. The son-of-a-gun really could cook.

When Leo served his *tour de force*—Hot Fudge Truffle Mousse Cake—Tess closed her eyes, knit her brows and savored the confection with such a throaty, sensual "ummm" that Cole's amusement faded. His temperature climbed and his body stirred with visions of what they could do with that chocolate....

Realizing that Leo also watched her with rapt attention, Cole shot him a forbidding glance. He hoped like hell Leo wasn't getting any such "visions." He'd hate to have to kill him.

But the moment Tess opened her dreamy gray eyes, Leo held up his paper to display his letter with such blazing pride that Cole knew he'd been too wrapped up in his artistic triumph to appreciate her astounding sensuality.

Good thing. Damn good thing.

"So what about it, Cole?" Tess was asking. "Does he get the job?"

Cole settled back and crossed his arms. He'd never hurried in a business decision before—especially not in front of the person most affected by that decision. Leo stood gnawing his lip, waiting for the reply. "There's more to this decision than just liking a few dishes," explained Cole. "There's the question of pay, benefits, training, work schedules, career goals...."

Tess uttered a scoffing sound. "Does he get the job, or not?"

Cole slanted her an admonishing glance. The woman had no appreciation for the fine art of negotiation. Then again, she *had* squeezed a promise of two million dollars and McCrary Place out of him. "Yes, he gets the job."

Her smile alone made the decision worthwhile.

Leo bounded around the work island, grabbed Cole's hand and enthusiastically pumped it. "You won't be sorry, Cole. We're gonna get written up in all those fancy magazines. Five stars, cousin. Five stars."

"I have no doubt, Leo."

Leo turned to Tess, a daffy smile loping across his mile-wide jaw. The lady had made a conquest. "So were you surprised when you found out I made all those dishes?"

"Stunned."

"You really liked 'em, huh?"

"Loved 'em."

"Hey, I'm sorry if I was...uh...you know, *rude*."

Tess lifted that arrogant brow of hers. "*If?*"

"Okay, okay. Sorry I was a horse's butt. Is that better?"

"Much."

He muttered beneath his breath as if disgruntled, but humor glinted in his gaze. From the corner of his mouth, he confided to Cole, "You know, she ain't too bad for a McCrary. Uh, I mean a McCrary-*Westcott*."

"Yeah, she's one of the best McCrary-Westcotts I know."

Leo guffawed and slapped Cole on the back. "Now you two sit down and finish eatin'. I promised you lunch, you're getting lunch."

They didn't argue. The food *was* damn good. And when Tess finally dug in to the remainder of her Fudge Truffle Mousse Cake and closed her eyes to savor it, Cole angled his face near hers. "What was that again?"

She opened her eyes in surprise.

"Did you say, 'ummm'?"

She smiled. "Mmm-hmm."

"No, no...*ummm*."

She said it, but with even more sensuality than she had before. He nipped at her lips, teased her into a kiss, savored the taste of her mouth as well as the chocolate, while the need within him grew stronger, hotter, to make love to her again.

"Hey, hey, take it to the bedroom," Leo yelled from the

sink. "I can't watch stuff like that. I've been without my wife for a whole week...and she won't be home until Tuesday."

Tess pulled away from Cole in surprise. Cole, too, turned to gape at him. "Tuesday?" they both repeated. "She's coming home Tuesday?"

"Yeah. She called this morning. Said she's dropping the divorce proceedings. She missed me."

Tess turned to Cole with a glow of gladness and wonder. "The curse," she whispered. "The curse is being lifted."

A sudden squeeze of emotion kept him silent. What was she hoping for right now? That her family would be free from a legacy of heartbreak...or that Phillip would come home to her?

Cole glanced away from her to marshal his thoughts. He wouldn't think about her longing for Phillip—at least, not any more than he had to. The knowledge of it already pressed like impending disaster at the edges of his mind; rode like deadweight in his chest. He had to make her forget him.

"If the curse *is* being lifted," he managed to say, "then we'd better not stop doing what it says to do."

She nodded, her silvery gaze warm and welcoming.

They came together for another kiss.

But the telephone rang, snaring Tess's attention. Leo answered the wall set beside him. "Cole, it's for you." With a brief, almost furtive glance at Tess, he muttered, "Better take it in the, er, library."

Cole frowned. He hadn't planned on taking any calls today. "Who is it?"

Leo's face grew ruddy and he hesitated. After a moment, though, he lifted his beefy shoulder in a what-the-hell shrug. "It's Ms. Lacey LaBonne. She says it's urgent."

9

FUNNY, HOW SOMETHING as insignificant as a phone call could burst a gal's bubble. Telling herself she was better off now that her bubble had burst, Tess watched Cole catch the phone Leo had tossed him while she concentrated on not reacting.

"What's the big emergency, Lacey?" Cole asked in that low, sexy voice that any woman would find devastatingly appealing.

Sitting beside him at the kitchen work island, Tess averted her gaze from him and watched Leo busy himself at the far end of the kitchen with dishwashing.

Cole, meanwhile, listened to whatever the gorgeous, leggy brunette was murmuring in his ear. "No, I'm not upset about the 'pig' thing. I guess some men *can* be pigs. I prefer not to classify myself among them, but—"

The wry humor in his voice only made Tess's throat tighten more. She'd been having so much fun, feeling right at home, enjoying Cole's company to the point that she'd forgotten a world existed beyond their little household. But the world did indeed exist, along with scores of women who had been—and would be—Cole's lovers.

Nothing had prepared her for the emotion gripping her heart. Was it jealousy, that he would want other women? Partially, yes. She couldn't deny that. But it was also possessiveness. A flat-out unwillingness to share. She didn't want him kissing, holding, making love to anyone else. Didn't want him indulging in intimacy or passion with any other woman. Didn't even want him holding another woman's hand, gazing into her eyes or flirting with her over the phone.

You've got to get over that, Tess! You won't be here long…and his love life will go on. For all she knew, his love life might "go on" before their five-month marriage ended. She supposed she should talk to him about that possibility. Remind him that the curse would not be lifted if he slipped out for a discreet rendezvous, and that he could lose his inheritance if he was caught.

But with all his money and connections, he probably had the means to keep from getting caught. Her heart ached at the very thought, and she slipped off the stool to leave the kitchen, needing to distance herself from him.

He caught her wrist and pulled her to him, his gaze connecting with hers as he continued to talk to Lacey. "Yeah, well, I'm sorry to hear you've been, uh, *anguishing* that way, but your interview on television had nothing to do with me not calling you."

Tess bit her lip and looked away. She didn't want him to see how much this call was affecting her. She shouldn't care on such a deeply personal level.

He slid his arm around her waist and trapped her between his knees. "You see, I'm a married man now," he told Lacey. After a pause, he responded, "No, the marriage isn't just a technicality. I didn't marry her just to get the money." The lie rolled from his lips so convincingly that Tess's heart slowed to a near standstill. He was terribly good at lying. "So I won't be calling you, Lacey. Our relationship is over."

Tess's heart picked up speed again, like a balloon lifting in a warm draft. She would *not* look at him. She would *not* let him see her acute relief. And that relief had nothing to do with curses, wills or any other practical concern.

"I don't owe you any more of an explanation, Lacey," he said, "but since you insist, I'll try to explain." After a long silence, he said in a soft but uncompromising tone, "My wife is the only one I want." Tess couldn't help glancing at him then. And his gaze embraced her—strong, steady and heated. "I've never known anyone like her. I've never *wanted* anyone like I want her."

Her heart tripped into a heavier beat, and intoxicating warmth filled her. She heard cursing from the phone, then a *click*, and knew that Lacey had hung up.

But Cole kept hold of the receiver, as if he hadn't noticed, his attention entirely on Tess. "I love kissing her," he went on in hoarse, slow whisper, his gaze burning into hers. "I can kiss her for hours and hours and still want more." He stroked her face, his thumb sweeping lightly across her lips. "And I love making love to her. I can't tell you how much. I want to take her somewhere—on a honeymoon—and keep her to myself for days, or weeks, or months."

A groan rose in her throat, and she caressed his face, needing to touch him. To kiss him. And *so* much more...

"And I'm going to do that," he swore, "even if I have to bodily kidnap her. But first we're going upstairs, to my bed, or the first bed we come to. We might stay there all day and all night...."

The phone clattered to the floor as she engaged him in deep, voluptuous kisses. He groaned, his hands coursing down her back every which way, pressing her body to his for a closer fit. She gave herself over to him entirely.

The annoying beep of a phone off the hook soon issued from somewhere nearby, and a deep, masculine grumbling drew nearer. Leo. She'd forgotten about Leo, and she believed that Cole had, too.

"See you later, you crazy Westcotts," he said on his way to the door. "Don't fall off that stool and hurt yourselves."

HOURS LATER, during a lull in their lovemaking, Tess lay beside him in bed and realized she should probably worry. He knew exactly which of her heartstrings to pull to get his way. He wanted to take her on a honeymoon. Crazy, of course, given that their marriage wasn't for real. That fact didn't deter him.

He suggested they go to McCrary Place—the house her ancestors had built after a fire had destroyed their rice plantation bordering the Westcotts' property. Legend had it that Cole's great-grandfather had set the disastrous fire, though no one had been able to prove it. McCrary ancestors had rebuilt on the coast, near Beaufort...far enough away from those damn Westcotts to give themselves peace of mind.

And now this Westcott owned the place—for the time being—and wanted to take her there for a week or so. How could she refuse? She'd spent every summer of her childhood at the big Victorian house on the beach, and when her father's finances had forced them into selling, she'd mourned its loss. She couldn't wait to stay there again.

And yet, she couldn't rationalize leaving the family business unattended.

"I'll have to find someone to work at the shop for me," she told him. "Maybe my mother. Or Kristen. Her spring classes have ended, and when I called home this morning, she told me that Josh has fully recovered the feeling in his leg and is being released from the hospital today. I suppose I could ask my mother and Kristen to run things."

"If they will, we'll leave tomorrow, around noon," Cole said. "It shouldn't take me much longer than a few hours in the morning to settle my business."

"My mother will be at the hospital when I visit this evening." With a glance at the bedside clock, Tess reluctantly withdrew from his embrace. "I told her I'd be there by seven. I'd better get dressed."

"You're going to the hospital to visit your father?"

Tess nodded, slipped out of bed and donned her robe. "My mother told me this morning that he's doing much better. He's out of traction. He wants to talk to me." Anxiety washed through her at the thought. She wasn't sure what her father had to say, but she knew he was violently opposed to her marriage.

"I'll come with you."

The offer stunned her. "To visit my father?"

"I was going to drop by there tomorrow," he said, rising from the bed, a splendidly naked Adonis, "but this will work out better in terms of my schedule."

"But why would you want to visit him?" The thought of Cole and her father in the same room shook her. "Surely you realize that he considers you *the enemy.*"

"We've got business to settle."

"Business? What kind of business?"

He hesitated. "I don't want to get your hopes up too high, but when I had a drink with the governor before his fund-raiser yesterday, I mentioned the assault charges, and he promised to call the district attorney about them. I have an appointment with the D.A. next Monday to discuss the whole fiasco. I'll need to arrange a meeting between Leo, Josh and your father before then to make sure we present a united front."

"Oh, Cole." She squeezed her hands together in hope. "Do you think the charges might be dropped?"

"Maybe, if we can get the D.A. to view the incident as a family matter."

Gratitude welled up in her. "Thank you." She slid her arms around him and showered his face with fervent kisses. "Have I ever told you how wonderful you are?"

Surprise flickered across his face, then his gorgeous green eyes smiled into hers. "No, I can say with absolute certainty that you never have."

"An oversight. A gross oversight."

Swaying with her in a full-bodied hug, he murmured into her hair, "This isn't just another attempt to satisfy my manly needs, is it?"

She blinked. Frowned. Pulled back to peer at him. Had she heard him correctly? No. Surely she hadn't. "*What* did you say?"

"I said, 'this isn't just empty flattery, is it?'"

Tess narrowed her eyes. His consummate innocence was

just a *little* overdone. "That's not what you said." At a slight quirk of his mouth, the truth slowly dawned, and she jerked away from him. "You searched my dresser, didn't you? You found that translation and read it."

"What translation?"

"Ohhh! You *scoundrel*." She threw a punch at his muscle-hard shoulder.

He caught her arm and swung her around until he held her from behind, her back lodged against his front, their arms entwined across her chest. "You brought it on yourself." His voice was low and soft with amusement. "You taunted me with that translation, then hid it from me."

"Of course I hid it from you."

He rubbed his beard-stubbled chin against the side of her neck, sending sensual tingles throughout her. "Why?" The word itself tingled thrillingly across her ear.

"Because I know what you'll do."

"I don't know what you're talking about." He feathered kisses along her jaw, then let her go. "But we'd better hurry. Let's get this trip to the hospital over with." He glanced at his watch. "My manly needs are already growing. You'll be sorely needed by nine."

She sucked in a hissing breath.

Wasn't he just *too* cute?

Before he saw it coming, she snatched a glass of ice water off the nightstand and dashed it squarely where he needed it most. "*That* should take care of those manly needs for a while."

THEY LEFT FOR THE HOSPITAL slightly later than planned—only after he appeased her by bringing out his family bible and swearing on it that he would strive with body and heart to satisfy her womanly needs wherever and whenever she wanted him to.

He then drove her to the hospital and held her hand in his strong, warm, steady grip, satisfying a need she hadn't even recognized. "You're worried about this visit, aren't you?" he asked.

"A little." Her father had been at war with the Westcotts his entire life, and he wasn't one to let bygones be bygones. He hated the fact that she, his daughter, had defied him by marrying the son of his worst enemy. What would he say to her? How would he respond to Cole?

"Are you concerned that I'll do some harm to your father with this visit?"

"No, I've been told his vital signs have been strong and steady. My mother said he's calmed down quite a bit since that fight with Leo at your place. Plus, the news you're bringing about the governor talking to the district attorney should make him happy. But still, he'll probably...well, *say* things. Insulting things."

"Even from the little I know of him, I'd be surprised if he didn't." He kneaded her hand and rubbed his thumb across her palm in soothing circles. "I'm not going to retaliate, Tess. There will be no battle."

With a jolt, she realized that her heart, her loyalties, had become divided. She was worried not only about her father, but about Cole, too. The thought of someone disparaging him— even if that someone was her own father—brought out her protective instincts. Imagine that. Tess McCrary, feeling protective of Cole Westcott. What had the world come to?

He needed no one's protection, let alone hers. Still, she hated that her father was at odds with him. Of course, the Westcotts and McCrarys always would be at odds. Her father would see to it.

As Cole pulled into the hospital lot and parked his long, low elegant sports car, apprehension filled Tess. "I think it would be best if you wait outside the room until I talk to him. I'll call you in if...I mean, when...I think the time is right."

Cole kept her hand in his as they walked into the hospital, rode the elevator and strolled down quiet corridors. When they neared her father's room, he gathered her to him in a fortifying hug. "Don't worry. Your father will be okay, and so will I."

He's reading my mind again.

She forced a smile and brushed the dark, springy waves back from his face with a tenderness she couldn't deny. "I know. But thanks anyway."

This wouldn't do. This wouldn't do at all. She was feeling too *tender* toward Cole. Because of the lovemaking, probably. She wasn't the kind of woman who could make love to a man without feeling *something* for him. Nevertheless, she couldn't just allow those feelings to run amok.

They seemed so damn close to running amok.

Gathering her poise, she withdrew from the sanctuary of his arms, prepared herself for battle, and left Cole in the hall while she entered her father's private room.

"About time you came to see me." Though he wore a back brace, her father looked robust enough to take on the world. His thick white hair glinted, he smelled of aftershave and his dark pajamas and robe lent him a sober, distinguished air.

Her mother smiled a greeting from the other side of his bed. The smile looked somewhat strained, though. Not a good sign.

"Last time I was here, you wouldn't speak to me," Tess reminded him as she kissed her father's smooth-shaven cheek.

"Sorry I lost my temper. You're a good girl, Tessie, and I know that. You married Westcott because you thought you had to rescue your mother and me from debt, and because you want to search for Phillip. All that takes money." His gray eyes, so much like her own, gleamed with concern. "I realize now that you're not betraying us or your fiancé. You're sacrificing yourself. And I can't let you do that."

"I'm not sacrificing myself. It's a business deal," Tess assured him, settling into a chair beside him. "A lucrative one for everyone concerned."

He held her hand between both of his own. "Living with the enemy for five months is not a business deal. I won't let you live with Westcott for your mother and me, or even for Phillip. We won't take any of the money. I won't let you pay off my bills. And you're not going to work in my store, either. You're barely earning a living there. It's time for you to get back to your own life."

"I'm living my own life, the way I see fit."

"You left your job at the university. I shouldn't have allowed it. I thought I'd be back on my feet in no time, but I wasn't."

"Until you are, I see no reason I can't help you out by—"

"No." His tone, his gaze, brooked no argument. She knew when her father had made up his mind, and this was definitely one of those times. "If you want that two million dollars and McCrary Place, it's up to you. But your money's your own. Your property's your own. Your time's your own."

She hadn't expected this. She felt cut off. Adrift at sea. Her life had been built around her parents' needs. With good reason. They needed her!

"I'm asking you to please put an end to this nonsense with Westcott," he said.

"I can't. I've made a commitment to stay with him for five months, and I will."

"You were forced into that commitment. I know what Westcott did with my business loans. He foreclosed on them to pressure you into marriage."

She couldn't deny it. He'd done precisely that.

"I won't have anyone playing mind games with my little girl." Her father's face flushed with anger. "That's why I'm suing him. I'm suing him for everything he's got. Cole Westcott, and his cousin, too—the cop who shot Josh."

"You're suing?" Tess jumped to her feet. She'd always known of the possibility, but she hadn't thought he would. "You can't do that."

"I can, and I will. I've got a lawyer who's sure he can make the case stick. He's even willing to defend me against the criminal charges for free. What's more, Tessie, you can walk away with more money than Westcott's giving you. This law-yer also represents his stepmothers in the inheritance case."

"Oh, Daddy, no..."

"I'd rather have you leave Westcott now and forget about the money. But if you want it that badly, come over to our side. His stepmother Deirdre is willing to pay you more, and all you have to do is be honest in court. Admit that it's just a business deal. Tell them how he pressured you into it. Keep your eyes open for signs that he's stepping out with other ladies. Get the specifics. Work with the detectives Deirdre has following him. Let's teach this Westcott bastard that he can't buy and sell McCrarys."

Tess felt as if she might hyperventilate. "You listen to me, Ian Patrick McCrary," she cried, brandishing a threatening finger at him. "If you sue Cole, you're suing me. Because I'm his wife. We're one legal entity."

"A divorce will take care of that. My lawyer will handle the divorce, too."

"I don't need your lawyer. And you don't, either. We'll have all the money we'll ever need, if you'll only—"

"We *will* have money—when I win that lawsuit. And if we play our cards right, we might get that damn Westcott put away on fraud charges. Or extortion, maybe."

"If you sue him or go after him in any way, I will never speak to you again."

He stared at her in hurt surprise, and a dull flush crept up his neck and face. "You would do that over some 'business deal'?"

Her throat closed so tightly, she could barely breathe.

"Oh, Tess," cried her mother, "please don't do this. Come home. You don't need that Westcott money."

"It's not the money. I've given my word. Doesn't that count? Doesn't honor and commitment and principle mean anything to either of you?"

"I've lived my life based on honor, commitment and prin-ciple." Her father's voice shook with emotion. "That's why I want you to turn away from the fast money that Westcott's promising you. He'll probably find a way to beat you out of it, anyway."

She gazed at her parents with a feeling of sick helplessness. How could she make them understand that they were reading Cole wrong, and that the money no longer played a big part in her commitment to him? How could she explain the change in their relationship when she didn't fully understand it herself? She certainly couldn't tell her father she was sleeping with him. He wasn't open-minded about things like sex—especially where his daughter was concerned. And she couldn't say that she and Cole had become friends. He wouldn't believe it. What kind of friendship grew so strong, so vital, in the space of a week?

For lack of a better plan, she acted out of impulse—the pure, simple need to have Cole with her, standing beside her, lending her his support. Swallowing the huge lump that threatened to choke her, she squared her shoulders and called on a higher power to guide her through this confrontation. "I brought someone with me," she announced. "Someone I'd like you to meet."

Her parents frowned at her, then glanced at each other in puzzlement.

Tess opened the door and gestured.

Cole stepped in. With one look at her face, he narrowed his eyes. "Tess?" He reached for her. She went to him. It seemed the most natural thing in the world—his arms enfolding her in a warm, protective huddle. She buried her face against him and absorbed his sureness and strength.

No one said a word.

Cole swore he'd never experienced silence quite as potent. The only sound he heard was the thudding of her heart and the drumming of his own pulse in his ears. What had her parents done, what had they said, to upset her so much? She'd looked on the verge of tears and felt stiff with tension. Anger stirred in him. *What had they said?*

Forcing himself to wait for her explanation rather than demanding one from her parents, he leveled a hard gaze at the couple who stared at them in open shock.

Tess soon lifted her head, met his eyes with a deeply troubled look, then turned to her parents. "Daddy, Mama," she began, "I'd like you to meet Cole Westcott. *My husband.*"

He didn't miss her emphasis on the last two words. The profound gratification of hearing her introduce him that way kept him silent for a moment—as well as the fact that her parents remained frozen and staring.

"Cole," Tess continued, her voice quiet and tight, "please meet my parents, Ian and Margaret McCrary."

"Ms. McCrary," Cole greeted with a nod. Even at her age, she retained a china-doll, blue-eyed prettiness that she'd passed on to Kristen. Not to Tess, though. Tess's beauty had more to do with fire and earth and all things powerful. When Margaret McCrary had gathered her wits enough to return his nod, he murmured, "I can see why my father never forgave himself for losing you to another man."

She blushed at the reminder of the fact that she'd been engaged to his father when she'd met McCrary. That fact had sparked the worst of their rivalry.

Her husband lost his frozen mask and scowled.

Cole extended his hand to him. "Mr. McCrary."

McCrary ignored his outstretched hand and glanced past him. "What do you mean by this, Tess? Are you trying to tell me there's something *personal* between you two?"

"Living together has a way of making things personal."

His annoyance slowly turned to dismay. "How personal?" Abject horror gradually set in. "Don't tell me you're *sleeping* with him!"

Her face warmed, but she maintained a steady gaze. "I believe that's between my husband and me."

His gaze lost its hard edge. Anguish replaced it, clearly shaking Tess all the more. "What are you doing, Tessie? You told me this was a business deal."

"It is."

"Since when do you do business in the bedroom?"

Her eyes widened. "It's not like that. It—" But her choked whisper couldn't sustain whatever she'd been about to say. Or maybe she simply didn't have more of an explanation to give. Her lips compressed. Her throat muscles worked.

Incensed by her father's implication, Cole slid his arm around her shoulders and held her close. "No matter how much you disapprove, Mr. McCrary, Tess *is* my wife."

McCrary shot him a loathing glare. "I wasn't talking to you, Westcott. I'm talking to my daughter."

Cole drew on every ounce of his self-control. And for the first time in his life, he didn't know right from wrong. Did he have the right to stop this man from upsetting Tess further? She was his wife. He had a marriage certificate to back up that claim. But only a certificate. And wedding rings. He'd bought her the nicest damn ring he could find—as if that meant something. No binding promises had gone along with it. No commitment beyond five short months. Four months and three weeks, to be exact. His claim didn't really amount to much.

This granite-eyed man glaring hatred at him was her father, tied to her with a permanent, God-given bond. Did that give him the right to verbally assault her? *Doing business in the bedroom.* If he'd been anyone else, Cole would have wrung a profuse apology from him. He wasn't far from doing just that.

McCrary turned his gaze to Tess, and the animosity softened to distress. "I should have known this would happen. You've been lonely for too long. You were ripe for the picking."

Ripe for the picking. The idea shook Cole. It was probably true. She *must* have been lonely, longing for Phillip all that time, determined to wait for him regardless of how long he stayed away. Cole examined his heart, his mind, forcing himself to look deep. Had he recognized her loneliness and taken deliberate advantage? Had he exploited her vulnerability...just because he wanted her?

"Don't let his looks and his sweet talkin' turn your head," McCrary implored her. "Westcotts have been known for their woman-pleasing ways for as long as I can remember. And they please as many as they can get their hands on, in merry little groups or one after the other."

The man had finally gone too far.

Cole dropped his arm from around Tess and shifted toward the bed, his hands clenching into fists. His common sense stopped him quickly enough, though. He couldn't very well pummel an old man in a hospital bed. But he wanted to. Just to stop him from talking. What if she believed him?

But then, was he saying anything that hadn't been true?

"He'll drink you up, Tessie girl, and throw away the empty carton."

"*You don't know him.*" The explosive force of her vehemence stunned McCrary into silence. "And you don't know me if you think I can't handle my own affairs. I'm keeping to my agreement with Cole. And he'll keep his promises to me. Beyond that, he owes me nothing. *Nothing.*"

"But Tess—"

"You've had your say. Now I'll have mine." She stalked closer to him, vivid and hot as a blazing flame. His face flushed from her heat. "If you carry out your plans to sue him or his cousin, you will contend with me. And when the fighting's over, one thing will be certain. You'll have one less daughter to worry about." Wrenching her glare away from her father, she whispered fiercely to Cole, "I'm finished here. If you have something to say to him, meet me at the car."

And she walked out.

"Oh, Tess, no," Margaret cried, leaping from her chair and dashing after her. "Please, honey, don't leave like this." She raced from the room.

The door closed behind her, and the two men were left

alone. Their gazes locked. The silence took on the quality of a ticking bomb.

"I'm going to say this only once," Cole said, "And I don't expect you to believe me. I won't hurt your daughter. Not now, not ever. And I'm going to see to it that she gets anything and everything she wants." He intended to stop there. Leave it at that. But he couldn't. "If it turns out that she wants *me*..." Emotion roughened his voice to harshness, "*no one* will take her away from me."

"I'll do everything in my power to make sure she leaves you."

"Then I'll fight you for her," Cole swore, "with everything I've got."

"That's exactly what you're doing, Westcott."

Cole stared at the man's implacable face and knew there was nothing left to say. The deal he'd come to offer, the truce he'd hoped to make, died an unsung death. He turned to leave.

"What I want to know..." the old man's hoarse words stopped him near the door "...is why."

Cole frowned and glanced back at him. "Why what?"

"Why you'd put yourself through a fight like this when you stand to lose forty million dollars. I might not be rich anymore, but I know how to inflict damage. I'll show no mercy. I'll take you down, son—unless you change your game plan and leave my Tess alone." His eyes blazed. His voice shook. He was ready to do battle from his hospital bed to protect her. Cole had to respect that. "So why don't you find yourself another McCrary wife. You've still got time." He leaned forward with a passion that Cole thoroughly understood. "Turn my daughter loose, Westcott."

As if it were that simple. "I can't do that."

"Why not?"

For all the times he'd spouted pretty nonsense, charmed the women, finessed his way through business transactions, earned a name as a consummate smooth talker, Cole found himself fresh out of words. The truth burned too hot and fierce for anything else to get through. The complexity of that truth, though, left him reeling and groping through unfamiliar territory. He couldn't show such vulnerability to anyone, let alone a self-avowed enemy like McCrary.

Cole clenched his jaw to the point of pain. "I want her."

"You *want* her?" McCrary repeated. "Oh, I know you *want* her. In your bed."

"Yes...in my bed." He wanted her with every fiber of his being. "In my home. In my life."

Something in his stare brought a deeper frown to Ian McCrary's face. "And how long do you suppose this *wanting* will last?"

"For as long as she'll stay with me."

"And when she leaves?"

He refused to think about that. Horrific emptiness waited just beyond. "I'll still want her." Realization unfolded with a clarity that shook him to the core. "Always."

"You Westcotts don't know the meaning of *always*. Not when it comes to love."

Love. He'd been so damn afraid to call it that. Because McCrary was right. Westcotts knew nothing about the "always" kind of love. A historical fact. A legacy. A tragic flaw. But if, by some miracle, Tess loved him, *she could teach him.*

And he knew then that she *did* have the power to revoke the curse. At least, for one sorry Westcott.

McCrary scowled at him, but a glimmer of uncertainty diluted his hostility. "What makes you so sure she won't come around to my way of thinking? How do you know that after you've settled all your eggs in our basket, she won't betray you?"

"Because I know her."

"You know her, do you? For what, all of a week?"

"For all of a week."

His age-spotted hands, still viable and strong, clenched

into fists against the bed covers. "You said you'd give her whatever she wants. What if she wants another man?"

Cole stared at him. A dozen answers ran through his head, but not the right one. He wasn't that good. He wasn't that strong. He couldn't willingly give her over to another man.

"You *do* know that she's in love with someone else, don't you?"

"Yes."

"That doesn't bother you?"

Bother him. Would someone gouging out his heart *bother* him? "He's gone. I'm here."

McCrary scrunched up his mouth and leaned back against the pillows. The measuring look in his stare troubled Cole far more than the rage and hatred had. "There's something Tess needs to know. You should know it, too. Go get her. Tell her it's *very* important."

Apprehension built in Cole's chest. He didn't want to cooperate. He wanted to hurry her to the car and keep her far away from this man...this McCrary. He couldn't, of course. He turned toward the door to get her.

It opened before he reached it. Margaret walked in, her eyes red-rimmed, her lip quivering.

Tess followed. The flinty quality of her gaze and the stiffness of her shoulders conveyed her reluctance at returning. "Mama says you need to tell me something."

"Sit down."

"I'd prefer to stand."

"Sit, Tessie," her father demanded.

Alarm flickered beneath the cool gray of her eyes. She sat. Cole stood beside her, his uneasiness growing.

"You remember the investigator you hired to find Phillip?" asked her father.

"Of course."

"When you ran out of money to pay him, I took up where you left off."

Tess stared at him. "You paid him to continue the search?"

He nodded.

Her lips slowly parted. "That's where your money went. You used your savings to..." Her eyes grew round, her face pale. "You went broke trying to help *me*."

"We're not talking about me. We're talking about Phillip."

Her breath audibly caught. "There's...news?"

"The investigator traced his movements to an island in the Pacific."

Her very stillness seemed to urge him on.

"Yesterday, the investigator called and said he learned about an American man being held there. The guy was caught with politically sensitive notes and photographs, and accused of spying. The detective has good reason to believe that prisoner is Phillip."

She half rose from her chair, looking dazed, pale, frightened. *Hopeful.* "Is he...okay?"

"From all reports, yes. And if it turns out to be him—" McCrary's gaze encompassed both Tess and Cole "—he may be home as soon as tomorrow."

10

SHE NEVER CONSIDERED not going home with Cole. They left her father's room long after visiting hours had officially ended for the night. Tess sat silently, stunned and dazed, in Cole's darkened car while he drove, her mind whirling with questions, emotions and prayers. She'd been waiting for news of Phillip for *thirteen months*. He seemed to have vanished into thin air. Most everyone had come to believe that he'd somehow met his death. She herself had begun to believe it. The news that he might have been found alive—in some primitive island prison, yet—had been a mind-numbing shock.

Was the prisoner on that island Phillip? Could he really be coming home? Though the news wasn't definite, she'd cried in her parents' arms—for joy that he might have been found, for fear that he hadn't been. She'd fervently thanked them for paying the investigator. Regardless of their protests, she would repay them every dime...and then some.

What would happen now? If the prisoner *was* Phillip, had he been harmed? What had he endured? What would he need, or want? There were too many questions clamoring for answers. If it hadn't been for Cole's strong, steady arms guiding her, she probably wouldn't have found her way out of the hospital, let alone to the car.

It wasn't until they'd climbed the stairway to Cole's bedroom that further implications of the news sank in. Phillip, the man she loved, could be on his way home. What was she doing in Cole's bedroom?

But Cole was her husband. *And her lover.* She'd spent most

of the weekend in his bed. And she'd promised to stay with him for five months. How could she break her word when his inheritance depended on their marriage? If Phillip returned, though, he would need all the love and support she could give to help ease him back into his life. To help him forget whatever horrors he'd experienced. She'd been engaged to marry him, committed to sharing his life forever. How could she stay with Cole?

The dilemma hit her in a blinding rush, and she leaned against a dresser for support. Cole stood nearby watching her, his face sober, his body tense. Although he'd been with her the entire time, a silent, supportive force in the background, she hadn't really been *seeing* him, thinking about him, until now.

"Cole," she whispered. "I don't know what to do."

He didn't ask what she meant. He searched her eyes and face with an intensity that told her he knew she was talking about them. "Then don't do anything."

Don't do anything. She supposed that made sense. It was certainly the easiest solution for tonight. But she quickly discovered it wasn't possible. Decisions had to be made immediately. Was she right to sleep with him?

Why not? You don't know if Phillip has been found. You might learn tomorrow it's all a mistake. And she felt a compelling need to immerse herself in Cole's passion now more than ever. She'd been emotionally battered by her father's frightening plans to destroy him, then jolted by the news of Phillip. She needed Cole tonight.

Phillip could be on his way home to you. She stood frozen and helplessly torn.

Cole didn't touch her, as she half expected he would. He simply held her gaze with grave intensity as he prepared for bed. He unbuttoned his shirt. Pulled it off his broad shoulders. Tossed it aside.

The sight of his muscled, silky-haired chest and sinewy arms infused her with emotion. *Emotion.* Not just sensuality, but an ardent tenderness for him that burgeoned inside her. He affected her too strongly. He always had.

He unbuckled his leather belt. Unsnapped his jeans.

And sensuality coursed along with the tenderness. But guilt did, too. Phillip might have been languishing in some prison while she'd been making love to Cole. Even now, Phillip could be suffering...or rejoicing, knowing he was coming home.

She'd never been more confused in her life.

Cole unzipped his jeans, his gaze still locked with hers.

Abruptly she turned away. Until she knew what was right, she couldn't sleep with him. *But she'd promised to sleep with him, not only tonight, but also for the next five months.* Conflicting ethics, conflicting emotions, overwhelmed her.

Cole loomed up behind her—near, but not touching. "Sleep on it, Tess," he urged softly. "We'll figure things out in the morning."

We, he'd said. As if he'd stand by her, regardless of what happened. His kindness was more than she could bear. Blinking back sudden tears, she nodded and lurched away from him.

Opening the closet, she reached for a soft, long nightgown with tiny faded rosebuds and scalloped lace around the demure neckline. It hung beside the candlelight-lace negligee Lianna had slipped into her suitcase. The sight of that negligee sent a pang through Tess. She'd made up her mind to wear it tomorrow, at McCrary Place. On their "honeymoon."

They couldn't go, of course. Not tomorrow. Maybe not ever.

Refusing to think past that curiously gut-wrenching fact, she headed for the bathroom with the nightgown. This would be the first time she'd worn any kind of night apparel to his bed. While she changed behind the closed door of the bathroom, she felt stricken. Why did it seem so wrong to withhold herself from him?

Determined to think with her head rather than her heart

and body, she stepped out of the bathroom in her modest floor-length nightgown. Cole lay in bed, propped against the pillows, his hands clasped behind his nape. With his dark, sun-gilded hair, chiseled jaw, gleaming musculature and intense green eyes, his virile beauty struck her anew. The power of his body, the thrill of his lovemaking, fresh and evocative in her memory, armed him with even more potent appeal. *She wanted him.*

And he wanted her. His gaze left no doubt of that.

How could she have believed that a prim nightgown would make a difference between them? She considered sleeping in another bed, but she wasn't that strong. She needed to be near him, even if they didn't touch. Too affected by his stare, she averted her eyes from his, crossed the immense bedroom, slipped beneath the luxurious comforter and satin sheets, and settled onto her side of the bed. Still and silent, she lay staring at the ceiling.

He clicked off the bedside lamp, throwing the room into darkness.

She closed her eyes. Held her breath. Felt the beat of his heart, the heat of his body, the tension in his muscles. Yearned for him.

He didn't reach for her.

A sense of loss gripped her. What difference would one more night of loving him make, she pleaded with herself. It might be the last chance she'd ever have.... But her ethics wouldn't allow it. What kind of woman had she become, wanting another man when her thoughts should be on her fiancé?

She tried to distract herself from her need for Cole with other concerns. Such as the curse. Had they succeeded in revoking it? Could the lifting of the curse have been a factor in Phillip's sudden rescue...if he had, indeed, been found?

She had no answers. Only more questions. And as they piled up, one after the other, weighing down her heart, she choked back a cry and turned toward Cole. She gazed at him through the darkness, and knew that he gazed back. She reached for him.

He let out a harsh breath and pulled her into his embrace.

"Just hold me," she whispered.

He did.

He held her. With everything in him, he held her. He shut his eyes, molded her body to his, absorbed her essence. And agonized. His desperation burned. He longed to kiss her until the taste and the feel of his mouth imprinted so deeply in her psyche that she would want no other man's kiss. He longed to thrust into her; to incite a hot, fierce craving that only he could quench. He wanted to bind her to him with primal need. To brand her soul with his fire.

He wanted to make her his.

He loved her so much that it hurt, and he didn't know what he'd do if she left him. And she very well could leave him. *Tomorrow.*

She wouldn't want to break her commitment to him, even if Phillip returned. Her sense of honor and fairness was too strong. She would try to find a way to keep their marriage intact for the specified period of time. But she couldn't continue to sleep with him. Her morals wouldn't allow it. Her heart belonged to Phillip, which meant *she* belonged to Phillip.

Pain sluiced through him. How could Cole keep her with him if the man she loved returned? Even if he could bring himself to be that heartless, he couldn't stand the torment of having her with him, but not having the right to love her. He couldn't tolerate the knowledge that she'd rather be with someone else who waited for her across town.

What the hell could he do? Not much. He couldn't even allow himself to hope that the man they'd found wasn't Phillip. He wouldn't hope against her hopes. He wouldn't hold her in his arms and wish for the very thing that would break her heart.

The night, for Cole, was hell.

But morning was worse. The phone rang early. Woke them up. He answered. A man asked for Tess McCrary. Cole handed her the phone. He knew who it was, even before she cried out his name.

She raised up onto her knees in his bed, then sat back on her legs, crying and laughing at the same time, choking out questions, murmuring replies. "You're okay? You're sure you're okay? Yes, yes, I'm fine. Where are you? *My parents' house?* God, Phillip...I can't believe it's you." And she cried some more.

The call lasted only minutes. Cole rose from bed and dressed while she spoke.

Before she hung up, she whispered into the phone, "I love you, too."

He knew then what he had to do.

A SENSE OF UNREALITY dogged her from the moment she'd heard Phillip's voice. When she'd hung up from the call, Cole had hugged her, murmured something about being happy for her, and told her not to worry—he'd take care of things here. She hadn't known exactly what he meant and hadn't been thinking clearly enough to ask, but she was grateful for the sentiment. And then he'd left the house, apparently in a rush to attend to important business.

She showered and dressed in an incredulous daze. Phillip was home.

He hadn't told her many details, other than he'd been arrested and imprisoned. He'd just arrived at her parents' house. The investigator had told him that she and her parents had paid for the investigation, and he'd gone directly there to thank them. They knew he'd lost the lease to his condo during his absence, and invited him to stay with them until he found a new place.

By the time Tess arrived, a small crowd of relatives and friends—both hers and his—had gathered at her parents' small suburban house to welcome Phillip home. He met her at the door, and her feeling of unreality deepened.

"Tess." With tears in his eyes, he caught her to him in a tight hug and kissed her. The intrusion of his wiry beard and mustache distracted her from the kiss itself. He'd always been clean-shaven. But then he whispered how much he'd missed her and that he loved her, which provoked more of her tears.

She examined his face in tender concern, searching for signs of trauma. He looked tired, and thinner, and half his face was hidden beneath the thick, unkempt facial hair. But his eyes were smiling beneath the glint of tears. He'd acquired a deep tan, his hair had grown long—almost to his shoulders—and had been bleached by the sun to a lighter shade of blond. His body felt more toned than she remembered.

His hug felt unfamiliar. She'd become used to a larger, more muscular build. But it wasn't fair to compare Phillip to Cole. Phillip was her loyal, steadfast partner for life. Cole was her fantasy lover come true...a shooting star, too fiery to last...

Family and friends gathered around them in happy celebration. Everyone talked at once. Tess wondered if anyone had told him about her marriage. She assumed that her parents had. They'd obviously given him Cole's phone number. He hadn't asked about the man who had answered. She had to talk to him about it, of course. Alone.

But others were clamoring for his attention at the moment, demanding to know what had happened to him. She, too, wanted to know. Urging her along with an arm around her shoulders, Phillip led the group into her parents' small living room, where he sat on the sofa, settled her beside him and explained what had happened.

"My note-taking started the trouble. Oh, and the photographs. The authorities confiscated my journal and camera, along with my passport and wallet. They charged me with spying and threw me in a prison. It was little more than a thatched hut, really." He shook his head in grim recollection. "That first week was hell. I thought they were going to kill me. But then the jailer's daughter took pity on me and helped me escape."

"Escape?" Tess exclaimed. "You escaped?"

A chorus of excited questions urged him on. He described how he'd hidden from authorities in the forested mountains with a primitive community of island natives. He had no access to modern facilities or technology. As a fugitive from the law, without money or his passport, he couldn't leave the island or communicate with the outside world. "What I wouldn't have given for a cell phone. And a cup of cappuccino from Campus Coffeehouse."

Everyone laughed, and he continued his narrative, which abounded with anthropological terms and observations. With growing enthusiasm, he described how the natives had helped hide him from the rulers whom they despised. He talked about the political unrest, and then the bizarre food, customs and beliefs of the people.

Tess gradually realized that the whole ordeal had been a supreme adventure. He'd mentioned a time or two that he planned to write a book.

"Then I heard about an American who was asking questions about me. I didn't know how to contact him without tipping off the authorities, but I watched and waited. Last Friday, the American spread the word that the authorities were willing to release me into his custody. So I turned myself in. And...here I am!" He held out his arms in a pleased gesture. The group responded with wild applause. "Now, if I can only get those photos back. I'll need them. They were incredible."

He launched into a detailed description of the photos and their anthropological importance. More friends dropped in, and he retold his tale. Tess soon noticed how often he mentioned the name of the jailer's daughter who had freed him. Kiki.

Kiki this, and Kiki that.

Interesting.

When he'd made himself hoarse with talking, friends filled him in on the happenings he'd missed around campus. His brother, a soccer player for the university, called out, "Hey, Phillip. Did you hear about Tess's adventures while you were gone?"

Everyone fell awkwardly silent.

Phillip glanced at Tess, whose face warmed with annoying guilt. As if she'd been deliberately cheating on him. As if she hadn't waited faithfully for thirteen months without hearing a word...while he played Indiana Jones. Probably with Kiki.

"Yes, I *have* heard." His gaze dipped to the fortune in diamonds on her left hand. When he met her eyes, he looked somewhat bothered, but not as much as she'd expected. Then again, he'd never been too emotionally riled by anything she did. "Your mother told me. I understand you're temporarily a married lady."

"Just since Friday," her mother assured him.

"And only on paper," Kristen said from her seat beside Tess on the sofa.

Tess cringed. She and Cole had agreed to make the world think their marriage was legitimate in every way to avoid problems in court. Hearing her sister announce that the marriage was "only on paper" unnerved Tess. Then, too, it wasn't exactly true. There was more to her relationship with Cole than paperwork.

Namely, sex. Wild, hot, passionate sex. And tenderness....

"Well, of course, it's only on paper," Phillip said. "And I fully understand why she's doing it." His expression warmed as he gazed at Tess. "She was trying to make money to keep the investigator on my trail." He tightened his arm around her shoulders in a fervent hug. "You and your family came through for me, Tess. You brought me home. I'll never forget that."

She smiled at him. And felt another stirring of guilt. No matter how she rationalized it to herself, she hadn't remained faithful. Maybe that was why she didn't feel completely comfortable sitting here plastered to his side.

"So what were those native women like?" his brother piped up. "Did they run around topless? Did they worship you as a golden-haired god?"

Phillip laughed a little too heartily, evaded the questions with a joke and went on to talk about the marriage rituals in terms that only an anthropologist could appreciate.

The phone rang. Her mother answered, then handed it to Phillip. He greeted an old friend with warm enthusiasm, chatted a few minutes, then gave the phone to Tess. "Kathleen O'Brian. She'd like to talk to you."

Kathleen O'Brian. The professor who had translated the curse from Tess's bible. "Tess, I've been looking at these two versions of the curse," she said. "The one you faxed to me, and the one Cole Westcott's lawyer sent." She hesitated. When she continued, she sounded distinctly uneasy. "I've realized that some of the phraseology is more modern than I'd first thought."

"Modern? What do you mean?"

"Both versions of the curse were dated 1825, so I assumed that was correct. But a few of the phrases wouldn't have been used before the early 1900's."

Tess frowned. "How can that be? The explanations written beside them clearly state that the curse was put on both families in 1825. The bibles themselves are dated even earlier."

"With the false date written in, I'd say the curse is a hoax."

"A hoax!"

"Someone found those two family bibles—maybe back in the early 1900's—and wrote the curses in them to persuade people that the families had been cursed for a century. Why anyone would do that, I don't know."

"But how could someone from either family write in both bibles if they were kept in separate houses? The families have always been bitter enemies. It makes more sense that in 1825, an embittered McCrary daughter wrote the curses in the bibles and sent one to each of the families—just as the explanations written beside the curses say."

"Sorry, Tess. The wording doesn't date back that far. It was a hoax. If you want more of an explanation, ask Cole Westcott."

"Cole Westcott?" At the very mention of his name, a pang of longing assailed Tess. She gripped the phone harder. "Why would I ask *him*? What does he know about ancient Gaelic?"

A dead silence answered her. The professor then stuttered, "W-well, I mean, he might be able to think of some explanation. He might...um...know about the family history. Look, Tess, I'm on my way to class and really have to run. Sorry that I didn't catch that dating problem earlier. Good luck."

Tess hung up the phone and stared blankly through the crowd of friends around her, all merrily chatting with Phillip about his island experiences. Could the curse really have been a *hoax*? Perpetrated by whom? And why had the professor said to ask Cole for more of an explanation? She'd then acted as if she'd said more than she should have. She'd sounded almost *guilty*. Why?

Regardless of what Cole knew, the professor believed the curse to be a hoax. If that was true, Tess's fear of the curse had been groundless.

As she pondered that realization, the door opened and her father limped in—a cane in his hand, a brace on his back, slippers on his feet and a bathrobe over his pajamas.

"Daddy," Kristen cried, "what are you doing out of the hospital?"

"They weren't supposed to release you until tomorrow," his wife exclaimed.

"Don't start in on me. I don't need to be in any hospital." He gazed past his anxious womenfolk to smile at Phillip. "About time you came home, son."

Phillip shook Ian's hand with profuse thanks for financing the investigation.

Ian didn't stay to hear the explanation of his absence, though. "I'll be in the den, on the phone. I've got business to settle. Important business." With those cryptic words, he limped off into the small office he called his "den" and shut the door.

Tess wondered what business was so important that he'd rushed from his hospital bed without changing into his clothes or shoes. Unease trickled through her. Did it have to do with the lawsuits he'd sworn to file against Cole and Leo?

Her suspicious musing was interrupted by Phillip's request that she come with him to retrieve his car from his brother's fraternity house. The ride there gave her time alone with him to talk about her marriage. She didn't tell him anything beyond basic facts—their prenuptial agreement, the five-month time span, the requirement that she live at Westcott Hall. Her mother had assured him that Tess had her own private suite. She didn't disabuse him of that notion.

The topic started her insides to roiling again. She was no closer now to knowing what to do than she had been last night. How could she live with Cole now that Phillip had come back? The prospect of returning to Cole tonight loomed largely in her mind, resurrecting all the ethical concerns and creating emotional turmoil.

She certainly couldn't sleep with him. Ever again. Not if she loved Phillip.

And she did. *Didn't she?* The question echoed through her as she drove to her parents' house and he followed in his own car. Had her feelings for Phillip changed?

By the time they reached the house, she wanted only to find a private place where she could be alone to think. But her father met her in the living room with a radiant smile. "I did it," he announced. "I've just wrung a deal out of Westcott that would make your granddaddy proud."

Everything in Tess went still. "What kind of deal, Daddy?"

He lowered himself and his back brace carefully into his favorite recliner, his smile beaming with triumph. "Westcott's going to pay the medical and legal bills for Josh and me, and compensate us for pain and suffering. He's having his no-good cousin write in his police report that our fight was a personal family matter, which should make the D.A. more open to dropping the charges. All I have to do is sign a waiver releasing Westcott and his cousin from legal responsibility. Josh will have to sign waivers, too. But the best part is—" he grinned at Tess and Phillip as if bestowing upon them a gift "—you don't have to live with him anymore, Tessie."

"What?" She nearly came off the sofa.

Her father motioned her back down with a gesture meant to calm, and Phillip put an arm around her and squeezed her shoulder—an annoying habit he'd gotten into. "A little rough talk from me made Westcott realize that it's against his best interests to tie up your time. We came up with a scheme, and it worked. I called his stepmother, Deirdre...the one who offered us more money than Westcott had if you'll testify against him in court. She knows I hate him. She thinks I tried to kill him with my hunting rifle. Saw it on the news, I guess. Anyway, I told her that you refused to cooperate with us."

"Of course I refused."

"I know you won't like this, Tessie, but I told her you wanted to stay married to him to get your hands on the full forty million. She didn't have any trouble believing that. She was mad as hell, thinking she wouldn't see a penny of that inheritance."

Tess found herself biting her nails and forced her hands to her lap, where she brutally clenched them. "I don't understand what any of that has to do with my agreement to stay with Cole."

"Now that Deirdre and the others believe that their strategies won't work, Westcott's lawyer offered them a last-ditch chance to get something out of the deal. Five hundred thousand dollars each—if they sign an agreement *today* to waive their right to contest his inheritance."

"And they agreed to that?" she asked incredulously.

"He said they did."

She sat in stunned silence, struggling to grasp the abrupt change of plans. "But I still have to stay married to Cole and live with him to satisfy the terms of the will."

"You *will* stay married to him, technically, for the full five months. But without his stepmothers looking to challenge him in court, nobody cares if you live at Westcott Hall or not. No one's going to be looking for loopholes. No one will challenge your marriage or his inheritance. When he inherits, his stepmothers get their money, Josh and I get our money, and you get two million dollars and McCrary Place." Her father drew two cigars out his robe pocket, tossed one to Phillip and lit one for himself. "Is that a sweet deal, or what?"

Tess's hands, though firmly clasped, had begun to tremble. *He'd ended it.* Cole had ended their time together without saying a word to her about it. Abruptly she stood up and reached for her purse and car keys. "I need to talk to him," she said, more to herself than anyone else. "I'm going home to talk to him."

"You're going *where?*" repeated her father.

She halted near the door. *Home.* She'd said she was going home. "To Westcott Hall," she amended, feeling thoroughly shaken. How could Cole have made such a serious decision without her?

"Don't bother. He's not there. Said something about business on the road. But he said you can call him on his cell phone if you have questions."

"I have questions," she whispered harshly. Without another glance at her father or Phillip who sat puffing on their cigars, she strode into the den, shut the door and keyed in Cole's number on the telephone.

At the sound of his rich, deep voice, a rush of emotion forced her down into a chair. "Cole." Nothing else squeezed past her tightened throat.

"Tess."

She realized then, with that simple exchange, that she desperately wanted to see him. *Be with him.* "Are you crazy? Do you really think your stepmothers will forget about forty million dollars for a measly five hundred thousand? If I move out of Westcott Hall, they'll persuade the court we're not legitimately married."

"They won't take the matter to court." He sounded calm and sure. "They believed your father when he told them that you're staying in the marriage. They also know that he told you about their strategy—hiring detectives to follow me. Paying women to trap me into compromising situations to prove infidelity."

"My father never told me about that."

"An acquaintance of Deirdre's warned me. Henry called Lacey today and got her to admit they'd approached her with money to get me alone. I mentioned the scheme to your father. He admitted it was on their agenda. As far as Deirdre and her cohorts know, your father told you everything. If you, he and Lacey testify to those tactics, my stepmothers would come across as ruthless home wreckers. The court wouldn't be sympathetic. Henry hurried matters along with talk about 'conspiracy to defraud' and bribery charges. Nonsense, but they listened. They'll take the five hundred thousand and be happy."

The effectiveness of his strategic dealings left her in awe. He really was a force to be reckoned with. In a matter of hours, he'd overcome every obstacle to his inheritance...*and eliminated her role in his life.* He obviously didn't want her there. "So, then," she whispered, feeling as if her heart was shattering, "you...don't need me?"

Silence stretched between them.

"I need you to stay legally married to me for five months. If the media approaches you, tell them we're doing fine. You can say I'm on the road a lot, which will be true." He paused, then added slowly, "It would be best if you keep your relationship with Phillip...discreet." Another pause. "And

I...well, I'm not going to take any chances with...women...until this inheritance issue is settled."

Astounding pain coursed through her. *He really was leaving her.* And when the five months were up, he'd go back to his many women.

"You can get your clothes from my house whenever you want. Tomorrow I'll deposit a few hundred thousand into a bank account that I've set up for you. It should see you through until the bulk of my funds are available. Then I'll transfer the rest of the two million to you, along with the deed to McCrary Place. If you'd like to stay there before then, I'll leave a key with Mrs. Johannsen."

Tess couldn't answer. Her insides were tied up too tightly in knots.

"We can file for divorce in November," he went on. "I'm sorry if the wait causes you problems with...your personal plans."

"It won't."

He didn't answer for a while. "Good." He cleared his throat. "Well..."

And she realized he was about to hang up, and she probably wouldn't talk to him again until their divorce. *Their divorce.* A fresh wave of pain hit her. "The curse," she murmured distractedly. "Did Professor O'Brian call you about it?"

"Yes. She said it was a hoax."

She wondered why the professor hadn't admitted talking to Cole. "She seemed to think you might know who perpetrated it." When he didn't reply, she prodded, "Why would she think that?"

"I, uh...might have mentioned that I planned to call my great aunt."

"Your great aunt?"

"Edna. I asked if she knew anything about the curse being a hoax. She didn't, but she remembered something about two teenagers—a McCrary girl and a Westcott boy—back in the

1920's. They wanted to marry, and their families didn't approve. We think it's possible that they wrote the curses in their family bibles to push their parents into allowing the marriage."

Something about that didn't seem quite right. Two teenagers, writing a curse in ancient Gaelic... "What happened to them?"

"They grew up and went their separate ways. The point is, the curse was just a ploy dreamt up by two kids. There was no vengeful, heartbroken woman involved, no Gullah maid with Lowcountry magic chanting spells while she wrote it."

Which meant there was no need for planting the seed. Or satisfying his needs. Or his keeping only unto her.

"So you don't have to worry, Tess," he gently concluded, "that our separation will cause repercussions. The curse isn't real. Our families will be okay."

A warm sheen distorted her vision. She stared at the diamonds on her left hand. "I'll leave the wedding ring at your house," she whispered.

"No." His voice had grown gruff. "Wear it until we...divorce. Then you can keep it, or...or sell it."

She violently compressed her trembling lips. When had she fallen so much in love with him?

"Thank you, Tess," he rasped, "for helping me keep my home. I wish you the best."

11

"HE'S NOT HERE for your sister's wedding? You've only been married a month, and Westcott's already found better things to do?"

Tess cringed at her Aunt Sophie's strident voice, which carried to the far reaches of even this massive, crowded reception hall. As other guests turned and glanced, Tess replied with a determined smile, "Cole's business keeps him very busy."

"I'll bet I know what kind of business he's up to." She did, at least, have the mercy to lower her voice. "If I were you, I'd divorce him and marry Phillip. You don't see *him* traipsing off and staying gone on business trips all the time."

Tess stared at her aunt in disbelief. Just because Phillip was here now—a highly visible member of the bridal party—she'd obviously forgotten that he'd spent a year "traipsing off" to godforsaken places in the name of anthropology.

Not that it mattered. Any of it. Aunt Sophie could say anything she liked. Tess would stick to the agreed-upon story, even if it killed her. And she was afraid it might. "Cole is on the road a lot, but we're doing fine. And Phillip and I are just friends."

"You were a fool to toss Phillip over for Westcott. He's playing fast and loose with you. I saw that interview you two gave on television, saying how you were in love. I know *you* don't lie, but those Westcott men are pros at it. You can't let a sweet talker like him sweep you off your feet. Mark my words—he'll divorce you as soon as the legal time period is up for his father's will."

Pain glanced through Tess. Aunt Sophie would be congratulating herself come November.

While Sophie sailed off in search of her next victim, Tess clenched her fists and headed for the back garden. She had to get out of here. She couldn't take any more interrogations or advice. She and her parents had agreed to present the story Cole had suggested—that his business kept him on the road. No one wanted to take the chance of endangering his inheritance. Her family had too much to lose.

The price, of course, was that Tess played the part of a newlywed left alone, spending a suspicious number of nights at her "sister's" apartment. Friends had come to believe the same as Aunt Sophie—that she'd fallen in love with a smooth talker who'd charmed her into marrying him, but wanted her only to satisfy his father's will.

But it hadn't been like that. *Had it?*

Her mother's most inquisitive neighbor loomed up ahead of her. Tess turned toward a secluded corner, desperate to escape notice.

"Forget about the potted palm. The leaves aren't thick enough." Lianna materialized beside her with a toss of her tawny spiral curls and an impish grin. "We could always crawl under the ice sculpture table, but we'd probably be dripped on."

"I'm willing to risk it." Tess turned her back to the crowded room and faced her friend as if in earnest private conversation. Not many people would intrude. "If Mrs. Laslow heads this way, let me know. That ice sculpture could drip all it wants—I'm under there."

"You're safe. Mrs. Laslow veered off toward the cheese ball," Lianna reported. As a waiter walked by with a tray of champagne, she grabbed two glasses and pressed one into Tess's hand. "Down this and you won't mind the questions as much."

Tess took a few sips, but the cool fizz resurrected memories of drinking champagne on her wedding night. Champagne that Cole had poured, in his bedroom. Wearing nothing but a green silk robe. Right before they'd—

Pain billowed in her, and she set the glass down on a nearby table. "I'd better not. Who knows what might come out of my mouth the next time someone asks a question."

Maybe the truth. That he'd left her. That he'd wrapped up his business in a tidy little package and hit the road. That she thought of him every day, every hour, but hadn't heard from him in a month. A whole month. Without Cole.

Excruciating.

"Tess, I know that you and your parents agreed to keep quiet about the deals with Cole, and you've been telling me that you don't mind him being gone." Lianna peered at her in concern. "You say you're fine with the divorce in November, but—"

"That's all there is to it, Li," Tess fiercely insisted. Shifting her gaze to the wall, she willed away an annoying warmth filling her eyes. She saw no use in burdening Lianna with her troubles. There was nothing anyone could do about the pain.

But every day *was* getting harder to bear, and today had been the worst. Not that she wasn't happy for Kristen and Josh. As their maid of honor—or "matron of honor," technically speaking—she'd stood near the flower-decked altar while they'd tenderly spoken their vows in the cathedral. A beautiful, glowing bride with her lovestruck young groom, they'd fervently promised each other forever.

Their happiness had warmed Tess.

But she couldn't help remembering her own wedding, a month ago, in a chapel of empty pews. A ceremony of empty vows. A kiss filled with passion that still burned in her heart. A ring imbued with memories that still made her throat tight with pain.

Lianna mercifully turned her gaze away from Tess and was distracted by something beyond her. "Oh, your poor cousin. Your Aunt Zoe's dragging her from guy to guy again, trying to find her a husband. She's zeroing in on one now." Lianna's tawny brows rose. "Hmmm. She doesn't have bad taste. I haven't seen his face yet, but the rest of him looks pretty darn—" Lianna broke off, and her brown eyes grew wide. "Oh...my...God.'

Tess frowned. "What is it? What's wrong, Li?"

"You won't believe who Zoe is trying to net."

Unable to resist, Tess peeked over her shoulder. And her heart turned over with a painful thud. *Cole.* Cole stood across the reception hall from her—tall, broad-shouldered and heartbreakingly handsome in an elegant black tuxedo, an ivory shirt and matching tie. His gaze raked the crowd.

What was he doing here?

Panic filled her. She couldn't deal with him now. She needed time to brace herself. Fortify her defenses.

"Uh-oh," Lianna warned from the side of her mouth. "Here comes your mother, and she doesn't look happy."

Her mother's perfume wafted to Tess before a hand grabbed her arm in a panicked grip. "What's *he* doing here, honey?" Her worried gaze was, of course, aimed at Cole, whose attention had been snagged by Aunt Zoe. "How did he even know about the wedding? I didn't send him an invitation. And I know that Kristen didn't."

No doubt about that. Her sister and parents were afraid she'd been taking her relationship with Cole too seriously. They wouldn't welcome the fox in the henhouse. Maybe they had a point. "I didn't invite him."

"I hope there won't be trouble," her mother fretted. "I know that technically he's your husband, and we've been letting everyone think that your marriage is legitimate, but you know how these McCrary men feel about Westcotts—especially if they believe one of their women is being taken advantage of."

Tess wrenched her gaze away from Cole and turned her back to the crowd again. Her heart was racing too fast, and her breath was coming in shallow spurts. At least he hadn't seen her. Thank goodness Aunt Zoe was distracting him.

"Someone needs to make him leave before your father comes in from the bar."

"Go talk to him, Tess," Lianna urged. "You know you want to."

No, she didn't want to. Her wounds were still too open. And she'd been such a fool, falling in love with him when she'd known it was only a business deal to him—with a little sex on the side.

"Zoe moved on," Lianna observed. "Cole must have told her he's married...or he's wearing his wedding ring."

He probably *was* wearing his ring. He'd asked her to wear hers until after their divorce. The thought of that gold band on his finger—the one she'd helped push into place—generated chaotic warmth in her stomach. And the idea that he had come, uninvited, to Kristen's wedding, churned that warmth into a glowing, painful force.

Why was he here?

WHY THE HELL was he here? He'd made up his mind a month ago to leave Tess to the man she loved. So what was he doing at her sister's wedding?

Standing beside one of the marble pillars in the posh, candle-studded reception hall, Cole searched the formally dressed crowd. She shouldn't be too hard to find, with that vibrant auburn hair and flashing smile.

Pain flickered through him and he cursed himself. He should have thrown the invitation away. But the fact that he'd received an invitation—not to mention the unsigned personal note inside—had piqued his curiosity beyond bearing. What had it meant? He had to find out.

And he wanted to see her again.

Just once. He'd settle for once. Unless something, anything, gave him the idea that she still wanted him. Then Phillip would have a fight on his hands. Figuratively speaking. Or literally, if it came down to it.

He'd spotted Phillip in the bar at the front of the complex.

He'd been laughing and smoking cigars with a group of men that included Ian McCrary. Cole recognized Phillip from Tess's photo. His hair was longer, and he'd grown a mustache, but he otherwise looked the same. His imprisonment apparently hadn't devastated him.

He was a member of the bridal party. An integral part of her family. And why wouldn't he be? After November, he'd be her husband.

Pain coursed in harder currents through Cole's chest. Was she sleeping with him these days? Playing, laughing with him? Cole thrust his hands into his pockets and clenched his fists. He shouldn't have come.

The band struck up a dance tune and the floor filled with couples, blocking his view of half the room. Edging between crowded, candle-lit tables, he scanned the faces.

Would Tess be happy to see him? Dismayed? Indifferent? He had no idea how she felt about him. The subject utterly confused him. How could she have made love to him with such passion and tenderness if she loved someone else?

Maybe that was why he'd let the invitation goad him into coming here tonight. Because the longer he thought about it, the less sense it made.

Curious gazes followed him. Recognition lit a few faces. Probably from his televised interview with Tess. Only one guest had spoken to him. She obviously hadn't recognized him. She'd asked if he was married. He'd brandished his wedding band.

The ring had come in handy over the past month.

"So-o-o, you finally decided to show." A short, bulky old gal with a crotchety frown blocked his path. "Don't think you're doing my niece any big favor. She's doing fine, just fine, while you're out carousing on your *business trips*."

Cole narrowed his eyes. She'd bellowed loud enough that others had turned to stare. At least he knew now that people believed Tess and he were still together. What role, then, did they assume Phillip played in her life? "I take it you're Tess's aunt?"

"Sophie. Sophie McCrary. That's *Ms.* McCrary to you."

He recognized her name. *You can ask my Aunt Sophie to marry you, but she'd probably hit you with her umbrella.* Now he understood the beguiling sparkle that had played in Tess's eyes. "Where *is* Tess?"

"Wouldn't *you* like to know?"

He'd had enough of Aunt Sophie. Leaning close, he peered sternly at her. "Yes, I would. And if you were twenty years younger, I'd turn you over my knee and teach you a lesson for butting into our personal business."

Her gun-gray brows shot up. "*Twenty* years younger?" A gratified flush rose into her face. "I'd like to see you turn a fifty-year-old woman over your knee, sonny."

Fifty. Right. Twenty years ago, she couldn't have been less than sixty-two. He winked at her. She scowled. But the ferocity had left her.

"Where's my wife?"

"Headed for the potted palm, last time I noticed." She jerked her head.

He glanced in that direction.

And he saw her, across the crowded room. Staring at him.

Her vivid auburn hair was caught up in sexy, loose curls, as it had been on their wedding day. She wore a shimmery bronze gown that he'd seen on the other bridesmaids. On Tess, it looked uniquely elegant. Sleek. Alluring. Thin straps crossed each shapely shoulder—shoulders he'd held and kissed... and lathered with soap suds....

The pain in him increased. She was too damn beautiful. And she wasn't his.

He stood, hands in pockets, without moving. Things were much worse than he'd thought. He'd convinced himself that in time, he'd get over her. He knew now that it wasn't true. Nothing, *nothing*, would stop him from wanting her. Constantly. Endlessly.

She started toward him, her progress slow and hesitant. As she drew closer, her wide, incredulous gray eyes answered at least one of his questions. She hadn't known about the invitation he'd received.

"What are you doing here?" A curious, breathless, astonished question.

Her nearness shook him. He'd missed her too much. Obsessed over her for too long. He had to push his hands deeper into his pockets to stop from reaching for her. "Same as everyone else," he replied, his voice hoarse with suppressed emotion.

"Everyone else was invited."

"So was I."

"By whom?"

He shrugged. "An invitation came in the mail." Seeing her disbelief, he reached into his vest pocket, drew out the invitation and flashed it at her.

She gaped in clear surprise. He'd done the same when he'd received it.

Before she asked for a closer inspection, he shoved the ivory linen invitation back into his pocket. "Besides, I have important unfinished business to settle."

The distraction worked. "With my father?"

"No. With you."

Uncertainty gathered in her gaze, as if she suspected him of meaning something intimately personal by "unfinished business." Which, of course, he did.

"What business?" she demanded.

"The money I put in your account. You transferred it back to me. Why?"

"I don't need it."

"Everyone needs money."

Defiance warmed her gaze. "I'll work for mine."

If he had to provoke her defiance to warm her, so be it. "What about McCrary Place? Will you give that back to me, too?"

"Yes."

He frowned. She no longer wanted *McCrary Place*? Was she that damn carried away with Phillip that nothing else mattered? Or was this one of those "honor" issues she could be so stubborn about? "Let's go somewhere and talk."

"I can't leave." The suggestion had rattled her. "And this isn't the time to discuss...business." She glanced around at guests who were watching them.

Cole leaned his shoulder against a marble pillar and soaked up the sight of her. If he couldn't have her to himself, he'd take what he could get, with the whole damn McCrary clan looking on. "Then we won't discuss business."

She didn't look reassured. "My mother's worried that your presence here will stir up trouble."

"Are *you* concerned about that, too?" He allowed his gaze to caress her face, her hair, her shoulders...her mouth.... "That I might stir up trouble?"

"No," she breathed. "Well, maybe. I don't know. I mean—"

"You look beautiful tonight, Tess," he whispered.

Her gaze meshed with his. She blushed, then looked away. A pulse throbbed at her temple, and her breathing deepened, ever so subtly...the way it used to when he'd rubbed his thumb across her mouth.

He wanted her so much he could barely breathe.

She nervously raked back a tendril from her face, and he noticed she wore his wedding ring. He'd asked her to wear it. She probably assumed he'd meant for appearances' sake. But appearances had nothing to do with it. He'd wanted her to think of him every time she looked at it. To think of their marriage, and their hot, frenzied kisses. Their lovemaking. He was fiercely glad she wore it.

She cleared her throat and squared her shoulders. Ah. She'd decided to take control. Direct the conversation into safer channels. "I guess I should thank you for getting my father, Josh and Leo to meet with the D.A. and having the charges dropped."

"It would have been less touchy defusing a bomb," he admitted.

Acknowledgement sparkled in her eyes. "I was impressed. No punches thrown, no guns fired. Leo even told my father and Josh that he wouldn't boot them out of his restaurant if they came in...as long as they didn't bring too many Mc-Crarys with them."

"A cordial invitation, coming from Leo."

Amusement bound them together for an instant and a smile flexed her mouth. The need to kiss her surged through him. And her gaze went to *his* mouth. He swore he wasn't imagining the answering heat....

"Tess. There you are. Your mother's been looking for you."

Startled out of their absorption, she greeted breathlessly, "Phillip." A flush had warmed her face—from the heat they'd been sharing or from Phillip's presence, Cole wasn't sure. She glanced awkwardly between them. "Have you met Cole Westcott?"

"No, I don't believe I have."

"Cole...Phillip Mattingly."

Cole shook his hand. As he'd expected, the guy's grip was a little firmer than necessary—a show of strength—and his gaze held cool appraisal. Cole understood that. The man felt that Tess belonged to him...and clearly knew that Cole wanted her.

"I hear you spend a lot of time traveling," Phillip remarked.

Aren't you glad? "I hear you've spent a little time on the road yourself."

Phillip gave a small, acknowledging smile. "Don't know if I'd call it 'the road.'" Cole sensed banked resentment in him, which led him to think Phillip knew of his intimacies with Tess. He went on, nonetheless, to talk about his most recent trip with a droll reference to his "forcibly extended vacation."

And despite the sharp, hot claws digging into Cole at the knowledge that she'd chosen this man over him, he soon noticed an interesting fact. Phillip didn't shift closer to her, or put an arm around her, or declare his ownership in any way. And she didn't settle closer to *him*, or gaze at him with intimate warmth, as Cole had been dreading.

But then, maybe that was part of the act. If she'd allowed the world to believe she was married to Cole and living with him, she couldn't publicly acknowledge Phillip as anything more than a friend.

That didn't mean the situation wasn't drastically different behind closed doors. But Cole couldn't tolerate that thought. It was torturous enough, seeing them together.

"So in September," Phillip was saying, "we'll probably head off to Zimbabwe."

Cole frowned. *What* had he said?

"Phillip, did my mother say why she was looking for me?" Tess cut in.

"Not really."

"Would you mind telling her where I am?" She smiled, and Cole realized that she *was* gazing at Phillip with intimate warmth. That intimacy had more to do with fondness than passion, though. Or was his perception warped by wishful thinking?

"Oh...sure." Phillip hesitated, nodded awkwardly at Cole, then loped off.

Relieved that he was gone, Cole turned to Tess. "Did he say *Zimbabwe?*"

She nodded. "He's going in September."

But Phillip had said *we*. Dread curled through Cole. Would Tess be leaving? For how long? He'd have no chance, then, of taking her away from Phillip. "Are you going with him?"

She shook her head with an odd little smile. "I don't think Kiki would like that."

"Kiki?"

"An island woman Phillip met. She's visiting to 'learn

other cultures.' She's been staying with me this week. I tried to get her to come tonight, but she was too overwhelmed by the crowd." Tess smiled, probably at the utter confusion in his gaze. "Phillip thinks of her only as a friend...or maybe a research project. But she adores him, and he's agreed to let her travel with him. I think he'll realize sooner or later that there's wonderful potential for them as a couple."

Cole's head was spinning. And his heart had picked up speed until it felt like it might explode. "I don't understand. You're matchmaking for *Phillip*?"

"In a way, I guess. I'd hate to see him...lonely."

He stared at her, transfixed. Things weren't making sense, but a blinding flash of hope forked across his dark horizon. And though he hadn't yet formed a rational picture of the situation, he'd clearly recognized the sadness that had shadowed her eyes when she'd said "lonely."

He knew that sadness. He'd lived with it for a solid month. He would live with it forever if she didn't come back to him.

"Tess." He reached for her. He couldn't help it. If he didn't hold her—hold *onto* her—she might disappear, as she had every night in his dreams.

A strangled sound rose in her throat and she pulled back from him. "I...I'd better go," she choked out. "I've got things to do."

"We have to talk."

"No, really, we don't." Tess turned to leave, but her path was blocked by chatting people. She felt trapped. She shouldn't have sent Phillip away! His presence had helped curb Cole's awesome draw. But she hadn't wanted to subject Phillip to further awkwardness. She had, after all, broken up with him because of her feelings for Cole—hopeless feelings, but undeniable. Phillip hadn't been happy about it. Then again, he hadn't been devastated, either.

"I envy Phillip," Cole called out, stopping her dead in her attempt to escape, "for having Kiki."

Tess shot him a startled glance. She'd known he'd traveled

to exotic islands, but what were the chances...! "*You* know Kiki too?"

He slanted his lips in sardonic response, which activated the sexy groove beside them. "No, I don't know Kiki."

Embarrassment warmed her. She hoped he'd thought she was kidding. But more disturbing was the pull of attraction she felt at his warm, wry enjoyment of her.

"But having someone to travel with would be a wonderful thing." His gaze grew serious, and his voice dropped to a reedy whisper. "Otherwise, it gets lonely."

Every shred of common sense screamed for her to walk away from him. But she couldn't bring herself to do that yet. "You've been...lonely?"

"Yes."

Haven't you learned not to listen to him? She couldn't, wouldn't, take his words personally. "I'm sorry. That 'forsaking all others' thing must be hard for you. November must seem very far away." Her throat tightened at that thought, but she forced a smile. "Once your inheritance is settled, you'll have plenty of travel partners."

"No one's going to challenge my inheritance, Tess. No one cares if I'm with a woman who's not my wife."

I do. And that was one reason she had to get away from him. Immediately.

But his hands swept up her arms in a gentle, kneading hold, and the imploring heat in his gaze held her captive. "I don't have to wait until November. I could find traveling partners now. But what I told you before still holds true." His hands tightened on her arms. "I want *you*, Tess. Only you."

And her defenses, never strong against him, crumbled a little more. To make matters worse, the lights dimmed, a spotlight lit the dance floor, and the singer announced a special dance for the bride and groom. A hauntingly beautiful love song drew Kristen and Josh to the floor—a breathtaking bride waltzing with her handsome, dark-haired groom.

Tess turned and stared at them with a slow, hot welling in

her eyes. Her emotions were too on edge for anything as heart-stirring as this.

Cole shifted behind her, slid his arms around her waist and held her against his warm, solid body. The feel of him, the scent of him, flooded her with agonizing pleasure. His embrace felt so good. So right.

"I remember my bride," he said in a hot, torrential whisper against her ear. "I remember dancing with her."

Tess closed her eyes, overcome by the memory of their wedding night. They hadn't waltzed on a dance floor, or even moved to music. Oh, but they *had* danced....

"Come outside with me, Tess."

Temptation surged with such compelling force that her defense system at last kicked into gear. He wanted her to go outside with him. If she did, she'd be kissing him. And then making love to him.

Oh, he was good. *Those Westcott men are pros.* He wanted her, yes...but only for sex, or he wouldn't have left her. He wouldn't have handed her over to another man at the very first opportunity. Did he think he could crook his finger whenever the urge struck and call her to his bed?

Of course he did. And it was too, too possible that she'd come running.

"Okay," she murmured, gritting her teeth, deliberately stoking her anger to hold back the hurt. "Let's go."

They hurried through the darkness, through the largely spellbound crowd, to the wide double doors at the back. Into the warm, star-studded Carolina night. Past another couple lingering on the spacious, red-bricked patio. Around a dimly lit corner.

And when they reached the secluded side of the building, Tess broke away from his hold and rounded on him. "Now you listen to me, you...you Westcott," she seethed.

He backed up a surprised step, confusion darkening his handsome face.

may not touch me, you may not hold me, you may

not whisper anything into my ear," she railed. "You lost those rights the day you gave me away."

"Gave you away?"

"Don't try to talk your way out of this. Just leave. Go ahead. Get out. I'll see you in divorce court—*if* a personal appearance is necessary."

Anger lit in his gaze. "Oh, so we're back to 'only what's necessary.'" He loomed closer, backing her against the smooth stone side of the building. "Well, open your eyes and see what that is. *We're* necessary, Tess. You and me."

Her throat clenched, and to her horror, liquid blurred her vision. "You left me."

"No, hell no. *You* left *me*." His whisper was scalding and bitter. "For Phillip."

"I would have come home by evening. You know I'd planned to stay with you."

"You left me the night before."

She stared at him, stunned into silence.

"You left me, Tess, when you turned away from me in our bedroom." His anger, his pain, smoldered with every word. Expelling a harsh breath, he glanced away. Only after he'd tempered his intensity did he return his stare to her. "It's not like I didn't know," he whispered. "You told me. From the very start, you told me. And you kept his picture in your drawer. When he called, you cried and whispered 'I love you.'"

She couldn't deny it. Any of it.

Cole shut his eyes, pulled her roughly against him and buried his face in her hair. And she held him. Tightly. Every muscle in his body seemed clenched, and his arms were bands of iron around her.

Her heart ached. *She'd hurt him.* She loved him so much, and she'd hurt him. The silence bled with regrets...but also with excruciating hope. She'd thought he hadn't cared. She'd been wrong. But how deeply *did* he care? Was she reading too much into his anger and pain?

No. For all the mistakes she'd made throughout her relationship with Cole, the biggest had been not trusting the evidence of her own heart. She'd felt the emotion in his touch, his gaze, his kiss. His lovemaking. *She believed he loved her.*

And if she was wrong, knowing the truth was worth any risk she could take.

He stirred in her arms. Loosened his grip. Rested his jaw against her temple. Softly, hoarsely, he asked, "What happened with Phillip, Tess?"

She swallowed hard, overcome by the most ferocious hope. "It...it didn't work out," she whispered. "I'll always care about him, but he...he wanted to kiss me. And to sleep with me." A stark stillness came over Cole—one that she sensed rather than felt. In a barely audible rasp, she explained, "I couldn't do that."

Slowly he drew back to see her face, his gaze blazingly intense. "Why not?"

"Because I'm married."

Confusion jammed Cole's chest with emotion—gladness that she hadn't slept with Phillip and fear that she'd refrained for the wrong reason.

Because I'm married. Did she mean that her legal status had kept her from going to bed with the man she loved? Was this another one of her morality issues—and all because they'd signed a few papers? Had the conflict broken them up?

Or...did she mean that she was *married* to him, in the truest, finest way imaginable?

"Tess." He searched her eyes, desperate for the answer. He was almost afraid to find it. He, one of those historically damned Westcott men. But he had to know. "Are you saying that the technicality of our marriage came between you and Phillip?"

"Our marriage," she replied slowly, "isn't a technicality...at least not for me." Her gaze followed her hand to his face, where she caressed him with a tender, lingering touch. "You see, my husband's the only one I want," she murmured.

"I've never known anyone like him. I've never *wanted* anyone like I want him." Intensity replaced the tenderness as her stare met his. "And I love kissing him. I can kiss him for hours and hours and still want more...."

Hot, incredulous elation surged from somewhere deep within Cole's heart. He drove his fingers into her lustrous hair, caught her face between his hands and consumed her with his gaze, feeding on the emotion he'd been starving for.

"And I love making love to him," she rasped, tears of sincerity welling in her eyes. "I can't tell you how much."

"I love you, Tess," he swore. "I love you." And he kissed her, saying it again, not out loud, but in the way he'd said it so many times before. He held nothing back, and neither did she. They took possession; marked their claim, in the deepest, most jubilant of kisses. A sensual celebration. A spiritual re-affirmation.

A homecoming.

When the need grew too great and practicality forced them to stop, Tess whispered fiercely, "I love you, Cole. I'll always love you."

That fact no longer scared her.

"Then you have to stay with me," he decreed. "No divorce. No living apart." In a touchingly fervent whisper, he added, "No hiding in the bathroom to change."

She laced her fingers through the thick, silky hair at his nape and smiled into his eyes. She'd have no problem complying. "We *do* have unfinished business, you know."

"A honeymoon," he said. Would he *forever* be reading her mind? "And then there's that negligee I saw hanging in our closet."

No doubt about it...the man saw clear through her.

A commotion from around the corner of the building drew their attention. "I saw Westcott bring her out here," came Aunt Sophie's strident bark. "And I'm telling you, Tess didn't want to go. I could see that, plain as day. She was about to cry. I think he *forced* her outside. He's a fresh one, you know."

A chorus of masculine mutters and oaths followed.

"Uh-oh," Tess breathed into Cole's ear. "A McCrary lynch mob."

He didn't seem particularly worried, and when he opened his mouth to reply, she shushed him with a finger over his lips. She wasn't ready to give up their privacy.

"You all turn around and march right back in here." The sharp command rang out into the night, effectively silencing the grumblings. Tess's eyes widened. She'd never before heard such strength of purpose in her gentle mother's voice. "Whether you like it or not, those kids are married. *Leave them alone.*"

Greatly subdued retorts and mutters answered her. The men were clearly not pleased. But the wave of noise receded, leaving silence in its wake.

Wonders would never cease!

"Brace yourself," Tess warned Cole, who hadn't loosened his embrace for a single moment. "My father couldn't have been with them. When my uncles and cousins advise him of the situation, he won't give in as easily."

"Oh, I don't know about that."

She frowned in question. He released her from his arms, drew something out of his vest pocket and handed it to her. The gold-embossed wedding invitation. She glanced at it in puzzlement.

"Open it," he urged.

She did, and was surprised to see familiar bold handwriting scrawled across the ivory linen. *I've known Westcotts to be shifty, scheming, unscrupulous and the lowest form of life on this earth. But I've never known one to give up on something he wants.*

Astonishment kept her staring at it. But then the happiest sense of well-being bubbled up inside her, liberating her heart from the last of its bonds. She beamed at Cole. "Gosh, what gave you the clue that it's from my father?"

They gazed with silent laughter.

But then his amusement faded, and he answered in a

hushed, solemn way, "Because I know that he loves you. And if he thought you were unhappy, and that I could make things right, he'd do whatever he could to see that it happened...even if it cost him everything he had."

The warm sheen returned to her eyes. And she smiled at him with a love that knew no bounds. "I don't think my great-great-grandmother had vengeance in mind at all when she wrote that curse," she mused. "I think she wanted to end the fighting between our families."

"I suppose that's possible."

The idea pleased her. But then a realization hit. "Oh, you suppose it's possible, do you?" She narrowed her eyes. "I caught you, you scheming Westcott."

He frowned. "Caught me?"

"You *know* that my great-great-grandmother wrote that curse—*not* two teenagers in the 1900's."

A barely detectable flicker of guilt rippled through his gaze. Not quite enough guilt to please her.

"I took the curse to another translator," she informed him, "and he had no idea what Kathleen O'Brian meant by 'outdated phraseology.' What's more, Kathleen has been avoiding me...as if she feels guilty."

Cole pursed his mouth and regarded her in secretive silence.

"*You* made up that story about the teenagers," Tess charged, "and you coerced Kathleen into cooperating with you."

"Coerced? I wouldn't say 'coerced.' I may have paid her fairly well for the time and effort she expended on my behalf," he allowed, "but—"

"You bribed her to lie to me."

Even a Westcott knew when he was caught dead to rights. He admitted it only with a shrug, though...and an unrepentant sparkle in his green, green eyes.

The scoundrel. "Why did you do it?" she asked in bewilderment. "Because you wanted to stop me from worrying about the curse?"

"Because...Ms. Tess 'Only-What's-Necessary' McCrary-Westcott...that curse was complicating things. I didn't want you to feel pressured into staying with me because of it. I wanted you to stay because you fell deeply, madly in love with me."

She held his hands, locking her fingers with his, and gazed at him with all the love brimming in her heart. "Fiendishly clever. Your plan worked." He drew her closer, clearly zeroing in for a kiss. She couldn't let him off *that* easily, though. "You realize, don't you, that this means the curse *is* real."

He maneuvered her closer, nodding in grave agreement. "The more I think about it, the more I believe we'll have to carry out its terms for the rest of our lives. The planting of the seed. The forsaking of all others. The satisfying of manly needs..."

She tilted her head in reflection. "You think?"

"Oh, I'm sure of it."

"Well, then. That settles it." She sank deep into his embrace, supremely resigned. "Till death do us part."

Duty was, after all, duty.

If you enjoyed what you just read,
then we've got an offer you can't resist!

Take 2 bestselling
love stories FREE!
Plus get a FREE surprise gift!

Harlequin is having a

Heatwave

Featuring *New York Times* **Bestselling authors**

LINDA LAEL MILLER
BARBARA DELINSKY
TESS GERRITSEN

Watch for this incredible trade paperback collection on sale in May 2000.

Available at your favorite retail outlet.